"You don't have to tell me," Captain Janeway said to Lieutenant Tuvok. "They've taken the computer core."

The optical data cables that once led from the core junction node to the processor were lying in a pool of blue nutrient fluid. The bio nutrient gel-pack had been severed. Most of the gel was dripping down the interior of the core.

"You know," Janeway said, with extraordinary calm, "at the Academy, they told us to maintain an impartial attitude. Not get personally involved with our decision making." She paused, then continued, her voice dripping with barely controlled fury. "But when someone does this to my ship . . . I take it very personally." The Captain's voice left no doubt. Someone was going to pay for leaving *Voyager* crippled, so far from home.

Look for STAR TREK Fiction from Pocket Books

Star Trek: The Original Series

Star Trek: The Next Generation

Star Trek: Deep Space Nine

Star Trek: Voyager

STAR TREK
VOYAGER™

VIOLATIONS

SUSAN WRIGHT

POCKET BOOKS

New York   London   Toronto   Sydney   Tokyo   Singapore

An *Original* Publication of POCKET BOOKS

POCKET BOOKS, a division of Simon & Schuster Inc.
1230 Avenue of the Americas, New York, NY 10020

Copyright © 1995 by Paramount Pictures. All Rights Reserved.

STAR TREK is a Registered Trademark of
Paramount Pictures.

A VIACOM COMPANY

This book is published by Pocket Books, a division of
Simon & Schuster Inc., under exclusive license from
Paramount Pictures.

ISBN: 0-671-52046-6

First Pocket Books printing September 1995

10 9 8 7 6 5 4 3 2 1

POCKET and colophon are registered trademarks of
Simon & Schuster Inc.

Printed in the U.S.A.

*For Lisa Wright DeGroodt
and Gwen Roberts Sherman,
who were there when the voyage began*

PROLOGUE

"I THINK WE'RE BIG ENOUGH TO HANDLE THE CARTEL," Captain Janeway told Commander Chakotay.

From his post at Ops, Harry Kim could see her smile, and he was beginning to recognize that expression on her face. *She wants to march us in there, bold as brass.* Kim had to admire her audacity, even as she confronted the doubts of her first officer. Everyone on the bridge was watching, except for Paris, who was sitting at the conn, acting as if he didn't notice them arguing right behind his shoulder.

"May I respectfully remind the captain," Chakotay continued, his voice taking on a warning edge that carried through the hush. "You're used to evaluating situations as a Starfleet officer, whereas in this case, guerrilla tactics would be more to our advantage."

"Are you forgetting that we are Starfleet officers?" Janeway asked.

"Not at all. However, I am basing this suggestion on my experience with the Maquis." Chakotay leaned closer, adding something that was too low for Kim to

1

hear. Bursting with curiosity, he reminded himself to ask Paris later if he'd been able to overhear what the commander had said.

"Come to my ready room," Janeway ordered. "Tuvok, you have the bridge."

As the door slid shut behind them, Kim slowly let out his breath. He hated it when the captain and Chakotay disagreed; he trusted them both implicitly, yet in this case, one of them had to be wrong.

The rest of the bridge crew seemed uneasy, as well, just as they had been ever since *Voyager* was drawn off course by a plasma storm that stretched across several sectors. It had taken weeks to get around it, bringing them within range of the Tutopa binary system— home of the legendary Hub. The Hub was on every star map and cartography survey they'd encountered on this side of the galaxy, and according to Neelix, it was "the information center" of the Delta Quadrant.

"Sensors indicate another vessel proceeding along this vector," Kim announced, noting the trajectory of the ship.

Tuvok confirmed the reading, as Paris grinned back at Kim. "That's the fourth ship to pass by since we've been here," Paris said. "This Hub must be some hopping place."

"Seems to be," Kim agreed, cautiously checking Tuvok's reaction. He was usually fairly strict about maintaining bridge protocol. Since this was Kim's first mission, he wasn't sure if all security chiefs were the same way or if it was because Tuvok was a Vulcan.

"Well, the Hub sounds like an ideal spot for some R and R," Paris added. "If we were in Federation space, I'd be due for shore leave right about now—"

"Lieutenant," Tuvok interrupted. "You are employing faulty logic. If we were in Federation space, you would not be assigned to this vessel. You would currently be serving your sentence in the New Zealand penal settlement."

An odd expression passed over Paris's face, reminding Kim of the first time Paris had breezily admitted lying about his pilot error that killed three fellow officers. When Paris had added that a fit of hallucinatory remorse had prompted him to confess, getting him cashiered out of Starfleet, Kim had nearly gotten up and left him sitting there alone. He was almost more outraged by the pilot's devil-may-care attitude than the deed itself, but he had stayed because of that strange smile. Staring into his soup, Paris had reminded him of Reggy, a guy he'd known in school who was always causing some kind of trouble. But once, when Reggy had made one of the younger girls cry by soaking her jumper with a stasis bubble full of water, he had looked exactly the same way as Paris did now—trying to smile because he couldn't back down now in front of everyone, while his eyes turned hollow as the little girl gazed up at him, her hands spread wide, innocent and hurting, wondering why anyone would do this to her. . . .

"For shame, Tuvok," Paris drawled over his shoulder at the security chief. "Eavesdropping on our conversation. Is that the sort of behavior you consider logical?"

Tuvok's hands didn't stop moving over the Tactical control panel, preparing the ship's defensive systems in case they entered the Tutopa system. "I cannot help hearing you, Lieutenant Paris, when you chose to broadcast your opinion to the entire bridge. I would suggest you refrain from doing so in the future."

There was a moment's silence as the rest of the crew pretended to be busy with their work. But their words hung in the air, making Kim feel even worse. He hated it when *anyone* argued, especially when they were hanging on the edge of a system that was reportedly one of the most powerful in the quadrant.

Paris never seemed to know when to give up. He grumbled something inaudible about, "Seeing nothing but the inside of this ship—"

The door to the ready room opened, cutting him off, as Captain Janeway and Chakotay emerged. Janeway nodded to Tuvok, officially taking command of the bridge.

"We're going to be discreet," the captain announced with a wry glance at Chakotay, acknowledging that she'd been convinced by his advice. "Plot a course for the secondary system of Tutopa."

Paris sighed, but he didn't hesitate to comply. "Course laid in."

Janeway noticed his reaction, just as she seemed to notice everything that happened. "Mr. Paris, we are attempting to acquire information about wormholes—we are not venturing into Cartel space so you can dive into the local gin joint." She glanced at Chakotay. "Where is Neelix, by the way?"

Chakotay was perfectly calm, despite the tension. "Apparently, he's been having trouble with one of his boilers. He should be here shortly."

"Tutopa secondary system within sensor range," Kim said, concentrating on his readings. "No class-M planets, but I'm reading at least forty ships and stationary platforms in the area."

"We need Neelix," Janeway commented.

Chakotay tapped his communicator. "Bridge to Neelix. Report at once—"

The turbolift opened before Chakotay could finish, and Neelix bustled in. His wispy hair was flying and his arms were waving, seeming to fill up more space than his compact body warranted. "Sorry I'm late, folks! Kes needed me."

"Glad you could join us."

His toady little face hardly flinched at her dry remark. He smacked his hands together, rubbing them briskly. "So what's on the menu today?"

The captain was obviously in no mood for jokes. "We're entering the secondary system of Tutopa."

That got his attention. "Are you sure you want to do this? *I've* never even been to Tutopa, in spite of the opportunities there."

"Why not?"

Neelix companionably hooked an arm over the back of the captain's chair, leaning in much closer to Janeway than Kim would have ever dared. "Let's just say that Tutopans tend to *acquire* vessels. Not that they're aggressive, mind you, but people usually leave only after they're working for one of the Houses or the Cartel, the conglomerate that runs the Hub and serves as the joint security force for the Houses."

"That is why we're avoiding the Hub." Janeway shifted away slightly. "Is there anyone we can negotiate with in the secondary system?"

Neelix's eyes lit up. "You know, you could probably get anything you wanted in exchange for that 'beaming' trick of yours."

"We cannot trade technology," Janeway told him. "That would break the Prime Directive."

"Ah, yes, that prime-thingy again." Neelix gave her a serious look. "It would be much easier, you know, if you could see yourself around that rule every once in a while. It certainly seems to get in the way."

Janeway made a sharp gesture with her hand. "I've tried to explain this to you before, Neelix. We simply can't hand over advanced technology that could cause a shift in the natural development of a culture. I'm sure there must be other ways."

"Oh, there's always other ways," Neelix quickly agreed. "It all depends on what you want to pay."

Chakotay considered the screen where the binary stars of Tutopa were growing larger as they approached. "What is the Tutopan form of payment?"

"That's the odd thing," Neelix told them, leaning forward again. "It's one reason why I never much bothered with the place. The Houses mostly deal in information—blueprints, technology, formulas, things like that. They play with stakes much higher than my reach, let me tell you."

"We don't intend to deal with the Houses or the Cartel," Janeway repeated patiently. "We're trying to keep a low profile."

"You don't have to go to the Hub, the Houses have adjuncts in the secondary system—" Neelix broke off at her expression, holding his hands up. "But you're right, Captain. There are other ways that won't attract as much attention . . . such as certain fringe elements who, shall we say, deal on the dark side of the moons."

"The dark side?" Janeway repeated dubiously.

Paris tossed over his shoulder, "Sounds like he's talking about the black market."

"Are these fringe elements engaging in illegal activities?" Janeway asked Neelix.

"The only law in Tutopa is the Cartel." Neelix shrugged as if that said everything. "Darksiders are fair game for the Enforcer patrols, but I doubt they'll bother with us. Their ships are maybe a quarter the size of yours." Neelix quickly corrected himself: *"Ours."*

"Where do we find these 'darksiders'?" Chakotay asked.

Neelix opened his eyes wide. "I told you, I've never been in this system before."

At the front console, Paris let out a snort. "Some native guide you are. . . ."

Tuvok's brows drew together, the only sign of displeasure he usually allowed himself. Kim figured he was itching to reprimand Paris.

"Do you have something to say, Lieutenant?" Janeway demanded, much more sharply than Kim had expected.

Paris checked his navigation display, as if his mind was occupied by more important matters. "If you ask me," he said. "This place looks like the Sassaniwan Cross—that binary system between Ferengi and Cordovian space. It's a hot trading spot, and they've got a healthy black market going in the secondary system, mainly in the asteroid belts."

"Don't tell me you've had experience with the Sassaniwan black market?" Janeway asked Paris.

"Enough to know what I'm talking about."

Janeway looked from Chakotay to Tuvok. "What do you think?"

"I am reading an asteroid belt in the secondary system," the Vulcan informed her. "However, this is not the Sassaniwan Cross."

Paris groaned, dropping all pretense of disinterest. "We wouldn't need to worry about finding wormholes if this *was* the Sassaniwan Cross—right, Tuvok? We'd already be in the Alpha Quadrant, safe and sound."

"I am simply reminding the captain of the unknowns," Tuvok replied. "However, in theory, it has been established that individuals who are desperate enough to endure conditions commonly found among asteroid belts are indeed more likely to operate outside the normal channels of society."

Paris didn't seem sure how to react to that. "It sounds like you're agreeing with me."

"He *is*," Kim murmured, too low for anyone to hear.

"He is," Janeway told Paris. "Lieutenant, set a course for the asteroid belt. Let's see if we can find a way home."

CHAPTER
1

JANEWAY TILTED BACK IN HER CHAIR, GAZING AT THE
ceiling of her ready room.

Chakotay was right.

What a way to begin the morning, but for the past
few days that thought had kept returning and intrud-
ing on her work—*Voyager* didn't have Starfleet to
back them up anymore. Intellectually, she was very
aware of the fact that they were a negligible force here
in the Delta Quadrant, yet for some reason, a feeling
of vulnerability had hit hard with Chakotay's quiet
reminder on the bridge.

The lights flashed as Chakotay's voice came over
the channel. "Yellow alert. Captain to the bridge."

"On my way," she acknowledged, hoping it
wouldn't be another false alarm. Despite of the days
of fruitless negotiations, she was determined to see
this through—if there were any wormholes within a
thousand light-years, the Tutopans would know
about it.

On the viewscreen, a bulbous freighter was slowly coming into sensor range. On the other side, the curve of the asteroid belt was spangled by millions of tiny flashes as dust and rocks turned and shifted, reflecting the light of the suns. Janeway had always thought asteroid belts were pretty, but that was until she was forced to sit next to one for four solid days with hardly a break in the monotony. But Chakotay was right. . . .

"Maintain course and speed," she ordered. "Let's see if they're serious about talking to us."

Janeway settled back in her seat, studying the screen. The rounded dorsal and front hydrogen scoop were similar in design to the other dozen or so ships they'd encountered in the secondary system, but this vessel looked particularly battered. Her eyes narrowed at the distorted bulkheads in the starboard hull, as she recognized the signs of a partial vacuum decompression.

Paris was shaking his head. "You couldn't pay me to fly that thing."

Janeway found many things to appreciate in her pilot's unique point of view, so she usually chose to ignore the fact that most of his comments were unsolicited. "Is she coming this way?"

"Their tractory would appear to bring them alongside," Tuvok replied.

"Very good."

"Shall I open a hailing frequency?" Ensign Kim asked.

"No, let's not scare this one off."

Kim subsided, frowning. When Janeway checked the Ops readout on her monitor, she saw that he had suspended all ongoing science projects in order to have maximum power ready to be routed to engines and weapons systems. A little extreme, under the circumstances. Janeway tried to suppress a surge of sympathy for the young ensign—this was hard enough on everyone, but it had been Kim's first posting, his first mission, that tore him away from everything he ever knew. No wonder he was nervous. But he was also a Starfleet officer, and as Mark would have pointed out, with that infuriating grin of his, "Don't you think your concern is edging *slightly* into the maternal, my dear Kate?"

Janeway banished the thought of her distant lover, sternly bringing her thoughts back to the present. "Is something wrong, Mr. Kim?"

"Not exactly . . ." The young man sneaked a quick look, making sure she was open to hearing more. "It's just that I don't understand why so many ships act like they're approaching, then suddenly veer off. Even some of the ones that do finally hail us."

"They're testing us," Chakotay said, philosophically enough.

"And word's getting around," Paris added. "Most people are smart enough to keep away if they don't have what we want. I mean, who needs to go looking for trouble? And we look like trouble—we could smash most of these vessels with hardly a ripple in our power grid."

Janeway didn't mind letting Paris reassure the ensign, while she was busy examining the welding seams that puckered the side of the freighter. It was barely as large as one of *Voyager*'s warp nacelles. "Report, Tuvok."

"The freighter is heavily shielded, as is usual among the Tutopan craft. However, their weapons systems are minimal."

Janeway considered the freighter. "That may be

true, but I think it's capable of making some speed. Their ramscoop looks as if it has a double compression chamber."

"I've seen one like that before," Chakotay agreed. "On an Orion courier—all legs with minimum cargo space. For fast delivery . . ."

"At least it isn't trying to scan us," Paris put in.

The freighter came to a stop and held position at thirty thousand kilometers.

"Hail them," Janeway ordered. Impatiently, she waited as Tuvok made the necessary adjustments in their communication frequencies. Apparently, no two Tutopan vessels used the same bandwidth.

"We have an audio channel only," Tuvok informed her. Janeway couldn't tell—despite their years of working together—whether the security chief was as irritated as she was by their paranoid refusal to return a visual transmission.

"This is Captain Janeway of the *Starship Voyager,*" she identified herself, leaving out her usual references to Starfleet and the Federation.

"Voyager, this is the *Kapon."* The voice from the freighter echoed flatly through their speakers. "We understand you are looking for a particular piece of information."

"Yes, I'm attempting to locate coordinates for wormholes." Janeway stood up, tilting her head in order to catch every nuance. The other Tutopans had also spoken with the same droning inflection, in the same middle register—practically indecipherable as far as emotional content was concerned. "Do you know of any wormholes in the area?"

"What is your credit?" was the reply.

Janeway stopped short—usually she was quizzed on exactly *why* she was looking for wormholes, not asked how much she could pay.

"We would give you, in exchange," she offered, "verified, accurate star charts of the other side of the galaxy, areas you call the Simari Cluster and the Trian Nebula."

"Star charts. Scientific curiosities," the voice said dispassionately. "Valueless."

"Not necessarily," Janeway quickly countered. "Plotting system motion and radiation disbursion rates is easier with verified points of reference. With these charts, and yours from your own sector, one can triangulate any system in the galaxy—an invaluable tool for navigation. It's also one that nobody else has. . . ."

There was a long pause, as Janeway hardly moved. The senior officers had agreed that star charts were simply an aid to technology already in use, and that to share such information would not violate the Prime Directive.

"This is confidential information?" the voice from the *Kapon* finally asked.

"Absolutely." Maybe she was getting better at their sort of negotiating. "Other than ourselves, only you would possess these charts."

"Then this would be information of acceptable value," the voice from the *Kapon* agreed.

"Good," Janeway said briskly, ignoring her rising excitement in order to close the deal. "We can transmit the cartography—"

"You would transmit sensitive information over an open channel?" the voice interrupted. "The value would be lost if it is intercepted."

"We have methods by which we can secure a channel. It will insure that no one can tap the transmission."

"I do not believe your methods could be superior to our own."

Janeway crossed her arms, nodding to Tuvok. The Vulcan thought about it briefly, then condensed the information into basic principles that didn't violate security procedures. "Our encryption protocols are handled by our main computer. Faster-than-light processors, augmented by bioneural circuitry, rotate and update the encryption algorithms randomly. In addition, we are capable of emitting a rapid transmission burst."

The *Kapon* didn't answer right away, as if they were considering the offer. Janeway held her breath, until the voice finally said, "Unacceptable. No channel of communication can be completely secured."

Tuvok tilted his head as if he was inclined to agree with that, but Janeway didn't want to hear about it. She wondered if Tutopans *enjoyed* making things difficult.

"What do you suggest?" Janeway asked, hoping she sounded patient. "A message capsule?"

"We prefer a direct exchange."

"You mean in person? You don't expect us to go to the Hub?" she asked.

"That will not be necessary. I see your ship maintains shuttlebays."

"You want me to shuttle the information to your ship?" Janeway wasn't sure she liked that.

"No, we could not take that risk. It is possible this is a ruse by the Cartel."

Janeway took a calming breath, trying to be reasonable. "Well, if we are the Cartel, aren't you already in a lot of trouble?"

"You will not be allowed to board our ship," the voice repeated. "We will come to you."

Janeway stopped pacing. "What makes you think we'll agree to that?"

"You require wormhole locations. We are the only ones who can supply this information."

"Why should I believe you?"

"That is unimportant. If you wish to purchase the wormhole information, you must cooperate with us."

Janeway clasped her hands behind her back, making them wait for her answer as she made a slow circuit around the bridge. Without a word being said, Tuvok's stiff stance indicated that he objected. Chakotay didn't seem pleased with the proposal, either. Janeway tended to agree with both of them—allowing unknown entities on board her ship was not something she preferred to do, and yet . . . there had been no signs of threat from any of the Tutopans thus far. Even Neelix said they weren't known for being aggressive people.

"You drive a hard bargain," she finally agreed.

"We can't afford to make a mistake." The voice from the *Kapon* could have been interpreted as sad. "Especially when it comes to the Cartel."

Tuvok had insisted that Janeway wait in the observation lounge, so she watched from the window overlooking the shuttlebay as the security team performed a sensor sweep of the yacht from the *Kapon*. Both the yacht and the four crew members had been thoroughly scanned by their ship's sensors before being allowed into the shuttlebay, but Tuvok apparently wasn't taking any chances.

The Tutopans didn't take offense at Tuvok's caution, but they did seem edgy, with their tall, slender bodies in constant motion as they fidgeted and nervously glanced around. It wasn't the sort of behavior Janeway had expected from their toneless voices. She was less surprised by their flattened faces and delicate features, which gave them a remarkable physical similarity. Their most distinguishing attribute was the hair clasps of various, shiny colors that gathered their receding, colorless hair into a fluffy bundle at the neck. From the brief orders, Janeway decided the Tutopan with the sunburst clasp was the leader.

"Nice ship," Janeway commented, knowing that Chakotay was watching from the bridge.

"Wouldn't Torres love to get her hands on that little number?" Chakotay answered.

Janeway nodded, pursing her lips. "Perhaps there's good reason these people are wary. Still, you have to wonder, what is a yacht like *that* doing in the hold of a run-down freighter?"

Down on the shuttlebay floor, Tuvok and his security team moved away from the yacht. Turning to the observation window, he tapped his comm badge. "Captain, all is secure."

"Very good, Mr. Tuvok. Please escort our guests to the lounge."

Janeway raised her hand to her chin, watching Tuvok and the Tutopans cross the shuttlebay. As the doors slid open, she took one breath and knew something was wrong.

"Chak—" she started to say, but her throat choked closed on her warning as her muscles seized in a wrenching spasm.

On the bridge, Chakotay had been growing more uncomfortable as he observed Tuvok's examination of the Tutopans. Something told him that these people were not to be trusted. Since there was nothing he could specifically point to, he wondered if he was merely feeling an instinctual distrust of the unknown. Still, his hand was moving to the comm panel to signal the captain, when suddenly Tuvok and the security team started jerking and falling like stiffened dolls.

Chakotay hit the emergency override. "Red alert! Close down—" was all he managed to get out. His eyes widened, filled with the sight of the *Kapon* crew members leaving the shuttlebay, as he pitched forward, his body wrested from his control.

In sickbay, Kes stood straight up, her blue eyes staring straight ahead.

"Kes?" the doctor asked. "Is something wrong?"

With a choking sound, Kes jerked back, her body convulsing.

The doctor's decision tracks were already working on the problem, and he had a medical tricorder in his hand before the patient was unconscious. Dilation of the arteries, accelerated heartbeat, and relaxation of the bronchioles. As the readings flowed by on the screen, correlating with his symptoms-decryption program, one of his subroutines noted the distressingly loud sound such a small humanoid could make when it hit the floor.

A compilation of the data indicated that the convulsions were not systemic but induced by an outside agent, triggering Decision Track 10. "Medical alert!" he announced.

Even as he scanned the ship's internal environmental readouts, he reached for a hypospray of condrazine for Kes. It wasn't that she was more important than any other patient, but he flagged a reminder to create a Priority Subroutine that would insure Kes was tended immediately whenever she was injured. After all, she was the only mobile medical technician the ship had.

"Captain Janeway, this is Dr. Zimmerman," he said calmly. "I have detected a large quantity of isoprenaline in the ship's atmosphere."

The hypo injected the neural-stimulator into Kes's neck. There was no response from the captain.

Decision Track 2112, a recent innovation, performed an emergency medical override, directly accessing the main computer and ordering atmospheric isolation of the areas infested with the isoprenaline. The subprocessors accepted the emergency medical override and directed all power toward cleansing the ship's atmosphere.

The doctor initiated an analysis of the toxin in Kes's system in the medical database, and requested an antidote to be processed immediately. He was returning to Kes, noting her flushed skin and rapid pulse, when his awareness was abruptly terminated.

CHAPTER
2

RED-ALERT KLAXONS SEEMED TO DRAW JANEWAY BACK TO consciousness, giving her a path to follow out of the confused tangle of dreamlike images.

When her eyes finally opened, she still wasn't sure she was awake. Aside from the red flashing, the lights were dimmed, as if the ship was running on emergency power. Janeway numbly tried to move, scraping her cheek against the rough carpet. Something was terribly wrong with her ship—she could feel it. A subtle vibration was missing, a comforting power that thrummed through the bulkheads.

A sudden surge of panic went a long way toward reviving her. "Bridge, this is the captain." Her words were slurred and heavy, like her thoughts, seeming to fall apart before they could fully form in her mind.

"The Tutopans!" she groaned, pulling herself up to the observation window. The shuttlebay was shadowed with dramatic spotlight cast by the emergency system. One glance told her it was empty. The *Kapon* yacht was gone.

"Tuvok . . ." Janeway knelt down next to her security chief. She was relieved to find Tuvok and the rest of his team lying in the corridor, as if the Tutopans had dragged them out of the shuttlebay before they'd left. When she didn't see them from the window, the alternative had been unthinkable, but it made her stumble into a run to get downstairs to find out what had happened to the security team.

"Captain," Tuvok said, sounding remarkably coherent for a man lying flat on his back, blinking up as if he couldn't quite focus. "We are in red alert."

"We certainly are." Janeway helped him sit up. "The optical data network is off-line, as are our comm badges. I can't tell how long we've been unconscious, so we've got anywhere from an hour to two seconds left in Emergency Environmental Support."

Tuvok stiffly got to his feet, surveying his groaning team, then the empty shuttlebay. "My security measures failed."

"They certainly did." The captain managed a grimace in place of a smile. They'd have to deal with that issue later—now, there was no time. She needed to know the status of her ship.

"You two go to sickbay," she ordered, gesturing to the members of the security team. "The rest of you secure the bridge. Tuvok, you're with me." Her hand closed around Ensign Navarro's arm as he went past—he was looking more alert than the others. "Report back to me as soon as you can. I'll be in the computer monitor room."

The ensign tried to stand a little straighter. "Aye-aye, ma'am!"

Janeway let it go. His enthusiasm was heartening.

"You believe the computer is malfunctioning?" Tuvok asked.

"It's more than a simple ODN failure if we can't

access the bridge. We'll have to directly access the main computer core to find out what's happening."

The crackle of forcefield energy could be heard down the corridor. Tuvok already had his tricorder opened to ready position.

Rounding the corner, Janeway came to an abrupt halt. The frame of the door had been cut away, removing at least two meters on either side. The pieces were stacked neatly against one wall. Tuvok scanned the razor-sharp edges of the bulkhead, then swung his tricorder into the monitor room. The rear wall shimmered with a blue forcefield.

"You don't have to tell me," Janeway said numbly. She took one more wondering step forward. "It's gone. They've ripped out our computer processor. . . ."

Tuvok went right up to the forcefield, holding out the tricorder. A gaping hole in the floor and the wall overlooked the three-level drop down the center of the cylindrical memory core. The optical data cables that once led from the core junction node to the processor were lying in a pool of blue nutrient fluid. Janeway saw the reason why—the bionutrient shunts leading to the banks of neural gel packs has been severed by the forcefield. Most of the leaking gel was dripping down the interior of the core.

"The integrity of the subspace field was lost when the junction nodes to the processor were severed." Tuvok snapped his tricorder shut. "The forcefield is experiencing minor power fluctuations. A secondary forcefield must be established before the subspace field can be stabilized."

Janeway nodded, waving him off, her eyes fastened on the dark hole in the center of the computer core. One of the most important rules of command she had learned in Starfleet Academy was how to maintain an impartial attitude in the face of a difficult situation. Janeway usually found that taking things personally interfered with decision making. Yet, faced with this wrenching hole, with her vessel disabled in one stroke from the removal of five square meters of computer processor. . . .

Yes, I take this personally.

Before she would work herself into a really satisfying, righteous fury, Torres arrived. As she skidded to a stop, her hair swung into her face and her arms shot out for balance. Her mouth opened and closed without a word, until she finally managed to blurt out, "Where is it?!"

Janeway was in no mood to endure anyone else's temper tantrum if she couldn't have one of her own. "I hope this means we still have our warp core?"

"They wouldn't dare!" The engineer gave her a quick look, before glaring at the hole in the deck. Even her hands were clenched.

Janeway wondered if the young woman knew how *Klingon* she looked when she was in a rage. "That won't accomplish anything," she said curtly. "I need to know what the damage is in here."

"I know what the damage is," Torres retorted. "Somebody stole our computer! That's some neat trick, cutting the processor right out from under the memory core."

"I don't care how it was done, Lieutenant, I want the ODN back on-line."

As usual, when directly confronted with a problem, Torres immediately went to work. "The auxiliary computer and dedicated subprocessors should be able to run primary operations once we reestablish the subspace integrity within these modules. But without the main processor . . . I doubt we'll have warp capability."

Tuvok stepped between them, setting down a portable forcefield unit. "You should not be standing here, Captain. The power failures could be allowing leakage of subspace radiation."

Janeway didn't move. "It's a dangerous universe, Tuvok."

Another forcefield glimmered on, this one tinged green as if indicating caution by its acid tone.

"Get that subspace field back in place, Torres, then report to the bridge." Janeway gestured helplessly to the hole. "And have someone clean up this . . . fluid, so we can see what we've got left in here."

"Aye, Captain." Torres smartly turned and ran down the corridor. She started to issue orders through her comm badge, but broke off with a frustrated curse when she remembered it wasn't working.

Tuvok made some final adjustments to the forcefield, then slowly stood at full attention. Janeway knew he wouldn't bring up his failure again—he would wait for her to chose the correct moment to discuss it. It was times like this she appreciated his rock-solid dependability.

"Is anything else missing?" Janeway asked.

"A tricorder scan reveals this is the only area that has been damaged." Tuvok turned to gaze at the ragged hole along with the captain. "Apparently, only the computer processor was removed."

"Only the processor," Janeway repeated. "Only the most important operational element on this ship."

Kes blinked open her eyes. "What happened?" she asked, but when she realized she could hardly move, she refrained from asking the other dozens of questions that immediately came to mind. Something was wrong, and she had to be quiet so the doctor could fix it. He leaned over her, reaching out with one hand, a concerned expression on his face.

Suddenly his body seemed to phase, disappearing in static lines, before popping back into position, exactly the same as when she'd first seen him. He was coming toward her and leaning into her line of sight. Then his image seemed to flatten, breaking apart, leaping backward several meters.

Kes pushed herself up. "Doctor?"

Zimmerman seemed unaware of her presence, as he repeatedly performed the same motions, trapped in a few seconds of time.

Kes reached for her comm badge. "Captain, this is Kes—"

The muted tone told her that it wasn't working. She tried a few more times without success, as the doctor repeated the same sequence of actions over and over again.

She got up to go get someone who could fix his systems, but for some reason she couldn't leave him like that. He would hate the distortion, its machine-like repetition and his loss of control.

She drew in her breath, aware she was making a big decision. But she liked making big decisions. "Computer, end program."

The image of the doctor disappeared.

Clutching her fist to her chest, she counted three heartbeats before ordering, "Begin program."

There was a momentary delay—maybe no one else would have noticed it, but she was familiar with every nuance of the doctor's existence. The telling pause penetrated down to her bones, and she knew something was wrong. . . .

Then Zimmerman appeared, his hands clasped in

front of him. "What is the nature of the emergency?" he immediately asked, glancing toward the red flashing lights.

Kes was delighted it had worked. "I don't know what's happening. I was knocked unconscious, and you were caught in some sort of . . . loop." She followed the doctor to the computer terminal. "The communication lines are down."

"The entire optical data network is nonfunctioning. Sickbay is currently operating under emergency power." Zimmerman picked up his tricorder. "You say you were unconscious? How do you feel now?"

She held still as he scanned her. "My head aches some."

He scowled at his readings. "Apparently you were scanned shortly after you were rendered unconscious. An antidote has been created to clear the degenerative toxins from your system."

Kes wondered why he sounded puzzled. "You must have done that."

"That is the problem," the doctor said shortly. "I don't remember performing the scan or entering the data into the medical database. The last thing I remember . . ."

"We were doing the crew reports," Kes prompted.

The doctor was motionless, apparently accessing. "My short-term-memory banks have been wiped. I don't remember the last thing I did."

"Maybe the neural toxin affected you, too."

"Impossible—isopropaline wouldn't impact my holographic systems."

"Something's interfering with the computer," Kes pointed out. "Even the chronometer isn't working."

"Yes, yes," the doctor brushed off, as if his condition was of no concern. Examining the comparative readings, he said to himself, "Neural gas, rapid dispersal . . . degenerative. I need to know the time that has lapsed to measure the dosage of the antidote."

Kes checked a chronometer. "One hour and thirty-two minutes," she said.

"Excuse me?" the doctor asked, looking up. "What was that?"

"That's how long we were unconscious."

"Impossible," the doctor said, giving her a penetrating look. Kes wasn't sure what he meant by that, but she didn't have time to ask as the first injured crewman stumbled through the sickbay door. She ran to help him, as the doctor ordered the medical replicator to process the antidote.

Kes overheard the doctor struggling with the replicator, making several attempts before the correct compound was processed. Then, in spite of her protests, the doctor injected her first, before treating the ensign. While she helped the young woman sit down, the doctor entered his findings on a padd. "Take this up to the bridge, along with enough antidote to inoculate the crew members you encounter. Then return here with a report on our status."

Kes hesitated, as two more people arrived, but the doctor turned away. The last thing she heard was his irritated voice. "I'd appreciate it if you hurried. I'd like to know what's going on, since as usual, I'm stuck down here."

Paris turned as the captain climbed up the Jeffries tube with Tuvok behind her. "Report!" Janeway called out.

Paris didn't want to admit how much he appreciated the sound of her warm, gravelly voice. He noticed Kim had no scruples about hiding his relief—the ensign was elbow-deep in the nutrient gel packs of the main bridge subprocessor, but he looked as if he could have jumped up and hugged Janeway. Paris turned away with a smile, which faded somewhat when he was confronted by the blank gray viewscreen.

Janeway strode into the center of the bridge as if ready to put an end to all this nonsense. "Where's Chakotay?"

"I guess I'm in charge," Paris finally answered, when nobody else did. "The security team just left with Chakotay, taking him to sickbay."

"He didn't regain consciousness along with the rest of us," Kim added.

Tuvok was trying to access the Tactical control panel. "Tactical station is off-line."

"I can't access the ODN to get the systems back on-line," Kim said, as if he was personally responsible. Paris almost felt sorry for the kid, except that the Ops officer *was* responsible for keeping the ship's systems integrated and functioning properly.

"The main processor was removed from the computer core." Janeway held up her hand to stop Kim's questions, while Paris felt a surge of admiration for her cool delivery. His own eyes were beginning to glaze as a cascade of implications piled on top of one another—no warp, no navigation, no sensors. . . .

But the captain spoke as if she'd always been prepared for this possibility. "Torres is reestablishing the subspace field of the main core, which should bring the auxiliary computer and the optical data network back on-line. You'll have to reinitiate the programs from this subprocessor."

Kim swallowed, then apparently remembered he was supposed to respond. "Aye, Captain."

Janeway was hardly listening. "I wonder what's keeping Torres." Her fingers tapped her comm badge, an abortive gesture, as if she knew it wouldn't work but she couldn't suppress the automatic motion that went along with the desire to speak to someone. "Is there any way you can route communications through the bridge subprocessor?"

"I'm not sure," Kim answered. "I'll have to see once we get power to the transceivers."

The captain's fist hit the arm of her chair as she sat down, a tiny sign of frustration that Paris found oddly reassuring. None of them were infallible, not even Tuvok, who insisted on acting so stiff and proper that Paris sometimes couldn't resist poking at that icy front. He sometimes forgot that they were all stumbling around in this alien quadrant, practically blind . . . which reminded him of the time he was lost in the wine cellars of the Trident Chin, an endless maze of tunnels and vats under the merchant complex. He had only gone down there to get a little nip on the sly, but it had taken him the entire night to contact someone to come find him—

"I know something that might work," Paris offered.

Janeway's eyes bored into his. "Well, out with it, Lieutenant."

"A tricorder has both a transceiver and a signal/encryption processor. If we leave our tricorders open to the same frequency, we can talk to each other without having to go through the ship's ODN."

Tuvok lifted one brow, and Paris could have sworn he was irritated that he hadn't thought of it. "The method would be highly inefficient, similar to ancient Earth devices which broadcast open signals, yet it would provide intraship communications."

"Then do it," the captain ordered. "Assign a different frequency to each department."

"Of course, Captain."

Paris could almost take pleasure in one-upping the

security chief, except for the situation they were in. Not that he disliked the dark Vulcan, but he'd been smarting ever since Tuvok's reminder that he didn't deserve to be a part of this crew. After all, how could he ever forget that? He was reminded every day, week after week in hundreds of subtle ways, that he had to earn the right to be among these people—both Starfleet and Maquis. Sometimes he felt as if he were still serving out his sentence.

Maybe that was why he'd been acting so flippant the past few days, setting up a booking operation and giving odds on holodeck rations that the captain wouldn't find wormhole information sitting next to these cursed rocks. He did it as much to shock Harry Kim as anything else, even after Kes embarrassed him by placing a bet of two hours of her time on the captain's success. Her eyes had glowed with belief as she did it. Even so, that hadn't stopped Paris from talking Harry into using his holo-ration last night to run the pool-room program so everyone could have some fun after their tedious shifts. It hadn't taken much to convince him, and then the kid had sat there all night with a tricorder, working on a new holodeck program to improve the place. As everyone offered suggestions, Paris had scoffed that one good way to ruin a holoprogram was to have too many parameters. But it had given him the idea to get together with Harry later to work a new program he had in mind— the kid was a genius when it came to computers.

Now Paris only hoped they'd have the chance. Adrift with minutes of life support left, he was sure this was the *last* place he wanted to be.

Torres arrived panting through the Jeffries tube. "I slipped on the rungs. Between decks three and four. I almost fell eight levels—"

"You can give us the dramatic details later," Janeway cut in. Kim cringed down behind the modules of bioneural circuitry even though her irritation wasn't directed at him. "Is the subspace field intact?"

"Aye, Captain." Torres quickly moved to the Ops station, her grace belying the strength of her half-Klingon body. After watching her work out, Paris had made a silent vow that he stay out of her way when she was angry. She could be downright vicious.

"I'll download from here," Kim announced from the subprocessor. "Let me know when that panel has access, and we'll do the diagnostics."

"Forget the diagnostics," Janeway told them. "We need to know what's out there."

"I should have visual in a few moments," Kim confirmed nervously. "And the most basic scanning procedures."

"I can tell you what's out there," Paris muttered, surprised they hadn't been boarded already. Only the intimidation of their sheer size must be holding the other scavengers at bay. "They're gathering out there, wondering how damaged we are, daring each other to make the first move. They could have scanned us already and found out we're sitting here helpless—"

"Shields?" Janeway asked.

"Shields at five percent," Tuvok informed her. "Near minimum levels for habitable environment, blocking EM and nuclear radiation."

An uneasy silence followed, and Paris focused his attention on Kim along with the rest of the bridge crew. Without panel displays, there was nothing else they could do, but Kim flinched when he turned to find every eye on him. "A-any second now . . ."

The lights sputtered, and somewhere in the distance a fan shut off, leaving them in perfect silence.

Paris suddenly realized he didn't know where the nearest emergency lifeboat was located—

"Got it!" Kim exclaimed, as the control panels began to glow. "ODN back on-line."

"Power up auxiliary generators," the captain ordered. "Maximum power to shields."

The viewscreen brightened, with horizontal lines scrolling upward in a dizzy surge before resolving into an image of the starfield. The focus and resolution was slightly off, reminding Paris of the screens he had used in middle school. Nevertheless, in and above the rocky swath of the asteroid belt, small geometrical objects could be seen. "There they are," he warned the rest.

Tuvok spoke right over him. "There are approximately eight vessels within one hundred thousand kilometers, and closing. I am attempting to widen the bandwidth of the sensors."

"The ship has stabilized into Reduced Power Mode," Kim announced, not bothering to wait for the captain to ask. "Deflectors and inertial damping at minimum power; communications and tactical systems off-line; environmental systems at thirty percent."

"Torres, can you get us moving?" the captain demanded.

"Warp and impulse engines are cold, but maybe I can get the Reaction and Control Assembly back on-line." Torres hurried over to the engineering control panel. "It's a good thing we were in drift mode when the processor was cut. I'd hate to imagine an unsupervised cold shutdown—we could have lost the whole core assembly."

"Vessels approaching at eighty thousand kilometers," Tuvok announced calmly.

"I'm having trouble with the guidance and navigation subprocessor," Paris called out. "Only partial data is being delivered." He concentrated on routing the sensors and deflector input away from the main computer. "But if you can give me thrusters, Torres, I'll fly this ship manually if I have to."

"Working!" Torres snapped.

Paris felt rebuffed, even though he knew she was in her usual "loose cannon" mode, firing at any target. "Of course, if you prefer," he added with elaborate courtesy, "I could take a shuttle out front and *tow* the ship."

"You'll do whatever it takes, Mr. Paris," Janeway told him. "To get us moving again."

"Aye, Captain." Paris wished he'd kept his mouth shut, as the RCS began responding, followed by a glare from Torres. "All systems go. Well, enough of them to get *us* going, anyway."

"Set a course for—"

"Captain," Tuvok interrupted, his rapid fingers betraying more urgency than his voice. "Infrared readings are detecting emission lines from the vessels, in wavelengths up to one hundred microns."

Janeway seemed puzzled. "Those sound like nebula readings."

"They are similar; however, these emission lines are created by the hydrogen-fusion engines of the Tutopan vessels. I have detected one set of lines that originates one thousand kilometers off our starboard."

"The *Kapon*," Janeway instantly agreed. "Very good, Mr. Tuvok. Give navigation the coordinates, and plot a course along that trail."

"Aye, Captain."

Janeway sat back, her lips tightening. "Let's go get our processor back."

"Ready when you are." Paris was also ready to sing

a silent Hallelujah—maybe things were starting to get better. He plotted a course right through the approaching vessels, figuring if they couldn't be fast, they might as well make it threatening.

"Engage," the captain ordered.

Paris boosted the main thrusters, smoothly routing plasma flow to hold them in a steady line. He fell into the complicated rhythms of manual navigation as if it were his natural element, as if the ship were an extension of his own body. Nothing else mattered when he could fly, not the Tutopans, not Starfleet—in spite of everyone, he was satisfied.

Really, I don't ask for very much.

He was sure the situation was improving when Kes arrived on the bridge to administer an antidote for their neurogenic shock.

"Chemical neuromolecular inhibitor . . ." the captain murmured, reading the padd. "That's why some people were more affected than others."

"Different biochemistry," Kes agreed, as she administered the antidote to Janeway.

"I don't wonder it happened so fast," Janeway commented. "According to the doctor, only one part per million was needed to affect the crew members."

Kes gave Paris a smile along with his injection, and his mouth puckered in a silent whistle. *Yes, sir, things are certainly looking up.* According to the limited sensor data that was available, the *Kapon* trail was heading straight for the primary system. He was going to get to see the Hub after all.

CHAPTER
3

TORRES WAS GETTING TIRED OF THIS. SHE HAD DONE everything she could to get impulse power back on-line, but the system kept getting shut down by minor fault errors and command delays.

"Status?" the captain asked.

Torres tried to think positively. "We're running power off auxiliary fusion generators now instead of depleting our reserves. And I'm almost done valving the surplus plasma flow to the ship's emergency utilities network to replenish what we used."

"Approaching another buoy," Tuvok warned the bridge crew.

The buoy emerged into view, marked by official codes and brilliant yellow lights as if warning off trespassers. *Voyager* had been skirting along the boundary of the primary system, marked by the line of buoys, following the trail left behind by the *Kapon*. Using only thrusters, it was slow going. It seemed to take forever just to pass the buoy.

Torres clenched her hands, trying to hide the frustration that was shaking her entire body. The situation was intolerable. How could everyone sit here, content to travel at forty meters a second? They should be doing something, *anything,* to get more power to the ship.

"Are they still back there, Tuvok?" the captain asked.

"Nine vessels maintaining pursuit."

"They're persistent, I'll say that for them," Janeway grudgingly conceded.

Torres could barely hear Paris when he said, "They're vultures." But Vulcans had superior hearing, and of course Tuvok couldn't let anything as important as protocol lapse, even when everything else was spinning out of control. "Did you have a comment, Lieutenant?" Tuvok asked.

"I said they're *vultures,"* Paris repeated. "Did you think I called them Vulcans?"

"It doesn't matter what they are!" Torres snapped, gripping the sides of her engineering console. What she really wanted to do was hit the sluggish panel with both her fists.

She was lucky she was braced when the ship lurched, coming to a heart-stopping pause, then leaping forward again. Kim wasn't as fortunate, and he let out a muted cry as he was thrown against the mainframe of the gel packs.

"Systems failure in the velocity indicator," Paris said, as if they couldn't tell for themselves. "I'm getting it back on-line. . . ."

Kim crawled back up to the Ops terminal. "I'm reading falling pressure within the bioneural masses of the main core. The tissue may have been damaged when the shunts were severed."

"I looped those shunts myself," Torres retorted. "Only the junction nodes were touched."

"That shouldn't affect the rest of the ODN or the circuitry in the local subprocessors," Kim agreed.

The ship lurched again, and this time, Paris didn't bother announcing the obvious.

"We have to do something," Torres insisted.

"I'm taking suggestions," Janeway retorted, her face flushed from the effort of staying in her seat. "Do you have any?"

"We could disconnect the main core from the optical data network." Torres took a deep breath, watching the captain's reaction. "For some reason the systems are still trying to access the main core, instead of defaulting to the auxiliary computer. It's causing minor failures and shutdowns as the ODN sends back null signals."

Kim gave Torres a dubious look, as if he didn't agree. "Computing speed is already down ninety-four percent, and even if local subprocessors can operate routine systems—"

"They can," Torres interrupted. "And network processing should improve overall system reliability."

"I can't advise it." Even in the face of her conviction, Kim seemed uneasy. "The control unit is gone, but the main core continues to regulate the ODN. If you isolate the core, there won't be anything to keep conflicting courses of action from shutting down individual systems."

"Isn't that what we want?" Torres demanded.

"We need the safety overrides," Kim insisted. "Even if the ODN is operating slowly with many fault errors."

Torres made a derisive sound in her throat, but she managed to stifle her sarcastic retort. She'd made her point; now it was up to the captain to take control or they'd never get the ODN back on-line.

"Sickbay to Captain Janeway," Kes interrupted, speaking over the open tricorder.

Janeway picked it up with an irritation that Torres could certainly sympathize with. "Go ahead, Kes."

The Ocampa's voice was high and reedy through the small speaker. "The doctor's holograph program keeps shutting off—" She paused, then added, "He's back on again, but it's interfering with the treatment of our patients."

"We'll give priority power to sickbay," the captain assured her.

The doctor's irascible voice replaced Kes. *"Captain, the computer seems to be down at the moment—perhaps you could get someone working on repairs for the medical unit. And my holograph projector is malfunctioning again. If you want these people taken care of—"*

He didn't finish, and the short silence was followed by Kes saying, "He's gone again."

As if shifting mental gears, Janeway asked, "How many are seriously injured?"

"We've got fourteen people down here right now. None are critical."

Janeway sighed, obviously relieved. "How is Chakotay?"

"He hasn't recovered consciousness, yet. They've all had a neural stimulant, and they're in stable condition. But these malfunctions are interfering with the replication of the antidote."

"Understood," Janeway said. "We'll do our best. Captain out."

Torres almost held her breath in anticipation, as Janeway slowly turned and considered her. She couldn't resist putting in one last bid. "Captain, if we cut the ODN link to the main core, the network has to default data to the auxiliary computer or the local subprocessors. We may even get impulse power."

"As long as we can follow that trail, that's all we need." Janeway braced herself as another tremor shook the ship.

Tuvok took the opportunity to say quietly, "The vessels are closing. Distance, under thirty thousand kilometers."

"Very well, Lieutenant," Janeway told Torres. "You may proceed."

Torres wanted to clap her hands, but instead channeled the surge of energy into taking her across the bridge to the Jeffries tube. "I'll have to disconnect the ODN at the main junction node under the core."

One thing she could say for Kim, he was a graceful loser. "I'll make sure the radio links are shut down," he called after her.

Kim tried not to care when Torres left the bridge without answering him. He had to admit, if only to himself, the woman was intimidating. He hoped he wasn't letting his personal feelings override his professional judgment, and wondered if he should have insisted that this was a big mistake.

"Captain—" he started, but the sight of the rest of the bridge crew preparing for the procedure made him hesitate.

"Yes, Ensign?" the captain asked.

"Radio frequency links are shut down," Kim finished weakly. The captain had already made her decision, and now it was his duty to support her.

"Torres should be in position shortly." Janeway settled into her chair. "Mr. Paris, I'd like to pick up some speed if this works."

"Aye, Captain!" Paris sounded as if he couldn't wait.

Kim crossed his fingers, carefully making sure no one else could see. He hoped Torres was right.

Torres crawled through the narrow access tube to the junction node at the base of the computer core. Through the wire-mesh catwalk above her, she could see the three-story shaft in the center of the core. Blue nutrient gel was slowly dripping through the mesh on one side, sliming the interior of the access tube.

It wasn't easy working in a space the size of a small doghouse. Wondering why the designers hadn't foreseen the need for easy access to this junction, Torres closed the top port using the manual wheel. When the bottom port was also sealed, she flicked open the tricorder. "Captain, I'm ready to shut down the subspace field."

"Proceed," Janeway ordered distantly.

Torres keyed in the long command sequence that overrode traditional, Starfleet fail-safes and redundancies. Too many, if you asked her.

"Junction closed—" she started to say, watching the series of red indicators flick on.

The next thing she knew, she was slammed against the rear wall of the Jeffries tube.

The viewscreen leaped, and Kim managed to grab hold before the ship shot forward. In rapid succession, it executed a bizarre series of maneuvers, then froze, shuddering. Abruptly, the lights shut off, leaving only the red wounded glow of emergency power.

Kim realized he was draped over his console. The captain was fumbling with the navigation controls, while Paris was crumpled against the front wall under the screen. Stars were drifting across the viewscreen in a lazy, oblique slide as the Tutopan vessels scattered out of their way.

"No response from helm!" the captain called.

"Captain!" Tuvok called out. "Phasers firing."

"Override!" Janeway ordered.

But it was too late to stop the iridescent phaser trail that shot out, disappearing into the distance. Kim's throat caught as several more bursts were sent out in erratic directions, narrowly missing the one of the vessels.

"We are experiencing a spontaneous discharge," Tuvok announced flatly. "The electroplasma system is overloading."

A gravity flux hit the bridge, mashing Kim's face against the plasteel surface of the terminal. He was stuck there, unable to move, his heart laboriously pounding under the stress.

Then it released.

"Inertial damping malfunctioning," he announced, breathless.

"We can see that, Ensign." Tuvok still managed to maintain his air of calm, even with his shiny hair sticking up on one side.

Paris crawled back to his console. "Plasma valving into the warp coils from the power transfer conduits. Automatic venting—"

A flash lit the viewscreen, practically blinding Kim with the blue-white brightness of precious energy being dispersed into space.

"—of plasma injection system," Paris finished.

Janeway leaped for her tricorder. "Torres—get that junction back on-line!"

Torres realized she was lying on her back, staring at the curved ceiling of the tube. She could actually feel the ship moving, straining against itself. *This shouldn't be happening. . . .*

The captain's order got Torres moving, but her mind was still reeling with denials as she tried to get up. Half-dazed, she bent over the control panel, trying to remember the codes.

The ship lurched again, followed immediately by the captain's query, "Torres, report!"

"I'm trying . . ." the engineer called out, righting herself. What she really wanted to say was—*this shouldn't be happening. . . .*

The Ops control panel was off-line again, just as it had been before they reestablished the subspace integrity in the core. Janeway met Kim's gaze as she hung on to the rail, the tricorder clutched in her hand. *I knew this was a bad idea. . . .* But Kim didn't have the heart to say it out loud.

Kes called through the tricorder. "Captain? This is sickbay. Something's wrong with the doctor—"

"Kes, we need to keep this line open," Janeway interrupted.

"But he's just standing there, frozen. I can touch him, but his eyes are blank."

"Stand by," the captain ordered. "The core will be reconnected any moment." The ship shook and accelerated again. *"Torres."*

Kim felt the ship lift beneath him, and knew exactly how helpless an earthquake victim felt. He couldn't hold on through the violent bucking, as the ship let off another phaser burst.

Then abruptly they paused, hanging motionless.

"No response from helm!" Paris called out, frantic.

Kim tried to ignore the sinking feeling in his stomach. As his grandfather would say, "Looks like the jig is up!" Kim wasn't sure what that meant, but if it didn't refer to a situation like this one—drifting helplessly in space as a pack of pirates prepared to descend on them—then he didn't know what it could mean.

Suddenly, all systems powered up, obliterating the emergency lights.

Kim's ears popped, and he had to open his mouth wide to equalize the pressure difference. When he could, he said, "ODN is back on-line. Systems returned to Reduced Power Mode."

Paris was sitting with his legs braced far apart, just in case. "I have thrusters."

"We lost almost a quarter of our energy reserves," Kim added.

The captain stood up, tucking a stray strand of hair into her bun. "Ahead, on our original course."

Kim didn't know how she could act so calm after all that. Then he wondered if maybe it was no act, maybe this was just par for the course in Starfleet.

"Ahead at forty meters per second," Paris confirmed.

Kim decided to emulate the captain, even if he felt like mush on the inside. He quickly completed a level-five diagnostic. "Basically, we're back where we started. Systems are functioning intermittently."

"Vessels are retreating," Tuvok announced.

"Wouldn't you?" Paris asked. "After that little display, they don't know *what* we could do next."

"Holding at a distance of one hundred thousand kilometers," Tuvok confirmed.

Janeway sat down gingerly, as if she'd pulled something in that last tumble. "Not exactly what I had in mind, but it seems to have had the effect we wanted.

As long as they think were unpredictable and violent, they'll stay away from us."

"Maybe that's not the reason," Kim said, staring at the readings. He hoped he didn't sound as frightened as he felt. "There's a large structure dead ahead."

"The Hub?" Paris asked.

"Confirmed," Tuvok said impassively. "We are approaching a space station approximately fifty kilometers in diameter."

"Fifty?" Paris repeated incredulously.

Tuvok ignored him. "There is a break in the outer defensive perimeter delineated by the buoys."

On the viewscreen, the two ends of the line of buoys came together directly ahead, narrowing into a funnel shape that joined with the end of a long cylindrical structure. The Hub loomed beyond it in the distance, with the movements of dozens of ships clear even from their position outside the perimeter.

"The emission trail is fading," Tuvok informed them. "Apparently due to heavy traffic in this area."

Kim decided he didn't like looking down the maw of that cylindrical structure. Its exposed girders and platforms were made of some sort of melted material, and it seemed raw and unfinished. Yet the brisk warning lights and the careful line of buoys leading to the opening indicated everything was in perfect working order.

"Looks like a huge construction dock," Paris offered.

"They don't want us to go through that thing," Kim protested, eyeing the threatening structure.

"We may have to," Janeway said grimly. "If we want to find the *Kapon*."

CHAPTER
4

JANEWAY GLANCED AROUND THE BRIDGE AND REALIZED the ensign was voicing doubts many of them had. It was no wonder—they'd been so cautious about entering this system, yet look where it had gotten them. If she had a counselor on board, he'd probably be ready to have a seizure over the ragged edges that were showing in her crew.

After everything that's happened, how can I blame them?

Especially when their only option seemed to be that intimidating structure ahead. She wondered if that was the effect the Tutopans had intended. If nothing else, the utilitarian severity certainly indicated a lack of concern for the technicians who must maintain it.

She stood up, facing the perimeter structure. She'd learned from hard experience that when all else failed, the captain must maintain at least the *illusion* of control.

"Our processor was taken in there," Janeway told the crew. "And we're going in after it."

"Aye, Captain!" Kim instantly replied, even though she hadn't given him an order.

Janeway suppressed a smile, pleased that some old tricks still worked, even if it was only on young ensigns. "Tuvok, can you give me ship-to-station communications?"

"Affirmative," he said, as if he had been prepared for her request. "In emergency mode, the tricorder will send burst data transmissions directly to the transceiver network of the ship. However, the Universal Translator is off-line, and the signal will be decrypted only if the lingual patterns have already been recorded in the dedicated subprocessor."

"We've been dealing with Tutopans for days, I trust we'll be fine." Janeway adjusted the tricorder's mode operation, and opened a channel.

After a few moments the tiny speaker echoed with a hiss-garbled drone, "What is your business at Gateway Pol? What is your business at Gateway Pol?"

Janeway readied herself to speak, but Kim interrupted in a stage whisper, "Captain—data storage will be reduced in burst mode, so keep it short."

Janeway knew she looked sour, but she spoke into the tricorder, "This is Captain Janeway of the *Starship Voyager.* We're looking for the freighter *Kapon.*"

There was a hesitation, as if switching recordings. "Place your engines on standby and await further instructions. Place your engines on standby and await further instructions. Place your engines . . ."

A slight jolt shook the ship.

"What was that?" Janeway asked over the sound of the tricorder.

"The perimeter structure has locked on with a tractor beam," Tuvok replied. "Holding position."

"Barely," Paris added, trying to make helm cooperate. "I can't get it to respond fast enough. . . ."

The recording continued to blithely order, "Place your engines on standby and await further instructions. Place your engines . . ."

"Auxiliary fusion generators are being stressed to red-lines," Kim warned.

"Cut power," Janeway ordered. Every instinct told her not to give into such preemptory action, but if the auxiliary generators blew, they'd lose their last source of power. She spoke into the tricorder. "Gateway Pol, please explain why you have locked on to us with your tractor beam—"

The tricorder beeped, interrupting transmission. The green power level indicator was all the way down, and the red warning signal was fading even as Janeway examined it. "You're right, Mr. Kim, it does use a lot of primary power."

Tuvok stepped forward to hand Janeway a different tricorder. "Science tricorders have secondary generators. This one should last longer."

"Captain!" Paris called out. "We're being drawn in."

Janeway glanced up as the structure loomed closer. The open mouth was big enough to swallow a ship twenty times the size of *Voyager,* and the interior of the cylindrical framework was lumpy with globular units, deflector dishes and emitter grids.

"Any idea of the function of those devices?" Janeway asked in general, adjusting the science tricorder for ship-to-station communication.

"They appear to be scanners of some sort," Tuvok replied.

When she opened the tricorder channel, the recording was repeating, "Stand by for processing. Stand by for processing."

"Please explain the processing procedure." Janeway hoped her voice would carry the weight of her her demand, even if she did have to keep it short.

The recording continued to blithely repeat itself as they neared the structure. Janeway didn't want to waste tricorder power trying to fight with a nonentity, so she waited impatiently until a bored voice broke through. "Present your House identification."

"We have no House identification," Janeway replied. "Please explain why are you holding us in your tractor beam."

"Did you not request entrance to the Hub?"

"No, I didn't," Janeway replied. "We're in pursuit of the freighter *Kapon.*"

"For information you must proceed to the Hub," the voice said. "Stand by for processing."

"Wait—exactly what does this processing entail?" Janeway broke off with an indrawn breath as the structure seemed to leap forward, sucking them inside. A fuzzy red haze obscured the interior walls.

"Deflectors and tactical systems are being scanned," Tuvok announced. "Down to quantum levels."

"Shields?" Janeway asked, even though she knew the answer.

"Unable to block the scanners."

Abruptly, the red haze dissipated, and *Voyager* shot out the other end of the structure, turning slightly as it slowed. Janeway felt no movement from her ship, and had to admit the Tutopans knew stasis fields. She could tell the moment when the stasis shut off and they were under their own power again.

"Thrusters back on-line," Paris exclaimed, busy regaining control of the ship.

The Pol voice intoned, "Unaligned vessel *Voyager,* processing code 07531TG6, proceed along the indicators to receive your docking assignment."

"They got everything," Kim groaned. "They might as well have our structural blueprints."

"They may be able to use this technology," Tuvok commented.

Janeway didn't answer with the obvious retort—*I tried to stop them*—knowing the Vulcan was simply noting the facts.

Suddenly the tricorder blasted out a melodic run of notes. Janeway flinched as it was followed by a recording at least ten decibels higher and far more animated than any Tutopan they'd encountered thus far: *"Welcome* to the Hub! You have entered through gateway *Pol. Please* have your House identification code ready for the docking official. And *remember* when you *leave,* process through gateway *Pol!"*

Janeway tried not to be annoyed by the smarmy tone, but she was silently fuming at the search and seizure of their defensive capabilities. When Paris slyly commented, "I thought we weren't going to call attention to ourselves," she had a hard time restraining herself to a look that clearly said she was *not* amused.

Paris turned and bent over his panel with renewed concentration. She knew he was only trying to relieve the tension, which was certainly running high right about now. She knew everyone was missing Chakotay and the effect his calming presence had on the bridge; the way he fluidly filled every gap, reassuring the crew with his steady eyes and even steadier belief that everything in the universe would work out exactly as it should. She reminded herself to check on him when things slowed down a bit.

"Proceed along the indicators, Mr. Paris." She wondered what Chakotay would have thought of the Hub, a roughly egg-shaped mass spinning alone in space. Even from this distance, it was huge. "I've never seen an asteroid shell the size of a small moon."

"You are correct, Captain." Tuvok raised one brow. "A solid core of titanium still exists within the asteroid shell. Infrared readings are off the scale. . . ."

"How many people are on that station?"

Kim sighed. "Uncertain, but I'm getting high activity in the microwave and radio wavelengths. . . ."

"Are we reduced to the industrial age?" Janeway demanded.

Kim acted as if he didn't want to admit it. "Basically, yes. But I'm working on it."

"Do that, Mr. Kim." *Patience,* she reminded herself. But she didn't enjoy being in such reduced circumstances—her ship should have the capability to do almost anything she wanted.

Speaking of patience . . . Torres popped up out of the access tube as if she'd been ejected. Janeway forced herself to remain motionless as her chief engineer dashed forward with her relentless energy, already talking as she crossed the bridge. "That shouldn't have happened, Captain! I isolated the junction and there was no damage to the circuitry below the primary node. . . ."

Torres trailed off as Janeway continued to look at her. "I want to know *why* it happened, Lieutenant, not the reasons it shouldn't have."

To Janeway's relief, Torres immediately shut up, but the engineer gave the viewscreen a lingering look on her way to the starboard console. As a new line of official, yellow and black indicator buoys swung in, the fuzzy outline of the Hub began to resolve into ships of all shapes and classes tethered to docking spires sticking out like spines from the hull.

Strung between the official buoys were larger, much

more eye-catching units. These were complete with fluorescent, flashing lights and universal picture symbols of containers with fluid pouring out, and various stylistic renderings of humanoids that could conceivably be viewed as erotic. Or maybe she was giving them the benefit of the doubt. There were also brief snippets of discordant notes that must be what Tutopans considered music, and various booming advertisements reminiscent of the Gateway Pol greeting. Some of the sounds were untranslated, apparently not logged into the dedicated subprocessor.

"I've got the sound level down as far as it will go," Janeway said. "But the buoys seem to be compensating. Is there anything you can do?"

Tuvok looked pained, which stood to reason since his hearing was so much more sensitive than humans. "Negative, Captain."

When they reached the end of the line of buoys, *Voyager* had to wait behind another vessel that was holding position next to a small outpost station. Enforcer patrol ships, their hulls painted rusty red, were docked to the long pier at the rear of the station, while the ship ahead of them had the bloated, luxurious design of an interstellar passenger liner.

When it finally moved off, sinking like a rock down to the Hub, another bored monotone interrupted the obnoxious advertising buoys. "Unaligned vessel *Voyager,* processing code 07531TG6, state your business in the Hub."

Janeway had an extra tricorder ready in case Tuvok's ran out of power. "We are pursuing a freighter known as *Kapon.* They stole our main computer."

For the first time, there was clearly a reaction from one of the Tutopans. "You mean your memory banks were absorbed?"

"No, the core was left intact," Janeway explained.

"But the entire processing unit was removed. It happened while we were in the asteroid belt of your secondary system."

The monotone returned. "State your business in the Hub."

"I told you, we're attempting to locate the freighter *Kapon*," Janeway repeated. "This is an emergency situation."

There was a pause as if the docking official was accessing data. "Vessel *Kapon* . . . aligned House Min-Tutopa. Arrived last shift, transporting salvage cargo. There will be no charge for this information."

"No charge?" Janeway repeated incredulously.

"You may file a request for an appointment with an agent of House Min-Tutopa," the voice continued. "For no additional charge."

"Yes, I'd appreciate that," Janeway replied. "Let me talk to someone who knows what's going on."

The official didn't seem to notice her tone. "Please follow the indicator beacon to your docking assignment."

As if in response, a yellow ball shot out of the front of the station. It took up position directly in front of *Voyager*, then moved forward as if urging them to follow.

Janeway pushed herself up. "I'd like to file a complaint with your authorities about the theft of our computer."

"You must appeal to one of the Houses to receive sanctions from the Cartel."

"According to what you've told us, one of the Houses is responsible. Can't we appeal directly to the Cartel?"

"For sanctions? Against one of the Houses?" The official broke from his routine. "Where are you people from, anyway? The other side of the galaxy?"

"Yes," Janeway snapped.

As if taxed beyond reasonable belief, the official's interest disappeared. "Please proceed to your docking assignment," he intoned. "You're holding up the line."

The yellow beacon danced in front of *Voyager*, leading them a leisurely spiral down and around the Hub, as a stream of falsely upbeat advertising rolled through the speaker. When Janeway closed the channel, the beacon froze and began flashing urgently. It only moved again when she reopened the channel, while a recording admonished them to "listen for further instructions."

"A captive audience," Janeway said under her breath. Rather than continue to fume over the delay or the noise, she took the opportunity to call sickbay. Kes reported that the doctor's programs were still suffering intermittent failures, and they had only replicated enough antidote for half the crew so far. Ever the optimist, Kes added that everything was basically under control.

"Chakotay is conscious and requesting to return to duty," Kes added. "But the doctor wants to observe the effects of the antitoxin for a few more hours."

"Understood," Janeway acknowledged, setting aside the tricorder that was tuned to the sickbay frequency. She was starting to be surrounded by open tricorders—perched on Chakotay's chair, on her monitor—and she was having trouble remembering which ones were which.

"I swear we've passed that docking spire already," Paris complained. "PTO-four-three, yes, I'm sure of it . . . only we were heading in from the port side last time."

Helpfully, Kim offered, "There's a lot of traffic

around here; maybe flight patterns dictate a spiral approach."

"More likely that docking clerk has a twisted sense of humor," Paris replied.

Janeway kept her eyes on the Hub, noting familiar vessel designs as well as far more numerous ones she'd never seen before. There must have been a few hundred ships docked at the station, and once again, she remembered Chakotay's warning that they were alone in this quadrant.

That reminded her of something else. . . . She took deep, calming breaths, imagining the beach where her spirit guide lived. She saw herself lying on the warm sand, with the sun beating down on her bare skin as the salty breeze refreshed her with its coolness. She liked to think of her spirit guide lying next to her, stretched out on a rock, its scales reflecting the strong light as its tongue lazily flicked out to sample the air.

Chakotay would be proud of her. As the ship neared their assigned pylon, she didn't say a word of protest as *Voyager* followed the docking instructions dictated by the beacon.

Up front, she overheard Paris say to himself, "There comes a time when simulations end, and you find out what you're made of."

The pilot was actually sweating as he completed the difficult maneuvers, but if there was one thing Janeway trusted, it was that Paris knew how to fly. Her confidence was rewarded when the ship docked to the Hub with a whisper contact.

"Docking joints coupled," Paris announced, with something like a sigh. *"Finally."*

"Nice work, Mr. Paris." Two other ships were tethered to the same spire—the one to starboard was a large merchant vessel similar to the ones they'd seen crewed by Yawkins, an interrelated family group. To the port, a stumpy freighter was connected to the spire with elaborate coils of electrocable.

The beacon bobbed, and a final recording informed them, "Docking complete. Welcome to the Hub."

"Thanks a lot," Paris retorted.

"We'd have been here ages ago," Torres added. "If they hadn't kept interfering."

"I've never heard of such rigid docking procedures," Kim agreed.

Janeway felt practically serene after her pseudo-meditation. "Now that we're here, take all nonessential systems off-line. Torres and Kim—I'll want a full report on the damage to the ODN and the main core as soon as possible."

Torres joined Kim at Ops. "Aye, Captain."

"Tuvok, you're with me," Janeway added. She refused to endure any more faceless manipulations. "I believe we have an appointment with an agent of House Min-Tutopa."

Paris casually turned to stop her. "Captain, navigation systems are locked down, and there's nothing I can do until computer control is returned so . . . request permission to go off duty."

"Request denied," she said instantly. "Paris, you have the bridge."

"Me?" Paris glanced around dubiously. "But we're docked."

"Make the most of it while you can," Janeway told him with a brisk slap on the shoulder.

Startled, he straightened up. "Aye, Captain!"

Paris pretended to jab at his control board, waiting until Kim and Torres followed Janeway off the bridge. Then he slumped back in his chair. The sound of Kim's nervous voice trying to placate Torres had been even more irritating than Janeway's refusal. He'd already told the kid to give up, but he figured some people were too nice for their own good.

Shrugging off his jacket, Paris sauntered over to the captain's chair. Ensign Yarro at the environmental station eyed his gray undershirt, but she said nothing. *Ah, the privileges of command. . . .* Paris took his time, settling into the seat of power.

But he felt nothing. How could he, when they were stuck to the station like some dying parasite? His chin sank into his hand, as he brooded on the image of the Hub on the viewscreen. He could almost feel the teeming life within it, all those possibilities barely within his reach . . . and he was stranded on the bridge, a puppet-commander in charge of a papier-mâché ship.

His eyes narrowed at the blinking lights of turbolifts transporting people to the interior of the station. Everyone knew the only realistic thing a pilot could do in spacedock was go on shore leave. He swore to himself that he'd get into the Hub somehow . . . it was only a matter of time.

CHAPTER
5

Tuvok deduced from the captain's relaxed gait on the way to *Voyager*'s primary docking port that Janeway had achieved a measure of calm, despite the series of unfortunate events. Complying with her silent request, he refrained from postulating about their circumstances, intending to file a complete security report later.

He confirmed that the hard gangway had automatically extended from the docking pylon, allowing shirtsleeve access to the service deck. As Tuvok opened the port, he instituted a security lock requiring an authorized access code before entrance or exit would be permitted.

The small service deck was empty, yet Tuvok noted the existence of umbilical monitors, indicating the Hub was capable of full external support. *Voyager* would benefit from such a service, and he intended to include that fact in his security report.

Entering the docking lift, they were carried rapidly down the pylon. After 16.4 seconds, the lift slowed and abruptly made a 180-degree roll. The gravity maintained a steady downward pressure, yet the captain emitted a sound that Tuvok associated with the tendency of human digestive systems to react adversely to unanticipated motions.

Tuvok prepared to administer whatever aid was necessary, when the lift came to a halt with a brief flash of white light.

A computerized voice announced, "Scan complete. You have been granted access to Lobby Five-eight."

"Scan!" Janeway exclaimed, apparently controlling her autonomic reflexes. "They've scanned us?"

The door slid open.

"It would appear so." Tuvok didn't appreciate the personal invasion any more than Janeway did, but he continued to shunt the negative associations to a portion of his brain that would not interfere with his performance. He had already been grossly derelict in his duty in allowing the Tutopans to render the crew unconscious, and he fully expected the captain to log a reprimand in his permanent service record.

Upon leaving the lift depot, they emerged into a vast chamber. The three slanting walls met in a point at the center, approximately fifty meters in height.

"A pyramid," Janeway said, craning her head.

"Technically, this would be considered a tetrahedron," Tuvok informed her. "If this room is a reliable indication, the interior framework of the asteroid is constructed on the geodesic principle."

Janeway nodded. "Good choice for what's basically a round structure. Our docking spire must be connected to the base of this pyra . . . tetrahedron," she corrected herself. "How disorienting."

Her comment was made lightly, so Tuvok determined it was unnecessary to respond. Surveying Lobby 58, he noted two other lift depots that were of much larger dimensions. The activity of orange-clad support personnel, moving bulky antigrav pallets, indicated those lifts were used to off-load cargo.

The lower portions of the slanting walls were pierced by numerous windows and doors, apparently leading to businesses that supplied whatever one might need when visiting a space station. Higher up, the walls were dotted with floating advertising buoys and communications boards with rows of brightly lit and moving symbols. Humanoids and aliens wandered among the businesses, and lounged on the two terraces of what appeared to be an entertainment center suspended in one corner—the miniature tetrahedron was upside down, its downward point mirroring the echoing space above.

"Rather tame," Janeway commented. "Almost sanitized, I'd say."

Tuvok attempted to scan the area with his tricorder. "I am reading heavy subspace interference, due to differential gravity bases. My tricorder is unable to penetrate beyond this immediate location."

Janeway approached a centrally located post approximately five meters from the lift depot. When Tuvok examined one of the screens mounted on the side, he quickly determined that it displayed a general menu of options.

"We have to enter our processing code," Janeway pointed out.

Tuvok keyed in the sequence the docking official had assigned to *Voyager*. He ignored the three-dimensional tetrahedron that tumbled disquietingly in one corner of the screen, each side flashing vibrant colors, as he keyed through the menus. Although he was unable to directly access an agent of House Min-Tutopa, his request was immediately answered by the appearance of a three-dimensional map of the Hub.

The interlocking tetrahedrons that comprised the interior of the asteroid shell swung into focus as the map rotated on the screen.

"It looks like a crazy quilt my great-aunt Hedra had on the bed in the spare room," Janeway said, attempting to gain control of the map rotation using the touch sensors. Their current location was indicated, followed by the appearance of a dotted line, cutting through the map in odd angles.

"I believe this is the path we are instructed to take," Tuvok said.

"Yes, but what is that symbol at the originating point?"

She glanced around, as Tuvok indicated the corner to their right. "I believe it is some form of expressway."

"Oh, right. But what do these symbols mean?" Janeway was shaking her head as they finally determined the station transfers, while Tuvok took the opportunity to record the map with his tricorder.

"It doesn't matter how many degrees in applied physics or quantum engineering you have," the captain sighed. "Trying to find your way around an alien transportation system is still the hardest thing to do in the universe."

"Perhaps you should reconsider the direct approach, Captain," Tuvok cautioned, as per his duty as security chief. "Space stations are typically dangerous places."

"Never say die," the captain responded enigmatically.

Tuvok debated several responses, attempting to determine which would be the most appropriate, as they went through the pointed arch into the expressway. A few other people were standing on the platform waiting for a car, including several red-clad Cartel enforcers.

Tuvok kept a vigilant eye on everyone. One of his early assignments was on Deep Space Four, as part of the security team. It had given him the valuable experience of applying his tactical abilities on the individual level, combating criminals who engaged in petty theft, brawling, assault, and occasionally even murder. It was an assignment that Tuvok preferred not to repeat. Yet during those two years, he had been able to cohabitate with his wife, who had taken a sabbatical in order to be with him. They had been young, then, beginning their family. . . .

A rush of air announced the arrival of an express-way car. Almost chagrined by the slip in his Vulcan control, Tuvok protected Janeway from the jostling that accompanied their entry into the transport. He ignored his distaste at being confined in close quarters with a crowd of humanoids, bringing his senses to full alert. He did not intend to disappoint the captain again.

Tuvok was cognizant of the fact that the lights in the office were too bright for the captain. Janeway was squinting even as the clerk—who had kept them waiting for several hours—performed a quick intro-duction to Agent Andross. A large hologram filled the wall behind the agent, in the most opulent display he'd seen thus far of the sunburst symbol associated with House Min-Tutopa. The sun moved as if with the coming of dawn, complete with complex atmospheric formations that changed as the star passed through a deep blue-green sky to finally set in a burst of dif-fracted light.

Agent Andross rose with a practiced smile that managed to greet them without any noticeable warmth. Tuvok was prepared to speculate that Agent Andross had been counting on them to give up and go away. He also noted that the agent was markedly shorter than most of the other Tutopans they had encountered. The presence of a raised platform behind the desk indicated that physical conformity was indeed a desirable attribute in this society, yet here was an individual who had achieved high rank in spite of his difference.

Tuvok committed this data to memory as Andross gestured for them to take seats. "What can I do for you today, Captain Janeway?"

"I would like my computer processor returned," she told him bluntly, placing her hands on her thighs. "The freighter *Kapon,* while in your employ, removed it from my ship."

The agent's delicate, flattened features remained motionless as he focused on the smoked-glass desktop. The surface reflected the strong lights, but his behavior clearly indicated that there were access nodes and readouts beneath the smooth top. Tuvok knew there was also a ninety-two-percent probability that scanners were focused on himself and the captain.

The Agent's eyes lifted. "According to your processing information, your ship is a derelict."

"It wasn't derelict until the *Kapon* stole our processor."

Andross smiled at that, a mere stretching of his lips. "The *Kapon* sensor logs record that your ship was drifting off the asteroid ring in the secondary system when they boarded. They performed a routine salvage of equipment."

"They requested that we take our engines offline, so they could shuttle over," Janeway countered. "Do the *Kapon* logs show that? They offered us information on wormhole locations in exchange for star charts, but instead they knocked out my crew and removed our processor."

"I'm sure you must be mistaken," Andross said mildly, clasping his hands together on the desk. "Who ever heard of taking hardware and leaving the database behind? Yet according to this file, your memory core remains intact."

The captain's control was admirable. Tuvok had spent the last several hours productively analyzing the data on the neural toxin, determining the cause of its rapid dispersal rate. Janeway had had no such activity to occupy her mind, yet her calm demeanor didn't falter. "We were informed that the freighter *Kapon* delivered their cargo to you. We would like that cargo returned to us."

"Salvage was conducted within legal parameters," Andross said, beginning to stand up. "However, if there is anything else I can help you with . . ."

"Certainly, there is," Tuvok spoke up for the first time. He had calculated the risks of more forceful persuasion, and found them to be acceptable. "We request the name of your superior."

Andross had the grace to look startled. *"I* am an official representative of House Min-Tutopa—"

"Yes, we understand that," Janeway interrupted, following his lead. "But we'd like to speak to your superior."

"I have no superior on the Hub. The Board is in the Seat of House Min-Tutopa."

"Where is that?"

"Min-Tutopa is the third planet from the sun." Andross made a gesture as if flicking an imaginary particle off the top of his desk. "Under present conditions, it is impossible for you to speak to the Board at this time."

Janeway turned to Tuvok. "At the information booth, I believe you mentioned there were other agents listed as official representatives of this House."

"That is correct, Captain."

She started to rise. "Good, I'm sure one of them will be able to help us."

"Agreed." Tuvok checked Andross's reaction as he joined the captain. "I suggest we do so immediately."

Andross reached out a hand to stop them, moving markedly faster than he had under his earlier deportment. "This matter wouldn't be in their realm of responsibility."

"You aren't acting very responsible," Janeway pointed out, turning away.

Andross almost sounded hurt. "I am uniquely suited to my position. All Tutopans are placed in their careers according to stringent psychological and aptitude testing."

Janeway told Tuvok, "Let's go find another one of these handpicked agents."

"You don't understand—the *Kapon* is under my jurisdiction." He quickly added, "If you'd like to take your seats again, I shall see what I can do for you."

Janeway feigned reluctance as she sat down.

"Now, let me see," Andross said briskly. "What sort of computer were you interested in?"

"It's a processor," Janeway corrected. "The unit which selects programs from the memory and interprets them so as to direct the movement of data through the system, transforming input into operational instructions. It incorporates five FTL nanoprocessing units, controlled by modules of optical transtator clusters."

"Hmmm . . ." Andross murmured, his eyes moving imperceptibly from side to side as he accessed information through his desk. "I can give you a new

FTL processor by the end of this quarter, at a total installation cost of 6.300. What is your current credit balance?"

"I don't intend to purchase new hardware." Janeway leaned forward as if to make sure she was understood. "If that's the sort of help you're going to provide, we aren't interested."

"I see." Andross tapped his finger thoughtfully against the edge. "Since you've been caused some distress by the salvage procedure, I'll reduce our price to 5.300 and not a ducet less. You can't beat that for brand-new hardware."

In the silence, Tuvok calculated the time expenditure thus far, and concluded the logical course of action was to persist even in the face of such irrationality. The alternative was to begin the entire procedure over again with another agent.

The captain was apparently aware of this fact, and attempted another line of inquiry. "You obviously received our processor from the *Kapon.* Can you tell us where is it now?"

"As with any salvaged goods, debris is sent to rendering for scans to determine its viability."

"Could you trace our processor to its current location?"

"I could try . . ." Andross said hesitantly. "But you'd be better off accepting my offer."

Janeway looked him right in the eye. "Agent Andross, I suggest you locate our computer processor immediately, or we will be forced to bring this to the attention of your superiors."

"Of course." His expression remained affably nondescript. "I'll conduct an inquiry into this matter right away."

"I would appreciate an answer from you within the hour." Janeway rose again, this time making it clear it was final. "If we don't hear from you, I'll take my request elsewhere."

"Certainly," Andross said pleasantly. "And if I may, allow me to have my clerk summon a private transport to return you to your ship. I must say, you both look quite weary."

Janeway appreciated the luxury of returning to the ship in an automated car instead of fighting the crush in the expressway. But she knew it was to Andross's advantage that they didn't stop at another agent's office on the way back. Andross reminded her of used-starship salesmen she'd encountered before—far too self-interested to be trusted. She didn't even risk discussing the interview with Tuvok in the car; it was possible that Andross was recording their activity in order to glean an advantage in their negotiations.

So she enjoyed the ride for what it was worth, dialing up a vegetable beverage for Tuvok from the dispenser, and choosing a protein mixture for herself. She needed the energy after combating all these inanities.

When they reached Lobby 58, a group of Yawkins were waiting in the lift depot to return to their ship. Yawkins were ungainly, green-tinged humanoids, and these individuals were noticeably darker than usual. The noxious fumes emitted from their neck gills made Janeway retreat from the depot.

Tuvok followed her. "Is something wrong, Captain?"

She gestured a denial. "Let's wait for the next lift, shall we?"

"Certainly."

Janeway appreciated his unquestioning assent. A screen on the side of the depot showed a real-time image of the three ships that were tethered to the docking spire. *Voyager* was just disappearing as the view rotated to show the pudgy freighter. At the bottom of the screen, the vessel was listed as the *Oonon,* with the processing code and House alignment following. The excessive coils of electrocable encircling the *Oonon* took on a new meaning in light of her frustrating encounter with Andross—it seemed as if the crew of the *Oonon* were afraid their ship would be stolen right out from under them, even while they were in dry dock. Janeway tried to suppress her feelings of persecution, knowing that was not a position of strength. She needed to deal from strength.

The Yawkin vessel swung into view, and she waited impatiently to see *Voyager* again. Her proprietary pride was rewarded when the sleek lines of her ship appeared, reminding her of the last time she'd seen *Voyager* docked at a space station. That was in the Alpha Quadrant, on Deep Space Nine. Tuvok hadn't been with her then—it was before they had located him and the Maquis, before they were transported seventy thousand light-years away.

Janeway didn't mention it to Tuvok. The one (if only) thing the Vulcan had in common with Tom Paris was a facade of indifference at being so far away from Federation space. Indeed, one could make the argument that Paris was better off in this quadrant, but that wasn't true of Tuvok. She knew he missed his family. They all wanted to return home, and she wondered if she had let her own desire lull her into taking unacceptable risks.

Tuvok glanced from her to the screen. "We will find a way home, Captain."

She had to smile at his perception—even in the midst of chaos, some things never changed. "Was I thinking that loud?"

His expression softened into what could almost be considered affection. "I know my captain," he said simply.

Janeway stared at the image of *Voyager*, curving out of view again. "I hope you also know the gift of prophecy, Tuvok."

CHAPTER
6

THE FIRST THING CHAKOTAY SAW WHEN HE RETURNED TO the bridge was Tom Paris in his undershirt, lounging in the captain's chair. He was surrounded by the power-dead husks of half a dozen tricorders.

Several hours later, Paris was almost done recharging the tricorders from a portable unit he had carried up six flights from storage. Chakotay wasn't surprised Paris hadn't thought of it on his own, but he did take satisfaction in watching the young man work so hard.

With one of the powered-up tricorders in hand, Chakotay was telling the Cartel clerk in Ship's Services, "I'll give you the entire Denarii subspecies *and* the Hoop-sted Marn for three cycles . . ."

The commander turned in time to see Janeway emerge from the access tube, followed by Tuvok. The captain's delighted surprise at his presence on the bridge was a stark contrast to the monotone reply over the tricorder: "Your credit-offer is being considered. Please stand by."

"Good to have you back, Number One," Janeway said, as Chakotay stood up. "How are you?"

"I could have returned to duty as soon as I regained consciousness." He didn't mention that his recovery had been accompanied by drawn-out, demonic hallucinations that had contained recurring symbols as well as some he'd never seen before. The doctor's delay in releasing him from sickbay had given him plenty of time to meditate on the dreams and come to terms with their presence in his life, if not their exact meaning. "I ordered everyone in sickbay to return to duty when I realized how badly the doctor is malfunctioning. It's a good thing Kes is there. I recommend putting her in charge of sickbay."

"Agreed." Janeway's gaze dropped to his unbuttoned collar. "Are you sure you're all right? You look feverish."

Chakotay rubbed a finger against his temple, below the tribal tattoo. "It's the climate controls. Logs show that internal temperature has been rising ever since the processor was removed. Manual realignments don't seem to have any effect."

"Now that you mention it, it does feel warm in here." The captain glanced at the other members of the bridge crew. Most of them had their jackets off or their sleeves rolled up.

"Kim says some areas of the ship have been more affected than others," Chakotay added. "Engineering, the bridge, and the computer monitor room are considerably warmer than anywhere else."

"Have Torres and Kim submitted a report yet?"

"They're still in the monitor room, and the only report I've gotten is that it's hotter than Vulcan down there, and that conditions are somehow worsening. Environmental controls in particular are erratic, with

almost all of the circulatory systems malfunctioning."
He gestured to the view of the Hub, arching away
underneath them. "In your absence, I've been negotiating with the Cartel for ship-to-station umbilicals. I
offered them some of our more exotic plant DNA."

"Seeds?" Janeway asked. "You're trading seeds for
life support?"

"It seemed appropriate." Chakotay grinned.

The tricorder beeped, prior to an incoming message. "Your credit-offer has been accepted," a detached voice confirmed. "Please transfer the information to the utilities representative in order to receive
three cycles of Series I shipwide life support, including atmospheric and water processing, system power,
and thermal and gravitational control."

Janeway nodded to Chakotay, who immediately
replied, "Agreed. I'll meet your representative on the
service deck." He closed the channel and tossed the
tricorder aside, glad to be done with it. "They've
agreed to supply direct communication units to the
Hub, as well."

Janeway lifted one corner of her mouth. "Very
good, Commander. Perhaps you ought to conduct any
further trade agreements."

"I've had practice. Remember the Cordone'ni?"

"True." Her expression said much more as she
remembered that experience. "You may proceed,
Commander. Tuvok, you better assist Chakotay. Try
to keep them from doing any more scans."

"Aye, Captain," Tuvok replied, as seriously as if
accepting a life-or-death mission. Chakotay wondered
what had been going on while he was held captive in
sickbay.

"Lieutenant Paris," Janeway added, taking one of
the renewed tricorders, "you have the bridge. I'll be in
the computer monitoring room if you need me."

The last thing Chakotay saw as he left the bridge was Paris crossing his arms as he leaned back in the pilot's chair. He didn't understand why Paris looked so irritated. After his checkered past, he should be grateful that Janeway trusted him enough to leave him in command.

"We've got a real problem," Kim announced.

Janeway had been hoping to hear good news, but she didn't let Kim know that. "Can't you stabilize the computer systems?"

"The ODN is functioning fine." Kim was looking up from the temporary scaffolding erected in the central shaft of the core. A white cloth was knotted around his forehead, and blue smears of nutrient gel darkened his gray shirt.

"We think the problem is in the neural networks," Torres agreed, glaring at the severed bioshunt she had repaired. The collar of her gray shirt had been ripped open, and her hair was tied back to get it off her neck. Janeway had a flash of an old clip she'd once seen of marines going through an obstacle course—all the Klingon needed was a projectile weapon to fit right in.

Janeway ran her hand along the bank of synthetic brain neurons suspended in the blue nutrient gel. It used to be next to the processor, when they had a processor. "Were the tissue masses damaged?"

"Not directly, as far as I can tell," Kim said. "But two of the shunts that supply nutrient to the main banks were severed by the forcefield. The loss of nutrient may have caused some problems."

Torres argued, "That doesn't explain why the neural networks are reacting as if the processor is still here."

"How can that happen?" Janeway asked.

"Like isolinear chips, the neural networks are

primarily a storage medium," Kim tried to explain. He climbed up through the severed floor of the monitor room, sitting on the edge next to Janeway. "In the same way the nanoprocessors of isolinear chips enable them to receive and store data, the neural networks manage data configuration independent of LCARS control, processing it in a way that's actually faster than the faster-than-light processors."

"The bioneural tissue can't select operational responses," Torres countered.

"But somehow it's responding to ODN input." Kim winced at her glare. "Only it's sending back nonsense signals. That's what causes the system delays, with operations canceled because of orders from the main computer that conflict with the auxiliary computer and subprocessors."

"That's why cutting the junction to the main core should have worked," Torres insisted.

Janeway examined the sharp edge of the severed bulkhead. "It looks as if the processor was removed with surgical precision."

Torres grudgingly conceded, "The mainframe was gamma-welded to the bulkhead, but it's been sliced as easy as if it was crem-bi-lange."

"They knew what they were doing," Kim agreed.

Janeway surveyed the gooey remains of what used to be their main computer. "You know something, it doesn't look like you need an engineer in here."

"No?" Kim asked.

Torres was starting to look offended.

"No." Janeway undid the neck of her jacket. "What we need in here is a doctor."

Kim raised his head. "It is *bio*neural circuitry. . . ."

"With this damage, we'll be lucky if we still have a doctor," Torres reminded them.

Janeway tried unsuccessfully to raise Kes on the sickbay frequency. Several sections reported that the medical technician had recently been in their area, administering the antidote to the crew members.

Impatient with the archaic communication system, Janeway muttered, "I don't know how captains did it in the old days."

"I guess it took a lot more time to get things done," Torres said flippantly.

"Maybe more time than you think." Janeway opened her jacket all the way, then gestured for them both to follow her. "Come on—we've got five flights to climb."

They met Kes in the corridor outside sickbay. From her weary smile and the size of the portable medical unit, she was apparently returning from administering the antidote to the crew.

"How is the doctor?" Janeway asked.

"He seemed to be functioning once the power went back on. He insisted that I finish distributing the antidote."

The main room of sickbay was empty, but a clutter of padds and tricorders indicated the recent activity. Inside the examining room, Zimmerman was alone, working furiously over the empty table.

"Quickly, Kes!" the doctor ordered, as soon as he caught sight of them. "I need a splatlian smear and the ion analyzer, right away. I'm having difficulty stabilizing his vital signs."

Kes drifted forward as he spoke, her confusion clearly growing as the doctor bent over the examining table. "Doctor, what are you doing?"

"Ensign Navarro has suffered an ion-phase infusion." The doctor injected hypospray into the area where a patient's neck would be. "The rest of you will have to wait."

Janeway entered the examining room as cautiously as if there was a dangerous animal inside. "I suggest you run a self-diagnostic, Doctor."

His expression said more than words. "No time for that. All of you, get out of here! Can't you see I've got an emergency on my hands?"

"No, we don't see that," Janeway told him. "I order you to perform a self-diagnostic."

Zimmerman hesitated, as if ready to initiate a medical override. Apparently Kes recognized the signs as well. "Doctor," she said gently. "Ensign Navarro isn't here. That emergency happened two months ago."

Zimmerman blinked down at her, then up at the monitor. "Impossible . . . the diagnostic database confirms my sensor readings of the patient."

"There is no patient," Kes repeated.

Kim was examining the medical scanner. "This is what I meant. It's like the main core is sending out impulse echoes."

"Can you stop it?" Janeway asked.

Kim tapped the readout. "We could turn off the diagnostic unit. That may reboot the entire system."

The doctor was searching their faces, as if trying to understand. "Ensign Navarro isn't here?"

"No." Kes moved forward, touching the doctor's sleeve. "Are you all right?"

Zimmerman looked back down at the table. "No, I'm not."

The words were hardly out of his mouth when everything began to flicker—the lights, the doctor, the diagnostic monitor. For a brief disorienting moment, everything went black.

What the . . .

Janeway blinked as the lights came back on, wondering if she looked as surprised as the others. The doctor was gone and the diagnostic readout returned to neutral settings. She'd never seen anything like that before—even the emergency lights didn't kick in.

"Did you see that?" Kim asked, an edge of hysteria in his voice. "Did I do that?"

"I doubt it!" Torres snapped.

Janeway was turning to the open tricorder on the monitor as it beeped for attention. "Chakotay to Captain Janeway."

She upped the volume. "Janeway here."

"Sorry about that, Captain. The computer tried to override the umbilical hookup. We've got it stabilized now."

"That was some power surge," Torres muttered. "I better check the EPS conduits."

"Was there any damage?" Janeway asked Chakotay.

"I'll have to get to the bridge to find out. I'll keep you informed."

Kes apparently had other things on her mind. "Computer, begin program."

Zimmerman shimmered into existence, looking exactly the same as usual. "What is the nature of . . ." The doctor began, then stopped himself.

Janeway pushed the tricorder away, as Kes asked the doctor, "Do you remember what happened?"

"Of course. You left to complete the crew inoculations and I ended my program in accordance with Reduced Power Mode."

"He keeps experiencing these memory wipes," Kes explained to Janeway. "Every time he runs a self-diagnostic, it says nothing is wrong."

"It's not his systems, it's that direct computer link we established," Janeway reminded her. "Whatever is causing the malfunctions is obviously affecting the medical program as well."

The doctor's expression was unusually vulnerable. "Is there something wrong with my systems?"

"Don't you remember?" Kes asked. "The computer processor was removed from the ship."

Janeway had to admit that whoever programed Zimmerman's life signs had done a good job. He truly appeared to be concerned. "I can't remember . . . how could that be?" He pushed though them, heading to main terminal. "Logs, I must have recorded something." As he read, he slowly sat down. "Here it is . . . administered a neurogenic antidote to counter shock . . . Why can't I remember?"

Torres turned to Janeway. "He's obviously malfunctioning. He won't be able to help us."

"Maybe the medical database can give us some answers," Kim suggested.

Kes shot the captain a worried look. "What are we going to do about the doctor?"

Janeway was still trying to figure out an answer to that one when Tuvok arrived. The security chief held up some kind of portable communications device. "Captain, Agent Andross is attempting to contact you through the direct link to the Hub."

"Excellent." Maybe they were finally getting somewhere. Her gaze swept over the other four, making it clear she was including the doctor. "Do what you can, while I take this in the office."

Tuvok didn't need to be told to accompany her. She wanted a second opinion on everything that little Tutopan had to say.

The communications unit folded out neatly to sit on the desk. "A viewscreen," Janeway noted. "Who would have thought Tutopans would include that?"

The youthful face of Agent Andross filled the small screen as soon as Janeway opened the channel. "Captain Janeway, how nice to see you again." He certainly sounded sincere. She wondered why she felt so cynical. "I hope you're doing well?"

"We're holding our own." She leaned forward. "Have you located our computer?"

"The processor salvaged by the *Kapon* was transported to Min-Tutopa, to be installed as a backup processor in one of the local communications centers."

"What?!"

Andross hurried on, as if to prevent her from interrupting. "Although I have been unable to contact my superiors, I took the liberty of shuffling some data and arranged for you to receive a new processor for a nominal installation fee." He beamed at her. "There, now, didn't I tell you I would take care of everything?"

"That is not acceptable." Janeway moved her hand to the communications unit, prepared to close the channel if Andross didn't cooperate. "Unless you agree to return our processor, then I must continue my negotiations elsewhere."

"That won't be necessary." Andross summoned up a smile. "I was merely trying to provide you with the best possible deal. If you want your old hardware returned, I'm sure it can be arranged."

"Who can arrange it?"

Andross glanced down at the desktop monitor. "The processor is currently in Seanss Province, under the jurisdiction of Administer Fee."

"I'd like to speak to Administer Fee at once."

Andross keyed up something. "The next open appointment is in sixty cycles."

"Whatever a cycle is, it's fifty-nine too many."

Janeway controlled her voice with effort. "My ship has been severely disabled by the *Kapon*'s actions and I hold *you* and your House responsible. I want something done right now."

Andross stared at her. "Please, there is no need for this."

"You're out of time," she told him.

Reluctantly, he met her level gaze with something like respect. "The quickest way to speak to Administer Fee would be for you to go to Min-Tutopa."

She frowned. "Surely a subspace communications link would be faster."

He dipped his head, as if admitting a flaw. "Our administration is undergoing some turmoil right now, what with the Supreme Arbitrator yet to be selected. Business has practically ground to a halt," he added, as if he couldn't quite believe it. "Administer Fee is usually the most generous of officials with her time, yet I'm afraid your request wouldn't be taken seriously unless you went in person."

"I could take one of our shuttlecrafts," Janeway started to say.

"That would be possible; however, it would take several cycles to obtain clearance from the Cartel. If you prefer, I could take you in my private transport. I have prior contacts with Administer Fee, and I should be able to obtain an audience for you upon our arrival."

Janeway could feel Tuvok radiating disapproval at the suggestion. "Is that the only option?" she asked evenly.

"Aside from House-owned transports, there are commercial liners." He concentrated on his desktop again. "The next scheduled departure is tomorrow, making stops at two other provinces before Seanss. My transport could be ready almost immediately."

"Then I accept your offer." She didn't want to imagine what Tuvok was going to say. "I would like to bring along some of my technicians."

"If you wish; however, if there are more than two of you, I would be forced to petition the House for permits. Commercial liners carry exo-insurance for their passengers, while the House is responsible for any individual who travels on its transports—"

"I understand," Janeway interrupted, unable to endure another lengthy excuse.

"Then everything's settled." Andross looked truly relaxed, not a good sign as far as Janeway was concerned. "I'll alert my transport crew, and we'll scoot over and pick you up. That way you won't have to venture out again. I know how intimidating the Hub can be to new visitors."

Torres glanced through the glass wall separating them from the captain. Janeway was apparently deep in an argument of some sort, while as usual, Tuvok's expression revealed nothing.

Torres crossed her arms, trying to imitate the Vulcan's composure, as the holographic doctor took his time examining the ODN/computer schematics and the sensor logs of their attempted repairs since the removal of the processor. He kept making thoughtful sounds like "hmmm . . ." and "ah-ha. . . ."

"This is useless!" Torres exclaimed, when she finally couldn't endure it any longer. "There's nothing he can do."

Zimmerman looked up at Torres. "Perhaps not. It looks as if you've almost destroyed this system."

"It wasn't our fault the processor was stolen," Torres retorted.

"Did you intend to finish the job when you cut the main ODN junction to the core?"

Stung, Torres protested, "It should have worked."

The doctor pointed to one of the experimental summations. "According to Utopia Planitia guidelines, it is not recommended to sever the ODN from the main control unit."

"That's what I said," Kim murmured.

Torres glared at both of them, feeling guilty in spite of herself. "Starfleet's fanatical about safeties—that doesn't mean they're right."

"If you chose to ignore the guidelines..." Zimmerman trailed off with an ominous shrug, as if the consequences were on her head.

"I've had enough of this!" Torres had truly made an effort to control herself, but these holographic interfaces were all alike. They were obviously programmed by supercilious stuffed shirts who thought they knew everything. The last one she'd tried to argue with was the tutorial program at the Academy, and when she punched the image, it calmly informed her that a demerit was logged in her file. So she kicked in the interface projector, shorting out the entire library system and ruining a good pair of boots.

"I thought you wanted my opinion," the doctor said.

She turned away. "I don't need some *machine* telling me how to do my job."

"Apparently you don't listen to anyone," he retorted. "More's the pity for those of us who have to suffer for your mistakes."

Torres almost shook with fury. "Computer, end—"

"Wait!" Kes interrupted, before she could finish. "He might lose all the information he's recorded."

"It can't hurt to get his opinion," Kim agreed. "What do you think, Doctor?"

Zimmerman apparently took that as enough encouragement. "From what I can see, the spasms and subsequent paralysis of the ship's systems—including my own," he added dourly for Torres's benefit—"are a reaction similar to spinal shock, resulting from the transection of the brain from the spinal cord. The abnormal impulse transmissions may be a result of this severance shock and will wear off with time."

"We were getting false signals before we disconnected the core," Kim said hesitantly.

"And in case you forgot," Torres couldn't resist adding, "this is a starship, not a living organism."

"Actually, it's remarkable how similar the computer system is to an organic nervous system."

Janeway emerged from the private office in time to hear the doctor's last comment. "Any progress?" she asked the collective group.

"It's no use." Torres appealed directly to Janeway, knowing that at least the captain would be sensible. "He's acting as if the computer network is a patient."

"And if you're asking my opinion," the doctor calmly told the captain, "I'd say your ship has been lobotomized."

Everyone began to talk at once, as Janeway tried to make sense of what was going on. Torres was practically shouting, and Janeway thought it was remarkable that Kes won out, making her defense of the doctor: "The analogy is correct if you consider that the processor acts like the cerebral cortex—formulating sensory stimuli into understandable images and determining the appropriate response."

Torres snorted, pacing back and forth on the other side of the room.

"Do you have a recommendation?" Janeway looked at both Kes and the doctor.

The medical program instantly resumed a professional demeanor. "I agree with Ensign Kim's hypothesis that the erratic impulses are originating in the damaged bioneural tissue."

"But I'm not even sure the tissue was damaged," Kim said.

"The evidence is right here, in the falling pressure within the subspace field of the main core."

"What does that prove?" Torres demanded irritably.

"Typically, a loss of pressure indicates degeneration of damaged nerve cells." He pointed to the next column of the readings. "As you can see here, the pressure is now starting to rise as the tissue begins to regenerate. We'll have to guard against increasing pressure in the gel packs."

"Why?" Kim asked, obviously intrigued.

Kes answered, "Because increased pressure in neural tissue will collapse the nutrient vessels, causing all functions of the cells to cease."

"Can you control the rising pressure?" Janeway asked.

"Nonsurgically?" the doctor asked. "The shunts can be adjusted, perhaps, to maintain a consistent pressure. And we may be able to use a chemical agent similar to corticosteroids to reduce swelling."

"We should also provide protein to aid in tissue regeneration," Kes added.

It sounded to Janeway as if they had a bigger problem than they originally thought. "Will we be able to reconnect the processor to the main gel packs once we get it back?"

"That is uncertain," the doctor said. "While neural fibers are capable of regeneration, function is usually only restored in the peripheral nerves, not those in the central nervous system or brain."

An unpleasant silence followed his words. Even Torres seemed taken aback by the grim diagnosis. Janeway actually preferred that to open hostility.

"But we'll see what we can do," Zimmerman added in that falsely cheerful tone that doctors assume when they're trying to keep up their patient's spirits. "First, every bank of neural gel packs must be tested for ion content. And I'll also need samples of the nutrient fluid."

"You want us to *test* the tissue?" Torres repeated. "With what, a medical tricorder?"

Zimmerman looked down his nose at her, not easy considering he was seated. "Obviously we'll need qualified personnel to perform the tests."

"I can do it," Kes quickly offered.

Janeway looked from Kim's expectant face to Torres, standing as far away from the doctor as she could. "Ensign Kim, you work with the medical team to get the computer systems functioning—with or without the processor. Torres, you'll come with me."

Torres turned. "Where are we going?"

"To Min-Tutopa." Janeway could feel Tuvok stiffen behind her. "To get our processor back."

CHAPTER
7

Tuvok paused outside the door to Captain Janeway's quarters. Usually when he had something to discuss with the captain, he requested an audience while she was in her ready room. However, these were unusual circumstances, and Janeway was not likely to go to the bridge again before she left for Min-Tutopa. If he admitted it to himself, he was hesitant to disturb her in her private sanctum, but he would be derelict in his duty not to warn her about the risks involved in going to an unknown location without a member of Security for protection.

That thought prompted him to signal for entry.

"Come in" was immediately called out.

Tuvok entered, standing stiffly at attention within several meters of the door. "Captain, forgive me for disturbing you—"

"I'm glad you're here, Tuvok." Janeway was packing a small case. "You can help me carry that stasis generator. Kim suggested we should transport the processor under stasis to keep it from being damaged."

"Indeed, that seems prudent." Tuvok carefully picked up the rectangular case.

"Has Andross's ship arrived?"

"Not as yet. However, Mr. Kim requested that I inform you the turbolifts are in working order."

Her delight was a welcome sight after so much stress. "How did he manage that?"

"The ensign ascertained that systems which do not incorporate neural banks in their dedicated subprocessors could be safely isolated from the ODN." Tuvok resumed his stance at attention, the stasis generator easily slung over his shoulder. "The turbolifts and the shuttlebay have been successfully isolated."

"At least something's working right," Janeway sighed in relief. "I was dreading carrying all of this down five flights."

"Kim is currently attempting to isolate Transporter Room Two. However, the biofilter will be inoperational, and targeting scanners may not be capable of creating a transporter lock."

"Then don't use the transporters unless it's absolutely necessary." He averted his eyes as she folded her silky nightgown, cramming it into a corner of the case. "You didn't come here just to tell me that, did you?"

"No, Captain." His chin lifted. "I must protest your going to Min-Tutopa without adequate security protection."

"Don't worry, Tuvok. I'll have B'Elanna Torres along, and you know nothing could possibly get near me without having to deal with her first."

"That is one reason for my concern." He phrased it

carefully. "Lieutenant Torres is an excellent engineer; however, I do not consider her to be a reliable officer."

"I need a computer technician, and it was either her or Kim. Besides, you saw the way Torres was treating the doctor, they'd kill each other before they solved anything." Janeway snapped the locks on her personal case. "No, Torres has to go with me. I can keep her in line."

"I would prefer to accompany Lieutenant Torres myself," Tuvok informed her. "The away team will be isolated, and dependent on outside communications."

"You're saying I'll be on my own." The captain lifted one hand as if to pat his arm, but she stopped herself. "I know, Tuvok. But we've been given this opportunity, and it's essential that I go to negotiate."

"I do not trust Agent Andross. He has cooperated only under direct coercion."

"True." Janeway slung her personal case over her shoulder. "It's fortunate we figured out how to apply leverage on the agent."

Tuvok considered her carefully, noting the signs that told him she had made up her mind. "The Theolsians have a saying," he told her. "Consider the vulnerability of your back before you corner a desperate man."

"I'll try to be careful," the captain sighed. "But, Tuvok, what other choice do we have? We must get the processor back, and as soon as possible."

Tuvok bent his head in acquiescence. He had known the captain was not likely to relinquish this mission, and he had prepared special security measures for that contingency. His hand closed around the hypospray in his pocket. "The primary offensive weapon of the Tutopans would appear to be chemical nerve inhibitors. I have taken the liberty of consulting with Kes and creating an inoculation which should neutralize any gas used against you or Lieutenant Torres."

Janeway raised her brows. "That's more like it, Security Chief. Something concrete, something I can rely on."

Tuvok stepped closer to inject her. "This is perhaps the only factor you can rely on when dealing with the Tutopans."

She touched her neck, apparently feeling a slight sting as the medication was absorbed into her bloodstream. "I'll remember that."

Janeway stopped in front of the turbolift, adjusting the strap of her case. She was glad Tuvok was carrying the heavier one. "Are you sure the turbolift system is reliable?" she asked. "I don't want to start playing chicken with other lifts."

"Chicken?" Tuvok enunciated clearly, as if he might have misunderstood.

"An old expression for an even older game of bravado." Janeway passed it off. "I just want to make sure we won't crash headlong into another lift."

Tuvok briefly shook his head. "The turbolift system is operated by the network control computer. There is currently no link to the ODN, except through the direct audio nodes."

"Fine, then," Janeway agreed, stepping into the small space. "We won't try to talk to anyone."

She ignoring the memory of the recent malfunctions, forcing herself to relax and enjoy being whisked to the shuttlebay. She almost felt like the captain of a starship again, instead of some rodent burrowing through tunnels in the ground.

Yet her first sight of Andross's transport gave her an unpleasant jolt. It was parked in the shuttlebay in exactly the same position as the *Kapon* yacht had been—was it only this morning? She tried to tell herself that the similarities between the designs were Tutopan in nature, not necessarily anything more sinister, but Tuvok's warnings rang in her mind.

Tuvok met her glance, noting the same thing. He looked about as displeased as a Vulcan could, but Janeway wondered if anyone else would have known.

Torres was waiting next to the loading ramp, holding a bulky tool bag in one hand and a cylindrical personal case in the other. Tuvok took the tool bag from the engineer despite her protests, and preceded them on board.

The transport was small, yet luxurious by anyone's standards. The padded floor absorbed the sound, while remaining firm beneath Janeway's feet. The arched walls were cool blue, fading to white overhead where it was lit by a diffuse source. A casual grouping of recliners and cushioned benches didn't come close to filling the space. In the front, the crew were readying the ship for departure, while a young, smiling attendant gestured toward the rear. "Welcome aboard! My name is Milla, assistant to Agent Andross."

Janeway quickly introduced herself and the others, noting the woman's carefully tended appearance and the way the cut of her jumper clung to her spare body.

Milla led them to the rear. "This chamber has been reserved for your use."

Tuvok went in first. Inside the narrow compartment, there were two low couches. Janeway wasn't sure if it was her own interpretation, but she counted on using one of those as a bed. She ran her hand along the plush teal fabric, as Tuvok set down their bags.

Torres stumbled in after them, gaping openmouthed at the silver scrollwork along the moldings.

"Looks like a fancy jewelbox I saw once. I hope it can fly."

"That will be enough, Lieutenant." Janeway reminded herself to instruct the Klingon later on matters of discretion. Tuvok narrowed his eyes at several key spots, while Janeway memorized his careful indicators—that's where scanners and optical recording devices were likely to be concealed.

Andross appeared in the opposite doorway, which obviously led to his private compartment. "My crew has signaled we're ready to depart. If you'll follow the assistant, Mr. Tuvok, we'll be able to close the airlock."

The captain accompanied Tuvok back through the main compartment. Watching his eyes, she noted various other locations the security chief considered to be suspicious. She stood near the hatch as it shut, and her last sight of Tuvok standing with his hands clasped behind his back, made her wish she could have accepted his advice and brought him along. The final muffled clang of the airlock severed her from her ship.

Tuvok returned to the bridge to find that the commander had called together the senior officers.

Chakotay nodded as he entered the conference room. "Have a seat, Tuvok. I was just informing everyone of our latest problem."

Tuvok accepted the news impassively, seating himself next to Tom Paris. His other choice was to sit next to Neelix, and he usually avoided the little alien's proximity whenever possible. Kes and Ensign Kim were closest to Chakotay.

"I've spoken to Cartel supply," Chakotay told them. "They are capable of providing us with chemical compounds once we determine the exact formula we need. However, in return, they want information regarding the situation on Min-Tutopa."

"What situation?" Kim asked.

Tuvok told them, "Agent Andross mentioned that his government was undergoing a crisis pending the selection of a 'Supreme Arbitrator.'"

Chakotay nodded. "I read your report. The Cartel probably knows more than we do, but they seem to feel we're neck-deep in whatever political intrigue is going on in House Min-Tutopa."

"We may be," Paris muttered. "Whether we want to or not."

"We've adjusted the bioshunts, but that's not relieving the pressure in the gel packs," Kim told them. "The doctor believes it'll be necessary to treat the tissue chemically, beginning with a huge dose of corticosteroids."

"I don't trust the medical replicators," Kes added. "They were barely able to supply enough antidote serum for the crew, and there were an unusually high number of single-bit molecular errors. Since we're dealing with neural tissue, any deviation from a precise chemical formula could cause irreparable damage."

"Understood," Chakotay assured them. "I've been trying to negotiate with the various Houses, but they all told me to go to the Cartel."

Tuvok believed he knew the reason. "The Cartel may be applying pressure on the Houses in order to compel us to come to terms with them."

"I agree, and I don't like it," Chakotay said deliberately. "I want to find some other way to get what we need."

"I already told you." Neelix rocked back in his chair. "Other than the Houses or the Cartel, that leaves the darksiders."

"Again?" Paris groaned. "That worked real well last time."

"We don't have to go back to the asteroid belt," Neelix said. "There's bound to be darksiders in the Hub. We just have to find them."

Paris let out an exaggerated sigh. "Then you better let me go. I should be able to wrangle a chemical-supply contact out of someone."

"That will not be necessary." Tuvok wasn't fooled for an instant. Paris wanted to enter the Hub. "I will endeavor to locate the chemicals that are needed."

"You?" Paris laughed out loud, almost insulting if a Vulcan could be insulted. "This isn't exactly your type of territory."

"On the contrary, it is my job as security chief to undertake a mission of this nature." Tuvok wasn't willing to explain his credentials to Paris. "If you provide me with the chemical formula, I will locate a supply."

Paris appealed directly to Chakotay. "You can't send a Vulcan to dicker on the black market! It would be like throwing Kes into a roomful of Cardassians—"

"Hey, wait a second," Neelix interrupted, glowering at Paris. "Nobody's throwing Kes anywhere."

"I was just making a comparison," Paris tried to explain.

"Well, don't." Neelix stroked Kes's arm. "I don't like to hear things like that. Even if I don't know what a Cardas . . . dassen, a whatever it is."

Chakotay held up his hands. "Please—let's get this settled so we can get on with the repairs."

Kim spoke up, "Kes and I were getting ready to test the bioneural tissue, but I can help get the chemicals—"

"No, you get back to work on the computer."

Chakotay turned to the other side of the table. "Tuvok, I want you and Paris to find these darksiders and locate a chemical supply. Between the two of you, you should be able to come up with something."

"If you say so," Paris grudgingly said.

Only a lifetime of control enabled Tuvok to nod agreement without discernible irritation. Even Paris's wry expression seemed specifically designed to provoke him.

"We will return shortly with the contact," Tuvok told Chakotay, attempting to set a good example. "If I may suggest, since our communications system is off-line, I would like to provide all personnel who leave the ship with closed-beam beacons in case there is need for emergency transport."

"Good idea," Chakotay agreed. "But use it only if you have to. We don't want the Cartel asking questions about our transporters next." The commander pushed away from the table. "Very well—let's get to work."

CHAPTER

8

PARIS COULDN'T BELIEVE IT—HE WAS INSIDE THE HUB AT last, and who did he have as a companion? An uptight Vulcan whose main goal seemed to be to avoid all of the really interesting places. Even now, Paris could have been in the midst of the market throng below; instead he was stuck on an upper terrace, ordered to wait there until Tuvok returned for him.

Paris leaned his arms against the dingy railing, vicariously enjoying the hum and bustle that echoed into the high pointed ceiling. There were voices pitching their products, snatches of music and song, plenty of shouts and laughter. It was much better than that starched lobby at the base of their docking spire, but even though this market held the best possibilities so far, it still didn't seem out-of-the-way enough for truly serious illicit dealings.

"I believe I have established contact with an individual who can help us," Tuvok announced, joining Paris.

Only Tuvok could make a drug deal sound boring. "Congratulations," Paris said dryly. "Where is he?"

If a Vulcan could be pleased with himself, Tuvok fit the bill. "He will be along shortly."

"Psst," someone hissed behind them.

Paris casually shifted, bringing his tricorder into view. None of the Tutopans would know it wasn't a weapon, and anything complex would be viewed with respect until proved otherwise.

A vague form drifted back into the shadowed hallway, one of the many openings to the endless warrens within the slanted walls of the Hub. *That's* where Paris would start his search if he was in charge.

"Is that the guy?" Paris asked from the side of his mouth.

Tuvok boldly stepped forward. "Mr. Ippi?"

"Ippi?" Paris repeated dubiously.

The figure beckoned, retreating farther. Clearly, Ippi wasn't Tutopan, but in the darkness, Paris couldn't tell what manner of humanoid he resembled.

"That is the contact," Tuvok calmly announced. "Proceed with caution."

"You bet." Paris followed Tuvok into the hallway, pausing to one side until his eyes adjusted. He could smell the nervous sweat on Ippi even from this distance, and his pointed face was gray with station grime. Obviously he wasn't one of the lucky ones who could afford regular water rations to wash.

"Do you have the corticosteroids I requested?" Tuvok asked politely.

Ippi held out his hands. "What—you think I carry ninety quants of a drug on me?"

"Then where is it?"

"I go get it." Ippi snuffled, wiping a hand across the tip of his beaked face. "You sure you want ninety quants? That a lot of drugs, spacer."

"At least ninety quants," Paris said firmly. "For a start."

"Ninety quants should be sufficient," Tuvok contradicted.

Paris tightened his lips. Tuvok had no idea how to barter with the underworld. You were always supposed to let them think you'd need them again, and again, and again. . . . "Let us know where to get hold of you later," he added, ignoring Tuvok's look. "Just in case."

Ippi grinned, and Paris wished he hadn't. His mouth was toothless and black inside. "What—you plan on dosing your ship water supply? Maybe someday when you out there, bored on a run? Maybe you get things lively?"

"Actually," Tuvok said before Paris could reply, "the chemicals are needed for the treatment of our computer core. Our processor was stolen."

"Computer . . ." Ippi drawled. "Huh! I got some thing to tell about computer. There been odd thing lately with computer, if you can follow."

"No," Paris said sharply. "What do you mean?"

"What you give me for it?" Ippi immediately countered.

Again, Tuvok stepped in. "We will provide you with sufficient reward for any information you can give us. However, we would first like the ninety quants of corticosteroids."

Ippi snuffled again, sneaking a look at Paris, having apparently identified him as the heavy. "I got to get it from Hummer, but *first* he need the credit."

"No deal," Paris instantly replied.

"Then no deal," Ippi echoed. "What—you want me to get strung up for bothering Hummer with no credit in hand? Uh-huh, for ninety quants, you got to hand over some real info."

"I will provide you with a list of the DNA catalog," Tuvok said quietly.

Ippi shook his head. "Not enough. I want few sample of the info to show Hummer."

"You may have one sample DNA." Tuvok held out a hand to silence Paris's protest. "I was assured this is the way business is conducted in the Hub."

Ippi reluctantly considered the offer. "Huh . . . I guess that a deal."

Tuvok manipulated his tricorder, recording the necessary information and removing an isolinear chip. "Is optical data compatible with your system?"

Ippi gingerly took the chip. "Why not?" He waved the chip in Paris's direction. "You wait here. I come back."

Ippi darted into the shadows, his toothless grin the last thing Paris saw. It was criminal, really, but there was nothing he could do with a Vulcan leading the negotiation team. He turned away, kicking at the debris in the corridor. "We might as well go."

Tuvok blinked over at him. "Mr. Ippi requested that we remain here until he returns."

"Yeah." Paris wasn't going to try to explain. "Believe me, we've just seen the last of Mr. Ippi."

Kim couldn't believe it: Paris and Tuvok were able to gallivant around the Hub, consorting with all kinds of interesting people, and B'Elanna got to go to an exotic world with the captain to rescue their computer processor—while he was stuck crawling around the bowels of the ship. It almost made him wish he'd pitched a fit at the holodoc, too; maybe then he'd be on an exciting adventure himself.

"This is amazing," Kes whispered reverently. "I had no idea these tunnels penetrated the entire ship."

"Ow!" Kim exclaimed, bumping his forehead on a

low-hanging conduit. He sat down, rubbing his sore skull. "I don't see what's so amazing about it, every starship has Jeffries tubes. If you ask me, when you've seen one, you've seen them all."

"I think it's fascinating." Kes craned her head to see up the vertical tube that led to the deuterium-matter tanks. "You can get anywhere in the ship and never have to go into the corridors."

"Sure, if you never want to stand up straight again." Kim started forward again. "There's the module housing the lower bioneural masses for the main core. The upper modules are in the monitor room."

"How do we access the tissue?"

Kim opened the magnetic constrictors of the bulkhead to reveal the primary bioshunt, a collared conduit with its own monitoring system in the main joint. "We can pull a sample of the nutrient from here."

"Get some that's being siphoned off, as well," Kes suggested. "If the neural cells are being stimulated, there should be an abundance of potassium ions in the nutrient."

"This'll only take a minute." Kim connected a siphon tube to the shunt, making sure the other end was tightly inserted into the collection jar. The last thing they needed was more blue goo leaking everywhere. His gray shirt was already caked with the stuff, and he kept scraping his fingers through his hair, trying to separate the strands that were clumped together. Very unpleasant . . .

"Is it possible to make direct contact with the tissue?" Kes asked.

"Only if the subspace field is off—and last time that happened, the ship was reduced to emergency power." He watched the blue gel slowly push through the tube. "Theoretically, we could create a stasis field isolating a sample section, and then go in."

"Would that inhibit the impulse transmissions from the rest of the bioneural mass?"

He almost laughed. "Definitely."

Kes frowned briefly, then shook her head. "That won't do. I want to measure the currents flowing across the nerve-fiber membrane. Usually, I'd need skin contact with an electrode stimulator."

"Can't you do it through the chamber seals?"

"I'm not sure. It might present a broader reading, more like an EEG, but that could be informative as well." She prepared her equipment, placing small nodes on the clear wall of the chamber. The lights of the stimulator blinked on.

"You're getting a readout." Kim checked the containment tube. Only a few more decigrams.

"Maybe I'll leave one of these units down here so we can get a continuous reading." She reached for the tricorder on her belt. "I may be able to scan for the level of sugar glucose and oxygen supply. B'Elanna had the right idea when she suggested we use a medical tricorder."

Kim contented himself with a noncommittal shrug. He didn't want to be the one to disillusion her—Torres had been ridiculing the doctor when she made that suggestion. But Kes could get very protective of the holoprogram, and there was no need to upset her over something that no longer mattered.

Hours later, in Engineering, Kim was leaning against one of the mainframe supports for the warp core while Kes finished her tests on the neural gel packs linked to the subprocessor. It had been a long day, even before they started the testing, but Kes had insisted on visiting every bioneural mass in the ship, including the auxiliary computer core, which had truly horrendous access tubes.

Kim was ready to slide into a hot bath and stay there until morning. Maybe that would keep him from being stuck in a hunched position for the rest of his life. Unfortunately, the way things were going, he'd have the rest of his life before he got back to the designers who had created those Jeffries tubes, so he could give them a piece of his mind.

Kes straightened up from the module. "That's should do it."

"Good," Kim sighed in relief. "Let's get these readings back to the doctor so he can analyze them—"

He was interrupted by red-alert klaxons, and a computer recording, "Warning—antimatter containment field breach imminent. Section sealing."

"Move, Kes!" Kim shouted, grabbing her arm.

"There's nothing wrong with the containment field," she protested. "The warp engine is off-line."

The double-hulled isolation door started to lower in front of them.

Kim broke into a run. "Do you want to stay and argue?"

She puffed along behind him, saving her breath rather than answering.

Kim slid under the door, feet first. His head barely missed the lower edge of the descending bulkhead.

He reached back to pull Kes through, but the isolation door closed at his fingertips. "Kes!"

"Here," she said, behind him.

Lying on the deck, Kim looked around. "You made it!"

"I went through headfirst—I figured that was the

most important part." She smiled wanly, holding up the tricorder with the hours' worth of information. "That, and the tricorder."

Kim's ears started to ring as the pressure abruptly dropped. His hands instinctively pressed to his head, trying to protect the delicate membrane of his eardrums.

The red-alert klaxons cut off in mid-wail, and the regular lights flashed back on.

The computer intoned, "Antimatter containment field intact. Warp core ejection terminated."

With a perky chime, the isolation door signaled that it was ready to be manually reopened. Engineering personnel were starting to move around again, cautiously, as if ready to run at the first sign of trouble.

Kim rolled onto his back, his chest rapidly rising and falling. "I need a hot bath."

Kim dropped the collection jar on the table next to Zimmerman, and collapsed into a chair. This was their last stop.

As the doctor correlated the data from the tricorder with the computer schematics, Kim wrapped his arms around himself, shivering. In spite of umbilical support, sickbay was freezing, and he'd left his jacket back in the computer monitor room.

"Interesting," the doctor murmured. "The EEG readings show pronounced fluctuations in the low-level spontaneous electrical activity of the bioneural tissue."

Kim wasn't even sure what that meant. "Is that normal?"

"How should I know?" the doctor retorted. "Where is that experimental information I requested?"

"I gave you everything I've got so far," Kim said defensively. "I'm still coaxing information out of the memory banks. It isn't easy using a remote processor to search through the isolinear chips."

Zimmerman made a disapproving sound. "Well, from what I've been able to gather, the electrical readings could be compared to the sleep/waking cycle of animal brainwaves. There are synchronized, slow waves that mimic sleep patterns, while the low-voltage, fast activity reflects waking patterns."

"Are these fluctuations connected in some way to the erratic impulses—"

Zimmerman winked out, and Kim found himself talking to nothing. He jumped up, his hands clenched. "Where'd he go?"

"He didn't do it on purpose," Kes reminded him. "Computer, begin program."

Zimmerman appeared, his hands clasped in front of him. "May I be of service?"

Kim sighed, slumping back down in his chair. "If this keeps up, we'll never get anything done."

Zimmerman pressed one hand to his forehead. Kim realized the doctor was trembling, and beads of sweat were running down the sides of his face.

"Is something the matter?" Kes asked.

The doctor seemed to be at a loss. "I'm not sure. Rapid breathing, cold, clammy skin . . . perhaps I am suffering from identification with my patients. I appear to have all the symptoms of shock."

"You don't have any patients," Kim pointed out.

The doctor gazed around, growing more puzzled. "You're correct. I don't understand this. . . ."

Kes patted his arm. "Why don't you lie down?"

He tried to pull away. "I am merely exhibiting the signs of shock, I don't feel the symptoms."

"I don't see any difference," Kes gently countered.

Kim sat down at the computer terminal. At least the data were still on the screen. "There's a raised level of potassium ions in the bionutrient fluid, as well as evidence of unprocessed waste buildup. Maybe that's what's affecting the computer."

Zimmerman sat down next to Kim, holding two fingers to his neck as if testing his pulse. "I thought the computer was gone."

Kim groaned, wondering if they were going to have to go over everything all over again.

Kes didn't seem daunted. "You were analyzing the nutrient fluid of the bioneural circuitry."

"Ah, yes." The doctor looked up. "I created a special memory file on our work, in case of accidental interruption. Accessing . . ." He seemed to grow stronger even as they watched him. "Yes . . . now I remember. I was performing a pneumoencephalography to determine if there are any intracerebral hemorrhages."

Kim rubbed a hand through his sticky hair. He almost couldn't blame Torres for blowing up at the doctor. "Well, Doc, do you have any bright ideas?"

"Once the pressure is stabilized, our primary goal is to reduce the conduction of nerve impulses." The doctor got up from his terminal, pacing with his hand on his chin. "Let's see, if we can find some way to block the ionic currents from passing through the cell membranes, that should prevent transmission. That would require neutralizing the salt solution in the nutrient fluid, or we could try adding calcium ions—"

"Simple ionic influx," Kim agreed. "I could do that with a opthiographic device."

"Not through a chamber seal," Kes denied. "It's made to block ion leakage."

"Then that leaves the nutrient fluid as the least invasive method." The doctor sat back down, his fingers moving faster as they canceled the errors that popped onto the screen. "In other words—we'll try a local anesthetic."

"What about denervation sensitivity?" Kes asked.

The doctor explained for Kim's benefit, "Damaged nerve cells are particularly sensitive to circulating or directly applied drugs."

Kim thought enviously of Tuvok and Paris down in the Hub. "They're trying to establish a chemical-supply contact right now."

The doctor ignored him. "Now, which anesthetic would be the most appropriate? It must be a local affect, or it will shut down the entire ODN. Lidocaine hydrochloride might be compatible."

"What about tetrodotoxin?" Kes asked.

"Could be," the doctor conceded. "That's a powerful poison; but in minute concentrations it blocks the nerve conduction of sodium ion currents." His eyes narrowed. "Tetrodotoxin also has a unique history. It's found naturally on Earth in an organism called a puffer fish. I have legends in my memory banks of people consuming these poisonous fish, despite a yearly death rate in the hundreds." His expression showed his astonishment. "Now, I ask you, is eating such a sensory pleasure that corporeal beings would be prepared to die for it?"

"Not me," Kes said seriously.

"Don't encourage him," Kim whispered in her ear. "He's rambling again, and we can't waste time—"

"I can hear you," Zimmerman told him in a singsong tone. "Don't ever try that with a computer-animated being."

"I'm sorry, but I'm tired and hungry and sticky . . ." Kim started to explain.

"Can you select one, Doctor?" Kes asked.

The doctor was starting to sag, but he managed to make a few notations on the tricorder. Kes took it from his limp hand. "That's the chemical we need, and the quantity that should suffice for the bioneural masses on the ship. . . ."

Kes reached out to grab the doctor, but his arm was blurring in and out of reality. "You need to lie down," she insisted, pulling on the parts of him that were in focus.

"I'm a hologram," Zimmerman protested. "I don't need to lie down."

"You're a sick hologram," she said, firmly pushing him onto a bed. "And you need to lie down."

Kim was ready to call it quits and join the doctor on the next bed, but he couldn't ignore the fascinating question of why the holographic simulation was exhibiting signs of distress. "I wonder if the erratic impulses are causing him to react this way."

The doctor had one hand on his forehead, mumbling, "A normal biological reaction."

"That would be great, if you were biological," Kim told him.

"The computer has biological tissue." Kes pulled a silver blanket over the doctor. "And we have a sick computer. No wonder he's not feeling well."

Kim noted that it was the peripheral areas that were fading on the holodoc—arms, legs, and feet. "Why don't you just turn him off?"

"No!" Zimmerman suddenly shouted, grabbing for Kes. "I may never come back on again."

"Shh . . ." Kes soothed, shaking her head at Kim. "We won't turn you off."

"That does it." Kim hated to be outdone by a slip of a girl, but enough was enough. "I'll see you in the morning."

As he was leaving, he heard Kes tell the doctor, "Don't worry about the analysis. I'll take care of it. You just lie there and rest."

When Paris and Tuvok finally returned to the ship, a security team was waiting for them on the other side of the airlock.

"Stand still," Tuvok ordered, while one of the members held out a bulky security tricorder, circling them.

Paris rolled his eyes. "I'm fine—"

The security guard showed Tuvok the readout, and the chief keyed in several commands. "Certainly you are. Only two microscanners were concealed on your person. They have been disabled."

Paris held his arms away from his sides, starting toward the turbolift. "I'm getting out of these clothes before they self-destruct."

"Sir!" The female security guard called after him. "Commander Chakotay wants you to report immediately to the ready room."

Paris sighed, but waited for Tuvok to catch up. "It's been a long day."

As soon as they stepped through the door of the ready room, Chakotay asked, "Did you have any success?" He was in his usual chair near the desk, rather than in the captain's seat.

"Minor," Paris said dourly.

"Locating a chemical supply has been more difficult than we anticipated," Tuvok explained. "However, our next attempt should prove to be more productive."

"I did get these," Paris offered, showing a handful of silver disks from his pocket. "They're passes to some of the private clubs."

Tuvok broke from his stance. "I was unaware you purchased these items."

"I had to do something while I waited for you," Paris countered. "I got in a *brateel* game with some of the core miners and won these."

"How did you learn how to play *brateel*?" Chakotay asked.

"I had nothing to do on the bridge but watch the open broadcast channels on the Hub communication lines. *Brateel* is no different from any other game of dice . . . and besides," Paris said, shrugging, figuring he might as well admit it, "I cheated."

Tuvok apparently took that as a personal offense. "Our mission was to locate a chemical-supply agent, not engage in shore leave, Mr. Paris."

"Important information is exchanged in places like these clubs," Paris insisted. "It's where people meet and do business. Besides, it was when I was playing *brateel* that I heard news about some recent computer thefts."

"What computer thefts?" Chakotay immediately asked.

With a sly look at Tuvok, Paris told him, "There's a bunch of beaked humanoids running around the Hub who are apparently the eyes and ears of the dark side. I met one called Rep, who told me there's been at least three other vessels that limped in here missing their computers. Most of them were smaller than us, and one was boarded with deadly force."

"Now, why would anyone want old computers?" Chakotay asked, narrowing his eyes.

"What makes it even stranger is that the Tutopans have a form of chemical replication technology that's even more energy-efficient than ours. Making new computers would take less effort than stealing them."

"So material goods are of little consequence,"

Chakotay murmured. "No wonder information is the valued commodity."

"From what Rep says, people usually deal in salvaged goods because they're much harder to trace than replicated material. Salvage can slip by the official channels."

Tuvok's lips were in a tight line. "We appear to be involved in a larger conspiracy."

Chakotay glanced at the empty captain's chair. "I hope the captain isn't in any danger."

"We won't know that until we find out what's going on," Paris warned.

"Very well," Chakotay said. "Get some sleep and you can go out again tomorrow. Kes has given me the chemical formula of an anesthetic that may eliminate the erratic impulses." Tuvok nodded shortly, turning to leave, as Chakotay added, "Paris, I'd like to have a word with you."

Paris was relieved that he didn't have to be the one to suggest a private talk. As door closed behind Tuvok, he could tell the Vulcan wasn't pleased, but he couldn't pinpoint exactly what part of his nonexpression gave it away. Then again, maybe he was imagining things.

"Why didn't you consult Tuvok on your *brateel* scheme?" Chakotay demanded. "He was in charge of this mission."

Paris didn't want undermine the security chief's authority, but he had to say it. "Because every time I *did* consult with him, he managed to mess everything up. Sir, meaning no disrespect for Tuvok's competence, he's impossible when it comes to bargaining with these lowlifes. He's too . . . *Starfleet.*"

"Aren't you Starfleet, too?" Chakotay countered.

Paris gave him a look. "Sure, I was trained Starfleet—so were *you.* But if I may say so, sir, both of us have seen the underside of Federation space, and we know how to use that experience."

"That is true." Chakotay bent his head, unsuccessfully hiding his smile. "What do you suggest?"

"Commander, you have to let me go alone. I could have made the contacts we needed in half the time without Tuvok."

Chakotay shook his head. "You can't go into the Hub alone, it's too risky."

"Then let me take Neelix, maybe he can help. Anyone, except for Tuvok."

"Perhaps this is simply a way for you to experience the wild side of the Hub," Chakotay ventured.

Paris had to grin. "I'm sure I'll get an eyeful, sir. But I'll also get your chemicals, and I'll find out more about these computer thefts. Isn't that what you want?"

Paris held very still, trying to look innocent, as Chakotay considered his suggestion. "Very well, Lieutenant, try it your way. But I expect results."

"You can count on me."

Chakotay didn't seem to be very reassured. "Don't take any unnecessary risks, Tom. And have Neelix go along with you. You may need someone to cover your back."

Paris wasn't bothered by Neelix going along. He waited until he was outside the ready room before he tossed one of the silver passes into the air, neatly catching it in his other fist. The jingling sound reminded him of Dabo markers, and he started to whistle as he stepped into the turbolift. Finally, things were looking up.

CHAPTER
9

JANEWAY HAD BEEN RIGHT—THE COUCHES DID MAKE FINE beds. Milla even provided them with light blankets, though the ambient temperature was perfectly comfortable.

When they woke, Milla offered them the "nourishment of your choice." With a straight face, Janeway asked for coffee. She didn't expect Milla to return with a steaming hot cup of the best Vienna Roast she had ever tasted.

"That's an indication that other people have come here from the Alpha Quadrant," Torres mused, deep into the Tutopan version of steak and eggs. "Or they wouldn't have the chemical specifications."

"I suppose." Janeway held the cup to her nose, inhaling the scent and thoroughly savoring it while she had the chance. She sometimes wondered how Torres could stay so slim with the way she ate. It must be that fantastic Klingon physiology—or else it was the endless exercises she did to burn off her aggression.

Agent Andross didn't emerge from his private room until they began their approach for a vertical landing. Looking down, Janeway saw the rooftop grid of an enormous complex in the center of an even bigger city. Transport lines converged on the complex from eight different directions, and it had obviously been built up over centuries, with towering spires marking every level change and corner. The transport was so smooth that Janeway could hardly tell they were descending as the points of the spires rose up around them.

Janeway waited until Andross had seated himself for the landing. Even though he hadn't been present, his subtle maneuverings had been clear—the interior lights had been dimmed to a more comfortable level for human eyes, and last night the assistant had served the same protein beverage she had selected in the private car. Janeway couldn't trust a man who was that quietly observant, that smoothly efficient and goal-oriented, making her suspicious of his every move.

"What is this place?" she asked Andross.

"This is the House Seat, Seanss Province."

Torres wandered out of the rear compartment at the sound of their voices, taking a seat nearby.

"When can we meet with Administer Fee?" Janeway asked.

"Your appointment is scheduled for tonight, after the Board adjourns."

"What about now?" Janeway asked bluntly.

The ship landed with a subtle jar, and the hum of the engines shifted as the thrusters disengaged. The smiling assistant opened the airlock and stepped to one side.

"Administer Fee won't be available until I've arranged a meeting," Andross explained. "Usually, petitioners make appointments several months in advance."

"But you yourself agreed that the situation is urgent." Janeway stood up, and Torres moved behind her, silently backing her up.

"That is why I brought you here."

Janeway stepped in front of Andross, blocking him from leaving the ship. "No, I don't think that is why you've brought us here. And unless you start being honest, I'm going to corner every Tutopan I can find and get some answers for myself."

"I don't understand—"

"Yes, you do."

Agent Andross was breathing faster, obviously chagrined at being cornered again. "If you insist." He motioned for Milla to step outside, then he closed the panel between them and the crew. "There is a rule for everything in Min-Tutopa, and a way to get around every rule. *You* are my way around a certain rule that has been . . . hindering me."

"Explain," Janeway ordered.

"Agents of the Hub are not granted leave to return to Min-Tutopa except in extraordinary cases. Otherwise, I too must petition to the House for a return permit, and under current conditions—with the Board in a stalemate over the Supreme Arbitrator— my request wouldn't even be considered."

His bitter undertone almost convinced Janeway. Until now, he had maintained a scrupulously professional facade, using his politeness almost as a shield.

Of course, Torres pointed it out. "You sound as if you don't like the way things are done around here."

Andross shrugged. "At times . . . I must confess, I am frustrated. We lose sight of why things are supposed to be one way and not another, such as allowing only two of you to accompany me. Yet, I've sworn to uphold the rules of our society."

"You just said you're using us to get around one of those rules," Janeway reminded him.

"I work from within the system to make change," Andross said evenly. "I don't apologize when I take opportunities that arise, even when I must acknowledge it is not within my right to do so. I serve, to the best of my ability."

Janeway wondered at the way he said it. . . . "Whom do you serve?" she asked.

Andross actually smiled at that. "I serve the Board. However, my patron to the Agency was Administer Fee, and the Seanss Province is my home. Bringing you here gives me the opportunity to visit my friends and family—I have not seen them for almost a rotation." He spread his hands wide. "So you see, you have caught me in a selfish act."

"An understandable desire." Janeway smiled in return, hiding her doubts. "However, we have our own needs. Has Administer Fee been informed of our situation?"

Andross gestured to the door. "If you will allow me to leave, I will let her know you've arrived."

Janeway gave him her most charming smile. "I'd like to accompany you since you're going to see Administer Fee."

"I wish that were possible," Andross said regretfully. "I myself will only be able to snatch a few moments of the administer's time until the Board adjourns. Rest assured, I will remind her of the gravity of your situation."

"I see."

Janeway realized she would get no further with him at this juncture, so she acted as if she had been convinced, allowing Andross to lead them from the transport and down into the bewildering passages of the complex. They walked for some time through white corridors, unbroken except for door after identical door. The assistant, Milla, and several attendants trotted behind them, carrying their baggage. Torres kept casting a wary eye over her shoulder, as if making sure the Tutopans didn't disappear with their things.

Finally, opening one of the doors, Andross gestured inside. On either side of the main room, Janeway caught a glimpse of chambers similar to those of his luxurious transport ship. "All your needs should be provided for," the agent told them, showing them the communications panel next to the door. "Please ring for one of my assistants if you require anything."

Smiling his way out, Andross briefly put his hands together in a triangle. Apparently, it was a Tutopan sign of respect. Janeway wasn't sure why this was the first time he'd given it to her.

When he was gone, Torres wasted no time in turning to Janeway. "This is absurd! Why don't we just get a new computer processor? It's got to be easier than *this.*"

"All of the ship's operations depend on that processor," Janeway countered. "We have a long way to go, and I don't want to rely on hardware we know nothing about. No, I intend to make every effort to have our own processor returned intact."

"Then why do you keep letting him get away with this?" she demanded.

"What do you think Andross is doing?" the captain countered.

"He talks as if he wants to help us," Torres complained. "But he always ends up saying no."

"Yes, he's quite good at manipulating the system to his own ends."

Torres irritably picked up a delicate blue vase, giving it a cursory glance before setting it back down. "I don't understand why you don't . . ."

"Don't do what? If I had kept protesting, I'm sure he would have found some way to confine us here. But *this* way . . ." Janeway went to the door and pushed the sensor pad. It slid open, revealing the empty corridor. "We can have a look around for ourselves."

Torres's eyes lit up. "Now, that's more like it!"

Paris glanced around the bar, figuring that darkness really was the universal bid for anonymity. He made a cautious round of the large three-sided room, avoiding the corners and keeping an eye on the shadowed nooks. There was a lot of activity near the rear doorways, apparently leading to private rooms deeper within the walls. He couldn't see the pointed ceiling, but he had to assume there were recorders and scanners trained on him from up there.

Paris had dragged Neelix into this particular bar after finding out it was known for attracting minor employees of the Hub, as well as various undesirables from within the Houses. This place was more his style than the last few clubs they'd tried—it was an old-fashioned "knock 'em down and drag 'em out if they can't take it" kind of bar. No talent trying to sing or dance on the flimsy stage, only hardworking locals in here. Paris had been able to make a chemical-supply contact in one of the fancy tourist joints, now he was going for dirt on the computer thefts, passing time until the contact confirmed their deal.

As if responding to his thoughts, the receiver chip his contact had given him buzzed against his palm. He slipped into a dark booth, motioning across the room for Neelix to join him.

Paris made sure the plasteel door was securely shut

before slipping the receiver chip into the slot. A nasal Tutopan voice informed him, "Your offer has been accepted. Ninety quants of corticosteroids, and three quants of Texteroxide will be delivered via runabout to *Voyager,* docking pylon BVO-nine-hundred." A string of code checks followed, and the time of arrival was vague, but Paris agreed, figuring that was as much as anyone was going to get.

The receiver chip was ejected in a smoldering ruin. Paris didn't bother picking it up, busy reciting the code checks to make sure he remembered them. He'd seen the beaked bums doing a brisk business in salvaging waste chips and returning them for recycling credit. Paris wasn't reduced to that, not yet. He still had a few credits from the last round of *brateel.*

The door banged open, and Neelix sang out, "You got it?"

"Shut the door!" Paris jerked the smaller man inside. "You'd make a lousy undercover agent."

Neelix seemed unphased. "Didn't the deal come through?"

"It did." Paris repeated the string of code checks. "Can you remember that?"

Neelix waved a dismissive hand. "No problem. Let's see . . . that was 'Oovi sentix denar' . . . or was it 'Oovi denar sentix'?"

Paris impatiently repeated the code, with Neelix mumbling it along after him. "It's our verification to receive the supplies."

Neelix brought his hands together with a sharp clap, grinning. "Then what are we waiting for? Let's get out of here!" He reached into the breast pocket where the small beacon cylinder made a bump. "They can *beam* us from here. No one can see."

Paris stopped him. "We've only accomplished one part of our mission."

"Tuvok told us to arrange for the delivery of the chemicals," Neelix protested.

"We need to find out more about this rash of computer thefts. Don't you want to know why it's happening? Captain Janeway and Lieutenant Torres could be in danger."

"Well . . . when you put it that way," Neelix agreed grudgingly.

"Good, you stay back and keep an eye on things." Paris narrowed his eyes. "I saw a Cartel janitor drinking alone. That's just what we need—if we can get a few minutes' access to one of their terminals, then we could hack into the computer—"

"We can?" Neelix stared at him. "Which one of us is supposed to do that?"

Paris frowned. "Okay, so my plan needs a little work. But you get the idea—at least it will get us access to their files. You've seen what happens when I try to buy docking and manifest information; people run away like we're spies." Paris opened the door to the receiver booth. "Just back me up—that's an order."

"Sure," Neelix agreed. "I just hope you know what you're doing."

Paris made another quick survey of the bar—you could never be too sure in a place like this—before sauntering over to the counter. He ignored the turned heads; he'd been getting a lot of attention tonight. Neelix had it easy—his species had been seen in these parts before—and he slunk off to one side.

Paris exchanged small talk with the tender while she poured his drink. She was almost pretty, to judge from Tutopan standards, with pale peach-tinged skin and white wispy hair. Her flattened features resembled a stylized mask to his eyes, but the look wasn't without a certain charm.

He overtipped her. Then he gestured with his chin to the Tutopan wearing the janitor's signet, slumped at a nearby table. "Looks like a regular in here."

The slightest backward move revealed her distaste. "What do you want with Tracer?"

"Someone told me Tracer might have what I want."

"Tracer doesn't have anything." Her monotone grated on his ears. "Will that be all?"

"Yes, thanks." Paris took a sip of his drink. Neelix had taken a seat near the back, where he could see both the counter and the janitor's table. His grin looked distinctly nervous.

I don't like this place, not one bit, Neelix was thinking. There was a lot of movement, as indistinct forms shifted vantage points inside the bar. And there were too many eyes watching him and Paris. The two of them obviously didn't fit in, despite the dark industrial-strength coveralls that Tuvok had suggested they wear in order to blend in with the Hub employees.

Neelix snorted. Lot of good that was doing.

Then he saw one of the beaked aliens who infested the dark side of the Hub. It scanned the room until it saw Paris, then jittered up and down in excitement before darting back outside.

As Paris approached the janitor's table, the beaked hominoid returned with a huge Tutopan following right behind. He looked as if he had just come off duty from construction mining, with his arms and face covered by stains of dark mineral dust.

Neelix quickly stood up, realizing it was one of the Tutopans that Paris had played the strange game with earlier. They were far too interested in Paris to be up to any good.

* * *

Paris stopped next to the janitor's table, holding his drink. "Hey, Tracer. How about a game?"

Tracer lifted his blank eyes from the holographic display of some version of solitaire. "I don't know you. In fact, I've never seen anything like you."

"I'm a human, from a planet seventy thousand light-years away."

"Is that far?" Tracer said absently. "You know, you look sort of like a Crestian, only your eyes and nose are squished together and you don't have enough hair."

Paris blinked. "I don't?"

"Yeah. It's weird."

"Gee, thanks." Paris sat down. Tracer seemed more curious than malicious, so he might as well take that for an introduction. "I bet you see a lot of aliens around here."

"Not like you. You're different."

Paris took a closer look. Tracer's dogged insistence on the obvious was either due to low brain power or the potent drink that was almost empty in front of him. Then he realized that Tracer didn't look like the typical Tutopan—his ruddy skin was mottled, ranging from dark reddish brown to white patches. Even in the dim light the discoloration was clear.

Seeing a possible opening, Paris hitched his chair closer. "You don't know what it's like, being different," he confided. "When I walk through a room, anywhere I go, people turn and stare. When I try to talk to them I can feel them looking at me, not really listening, while they're thinking how strange I am and wondering how awful it would be to look like me."

Tracer's eyes widened, his flat face taking on a pathetic eagerness. "Yeah . . . always looking at you. Staying far enough away to keep from getting contaminated . . ."

"Like they might catch something from me," Paris finished for him. "As if I've got some kind of sickness."

"Yeah . . ." Tracer mumbled soddenly into his drink. "Nobody gives you a chance."

Paris put his hand on Tracer's arm, ignoring the greasy stains on the worn sleeve. "We just have to face it, Tracer, the universe is filled with idiots." He lowered his voice. "This Hub is filled with idiots."

"Tha's right!" Tracer lifted his glass and downed a swallow. "Tutopans are vacuum-suckers! Only aliens are worth spit. Even weird-looking aliens like you."

"That's right," Paris echoed agreeably, ignoring the gibe. Maybe he'd be able to use that curse someday—vacuum-suckers. "We've got to stick together—"

"Hey, spacer!"

Paris shot the big Tutopan an irritated look, hating to break his roll with Tracer. Then he saw Neelix stumbling through the tables, pointing frantically behind him. Paris turned to see one of the beaked humanoids they kept running into—what was his name? Rep. The one who told him about the computer thefts last night.

"I'm talking to you, spacer," the Tutopan said ominously. "Cheat anyone else at *brateel?*"

Paris realized he was in the middle of a Situation. "I know you—you're Bladdyn, right?"

The threatening glare on Bladdyn's face was answer enough.

Paris's chair toppled as he stood up. "Relax, big guy. Let's go where we can talk about this." Paris grabbed Tracer's arm, hauling him to his feet. "Come on, buddy."

Tracer mumbled something in surprise, but followed Paris a few steps before trying to pull free. "Hey, what's this got to do with me?"

Neelix pushed the janitor from behind, pressured by Bladdyn breathing down his neck.

Paris murmured, "It's an opportunity you won't want to miss—"

"You cheated me," Bladdyn hissed past Neelix, shaking a fat fist at Paris. "A whole night's worth of R and R."

"We can work this out," Paris said soothingly, hoping he'd make the last few steps to the receiver booth before Bladdyn blew up.

"I'll show you!" Bladdyn's flat face wrinkled at the nose.

Paris wasn't sure what was coming next—more threats or a maniacal rage that would leave him pulp on the floor of the bar. He didn't wait to find out. He thrust his hand into Neelix's pocket, snatching the beacon cylinder and ripping his coverall in the process.

Neelix was thrown off balance, stumbling in front of Bladdyn and giving Paris time to shove Tracer into a receiver booth. Paris dove in on top of him, kicking the door closed as he activated both beacons. Before the lock could hit, he dropped one of the beacons down Tracer's neck, trying to keep the door closed against Bladdyn's pounding.

As he dematerialized, he hoped Neelix had the presence of mind to get out of the bar while Bladdyn was busy trying to figure out where he had disappeared.

Paris and Tracer materialized on the transporter platform.

Paris smiled at Tala, the Bajoran ensign at the console, glad to see a familiar face again. He had never noticed how cute those nose ridges were, until he'd been inundated with flat Tutopans. "Good thing the transporter works through those gravity bases."

"Where's Neelix?" Tala asked.

"He'll be along," Paris said shortly.

"Who's that?" she asked next, pointing to Tracer.

Tracer shuffled to the edge of the platform, his eyes bleary and his mouth pursed into a tiny round opening. "I think I'm gonna be sick."

"Sit down," Paris told him, hoping it was a false alarm. "Before you fall down."

Tracer had trouble lowering himself. Then his feet shot out from under him, and he landed hard on his rear end. "I mus' be ripsy, I keep passing out. Where am I?"

"You came with me to my ship," Paris told him. "Don't you remember the expressway ride?"

Tracer swayed slightly, obviously trying to think.

"Lean back, and close your eyes for a minute." Tracer immediately did as he was told, as Paris went to the transporter console. "Do you have a map of the Hub?"

"Yes, Tuvok recorded a three-dimensional diagram while he and the captain were in the Hub." Tala called it up before he had to ask.

"I need to go there," he indicated. "Keep an eye on Tracer here, and I'll be right back."

"Don't forget to report to Tuvok!" she called as the door slid shut behind him.

After putting out an all-points bulletin on the open tricorder channel, Paris finally located Harry Kim in the computer monitor room. The ensign was scraping blue gel off the walls. "Nice job you got, there, Harry."

Kim frowned up at him. "Don't ask what I was doing this morning, you don't want to know."

"I've got something that will cheer you up," Paris told him.

"Oh, yeah?" Kim asked. "I hope it's the anesthetic."

"It's on the way. Which reminds me, do you have a tricorder?"

Harry climbed up from the core, handing over his tricorder. Paris recited the code checks into it before he forgot them. "We'll have to get this to Chakotay. He'll need it when the runabout arrives with the chemicals."

"It better get here soon—"

"Stop complaining, Harry." Paris gave him a little shove. "You're coming with me to the Hub."

"Me?" Now the kid was looking sharp. "Why?"

"I need some computer help. Come on."

"Now?" Kim glanced around. "We're barely keeping the ODN going as it is."

"I'm trying to get our processor back," Paris tempted him. "But if you prefer this . . ."

Kim wiped his hands on a rag. "I'm coming."

When they reached the transporter room, Tracer was softly snoring on the steps of the platform. Paris glanced at Tala, who shrugged in return. "He hasn't moved."

"Who's that?" Kim asked.

Paris shook Tracer, waking him up as he pulled the janitor to his feet. "A local contact who's willing to get us into an office with a computer terminal. But we've got to get back before he starts sobering up."

Kim examined the sodden, snorting Tutopan. "You brought him through the transporter?"

"He's drunk—he won't remember a thing." Paris positioned Tracer in a wilting heap on a disk. "Let's go."

"I need clearance from Tuvok," the Bajoran protested.

"It's all clear," Paris said, definitely and without qualification. Tala's hand hovered over the controls as he ordered, "Transport, Ensign."

His slight emphasis on rank did the trick. "Yes, sir."

Kim asked, "Hey, aren't I supposed to have a beacon?"

"It's down his shirt." Paris gestured to the dematerializing Tracer. "Don't worry about a—"

CHAPTER
10

B'ELANNA TORRES COULD REMEMBER NIGHTMARES LIKE this—wandering in a maze of bland corridors and endless doors leading to more endless halls and archways. The textured walls glowed with an unseen light source, casting no shadows and leaving her with few points of reference. Everything was so repetitively similar that she started to wonder if they were going in circles. Even the people they encountered looked alike, with their expressionless faces and beige, draped clothing. Her dark hair and forehead ridges were getting a lot of attention, and she felt as if she were back in school, when the other kids had called her mutant and ugly. That was before she learned to strike out first, before they could hurt her.

Apparently, Janeway wasn't disheartened. When Torres expressed her doubts, the captain grinned and told her, "Tuvok and I found our way through the Hub, and nothing could be as difficult as that."

"We've been walking for hours. Are you sure you know where we're going?"

"Absolutely," Janeway replied. "We're going to the center of things."

Torres thought about that a moment. "How do you know that's where we want to go?"

"Because Tutopans have a remarkably symmetrical view of life. I'm sure we'll find what we need when we reach the middle of this complex."

Torres shut up after that, contenting herself with following the captain. Despite the shock factor of their appearance, none of the Tutopans tried to say anything to them until they reached a busy reception hall. From Janeway's discussion with the guard, she gathered this was where the Tutopans conducted their "testing" and they wouldn't be allowed through.

Janeway finally gave up trying to convince the man, and turned away. "Onward," she said with a sigh.

"But he said we couldn't," Torres pointed out, trying to hold her temper.

"Then we'll have to go around."

They had to climb almost to the top level to get past the restricted area, but their perseverance was finally rewarded when the corridors widened and gradually became more busy. Torres was frustrated by the leisurely pace of the Tutopans, but Janeway fell in with the crowd, and she was forced to do the same.

A slight crush at an archway momentarily blocked their view; then Torres stepped forward onto a terrace overlooking a vast atrium. She could see numerous other corridors opening onto the atrium from every level, and the terraces seemed alive with people. A small structure was in the very center of the ground floor, but there seemed to be no other reason for this much open space.

"Look!" Torres exclaimed, pointing down. "Isn't that Andross?"

Janeway narrowed her eyes. "That's him, all right."

His legs rapidly scissored as he crossed the floor among a group of people, going away from the central structure. It was difficult to keep sight of the little Tutopan, but the woman in the middle was impossible to miss. She was taller than nearly everyone, and her slender, erect carriage took her through the confusion with a direct purpose that the others didn't possess.

"Now how do we get to him?" Janeway tried to see where the stairs led down to the floor.

"Easy." Torres leaned over the railing, putting her hand to her mouth. "Andross!" she bellowed. "Hey, Andross, up here!"

Janeway grabbed her arm, but it was too late. The noise level abruptly fell as every Tutopan in the atrium turned to look. Torres hadn't expected that.

Andross was staring up at them as if horrorstruck. People were starting to make the connection between them and the agent, and a subtle hum rose as they commented among themselves.

"Come on," Janeway said. It sounded like her teeth were clenched. "Might as well bull it through."

"I thought that's what you intended from the start," Torres said defensively.

"Not quite," the captain said dryly.

When they reached the bottom of the stairs, Andross was waiting for them. "What are you doing in the Council Chamber?"

"We were curious," Janeway said lightly. "So we decided to take a walk."

"You managed to get all the way from your lodgings to the Chamber without being stopped? That's unheard of!" He looked from the captain to Torres, incredulous.

Torres shrugged. "We acted like we knew where we were going."

It was almost worth everything to see the way he struggled to maintain his composure. "I know where you're going now—back to your lodgings."

"Aren't we free to look around?" Janeway asked innocently.

"Nobody is!" he bit off sharply.

The captain considered him closely. "I think I like you better this way, when you aren't trying to sugar-coat things."

Andross stiffened, a defensive response that immediately brought Torres to full alert.

Janeway saw it, too. "Was that Administer Fee?"

"Yes, and you can rest assured, you made your presence known." He glanced around, lowering his voice. "Do you know how many regulations you've broken? If someone decides to detain you, there's little I could do."

"When do we get to see Fee?"

"Not until tomorrow—"

"Tomorrow!" Janeway dropped her good-natured pretense. "You said we'd see her tonight."

"That's impossible. She has prior appointments."

A slender man, not much bigger than Andross but considerably older, was approaching. His arrogant swagger was accented by a slim black stick he used as support, and he was surrounded by people in the same way Administer Fee had been.

"Oh, no, here comes Hamilt." Andross turned, trying to get them moving. "Let's go upstairs, and I'll explain."

Janeway resisted, and Torres already knew she wasn't going to budge until they had convinced this twisty little man to keep his commitment.

When Andross realized they weren't going to be able to avoid Hamilt, his flattened features slipped into pleasant lines. "Board Member," he greeted. "How gracious of you to take time to speak to me."

Hamilt's lips stretched, and a delicate hand smoothed his sparse hair against his head. Torres defensively met his narrow black eyes, and she didn't like the way he dismissed his followers with a negligent wave of his stick. The other Tutopans instantly scattered.

"I heard that you'd come back," Hamilt told the younger man.

"There was some trouble I had to attend to," Andross explained, gesturing vaguely in the direction of Janeway and Torres.

"Of course there's trouble," Hamilt agreed, his focus completely on Andross. "And I'll not have you come here and make matters worse, my boy. Your work with the Eldern was done when you persuaded him to sponsor those debates."

"I am here at the behest of Captain Janeway," Andross informed him. "I didn't intend to make an appointment with Member Eldern."

Janeway took advantage of the pause to step forward. "I'm Captain Janeway of the United Federation of Planets. I'm attempting to locate the computer processor that was stolen from my ship. We were in the secondary system—"

"The request came through Cartel channels," Andross interrupted. He spread his hands wide, smiling at Hamilt. "I'm simply doing my job."

"Buying salvage, is that it?" Hamilt asked. "My boy, it sounds to me as if you should pay more attention to business and less to policy, or you'll be collecting junk for petty credit the rest of your life."

Torres blurted out, "Junk!" But Janeway shook her head, and she managed to choke off the rest of her protest.

Hamilt ignored them, seemingly amused by Andross. "However, I'm sure this is a matter of considerable importance, as is everything you do."

Andross shifted slightly. "I'm dealing with it in the most expedient manner, Member Hamilt."

"I'm sure you are."

Andross simply smiled in answer, trying to usher Janeway forward as if to continue on their way.

Again, the captain resisted, planting her feet firmly in front of the board member. "We had intended to see Administer Fee tonight, but apparently she's occupied."

"Indeed? Administer Fee?" Hamilt intently turned, directly addressing her for the first time. "You have business with Fee?"

"Our computer processor is in her possession."

"Imagine that," Hamilt said lightly, but his thoughtful glance at Andross said far more. "As a matter of fact, Administer Fee will be at the tournament tonight. Perhaps you'd like to come as well. I'm sure you'd find the opportunity to speak with her there."

Andross's mouth opened, but nothing came out.

"Certainly, I'd appreciate that," Janeway quickly agreed.

"But, it's a tournament," Andross started.

"It's no bother," Hamilt assured him. "I want you to come, my boy. And bring that pretty lady assistant of yours. I haven't seen her in far too long."

Andross was breathing faster, and Torres knew from personal experience the signs of someone trying to control himself. "How can I refuse?"

"Then you'll come, and by all means bring these important business associates." Hamilt gave Janeway a slight nod. "Federation of Planets, did you say? Always welcome, anytime . . ."

Torres could tell Janeway was only waiting until the board member drifted away. It was nauseating the way his supplicants immediately returned, gathering around him until he was hidden from view.

"Why did you lie to Hamilt?" the captain immediately demanded. "The Cartel didn't intervene on our behalf."

"No, they didn't." Andross relaxed his shoulders, as if giving up. Torres wasn't fooled for a moment. "Our House is in a desperate situation with the Board in a stalemate over the choice of the next Supreme Arbitrator. I couldn't resist the opportunity you provided to return here."

"I couldn't care less what your motives are," Janeway told him. "I only want to know if you intend to help us get our computer back. Or was that a ploy, too?"

"How do we even know it's here?" Torres put in.

"I told you," Andross said sharply. "Tomorrow, I'll take you to examine your precious computer. I'm doing everything I can to make sure it's returned to you—but you must cooperate. By blundering around the Seat and letting officials like Hamilt know exactly what you want, you put everything at risk."

"Why would he try to keep us from getting our processor back?"

"There could be a hundred different reasons," Andross said, as if it was obvious. "Whatever ways he could use to his advantage. He would do anything to interfere with Fee's business, and since I openly began supporting Fee for the Arbitrator's position instead of him, Hamilt has been hindering my operations as well."

Torres shook her head. "That's disgusting."

"That's business," Andross corrected. "Everyone

manipulates the information they have in order to get what they want. *You* understand that."

"You're right, I do," Janeway told him. "The question is, are you going to help us or not?"

"I'll arrange for you to speak to Fee tomorrow morning, first thing, but you can't go to the tournament tonight."

Torres made a sound in her throat, but Janeway didn't need prompting. "Not good enough. You promised us that we'd see Fee tonight, and since you weren't able to arrange it, I'm accepting Member Hamilt's offer."

"You saw Hamilt's reaction," Andross protested. "Your sort of business means nothing among these high-level officials. He intends to shame me in front of my colleagues who still make policy, while I have been exiled to an Agency in the Hub. If I lose power, my ability to help you will be directly affected."

"All I want to do is talk to Fee tonight," Janeway insisted. "And work out some way to get our processor back as soon as possible."

Andross threw up his hands. "If that's the way you want it, but please, do me the favor of keeping your mouths shut about the salvage to anyone else. Especially to Board Members Hobbs and Sprecenspire, the Cartel supporters. It sounds more legitimate if you keep your purpose here vague. Just say it's province business with Fee, you understand the sort of thing I mean."

Janeway frowned at the agent. "Is it that important?"

"You're in the House Seat, now, and the tests can have serious consequence." He stepped back to consider them from head to foot. "Do you have anything more . . . refined to wear?"

Torres let out a snort. "You call *that* a serious consideration?"

Andross's gaze lingered for a moment on her forehead ridges, before turning away with a slight shudder. "I'll have Milla find something acceptable for you both to wear, or you'll stand out terribly."

"We will anyway," Janeway pointed out. "You don't let many aliens on your planet, do you?"

"No," Andross said shortly. "And I'm beginning to understand why."

As the slanted walls of the Hub materialized around them, Paris heard Tracer cry out in terror.

"No! No, I'm sorry," Tracer wailed, his mottled hands hiding his face. "I won't do it anymore! I swear on the three Kisars, I'll never have hot wisto again—"

"Take it easy, there, buddy." Paris tugged Tracer's arm, dragging him through the corridor as he quickly scanned the door signets. "You just blacked out again."

"What are we looking for?" Kim whispered, glancing back along the empty corridor.

"This one," Paris said, stopping in front of the correct symbol. "Waste Reclamation, auxiliary control."

"Waste?" Kim asked. "Why this?"

Paris drew Tracer closer to the door, and pressed his wrist badge to the identification pad. A loud ping and a blue glow announced the door had been unlocked. "It's a low-security area, but the terminals must be tied into the main computer to coordinate with the other systems."

"Good thinking," Kim told him, as Paris opened the door. A puff of chemical-tainted air hit them in the face. "I think," he added dubiously.

"It's perfect," Paris insisted. "You should be able to access manifest records, and anything that has to do with computer salvage."

It was dark inside, except for the control panels glowing amber and blue. Kim quickly located the main network terminal. "I hope you know what you're doing."

Paris winced, remembering Neelix had said exactly the same thing. Where was Neelix now? Instead, he said, "I got us in here, didn't I?" as he pulled Tracer farther inside.

Tracer was looking around as if he was starting to sober up. "How did you get in here? This is a restricted area—"

"You let us in, remember?" Paris checked behind a few doors, until he found a storage closet. "You wanted to help us."

"I did?" Tracer's eyes were still uncomprehending.

Paris gave him a hearty shove, right into the tiny closet, slamming the door shut behind him. With nothing else handy, he turned and swung his elbow back into the touch pad. A spray of sparks lit the room as the cover plate smashed, shorting out the electro-magnetic field.

After a shocked moment, sounds of muffled knocking came from inside the closet. It grew more frantic as Tracer realized he couldn't get out.

"Did you have to do that?" Kim asked without looking up from the terminal.

"You heard him. He was going to make trouble." Paris checked the door. "Would you hurry?"

"I'm trying . . ."

"Try faster."

Kim scanned the readout with his tricorder. "I'll have to copy everything and sort through it later."

The pounding grew louder.

"Do something," Kim urged. "Before somebody hears him."

Paris banged his fist against the door, drowning out Tracer's noise. "Shut up in there, or I'll . . . I'll shoot!"

"You don't have a phaser," Kim pointed out.

Tracer must have come to the same conclusion because he started his rhythmic pounding once more. The door bowed out under every impact.

"Harry, any time now . . . We can't keep him in there forever."

"I've almost got it—"

It sounded as if Tracer was throwing his body against the door. Paris hoped the guy wasn't hurting himself in there, when a squeal of stressed metal made him cringe. The closet door banged open, and Tracer tumbled out.

Paris and Kim froze in surprise, staring at the Tutopan sprawled on the floor.

Tracer let out a squawk of fear, as Paris started toward him. He bobbed to his feet, making that strange squawking sound with every breath, as he darted out the door.

Paris tried to grab him, but the janitor was obviously running for dear life. "We've got to get out of here," he called back to Harry, watching Tracer's heels kick up as he scrambled down the corridor.

"Wait!" Kim exclaimed. "I've found something. . . ."

Paris leaned out the door, listening to the dying echoes of Tracer's cries. He thought he could already hear Enforcers coming.

"It's a report on Andross by the Cartel," Kim said, scanning the file. "They've been recording his communications—"

"Tell me about it later, pal," Paris interrupted. "Enforcers are coming."

The stomp of antigrav boots grew louder.

"There, I've got the manifests for the past half-rotation," Kim said. "I think that's everything. Now what?"

"Now, you get back to the ship." Paris activated his beacon and tossed it to Kim.

Kim caught it neatly, meeting his eyes. Paris gave him a mock salute as he dematerialized with the tricorder full of information.

Might as well make the best of it.

Paris put on his most cocky grin, turning to face the Enforcers. Their red armor made them look twice as big as they should have.

"I thought you'd never get here," Paris told them.

One Enforcer raised his fist, and Paris got a faceful of burning gas for his smart remark.

CHAPTER
11

CHAKOTAY POURED HIMSELF A CUP OF NEELIX'S POTENT pick-me-up from the container he'd brought to the bridge. This version was as thick as the last brew, but there was still something missing. Chakotay managed to be grateful for it, since it was all they had—replicator use was strictly forbidden until the ODN was functioning properly. Lieutenant Collins had destroyed the replicator in his quarters when he requested a grilled cheese sandwich and got a mass of indistinguishable substance that was too big for the unit to hold. Chakotay wondered if Collins would ever get his quarters clean.

Chakotay hadn't told anyone, but he had dreamed about exploding replicators last night. He didn't tell anyone about the other dreams, either, the ones of Janeway and Torres stuck in a bubble in the sky, calling for help, or of Paris searching through the ship, begging for water. But he took them as a warning.

"Incoming message from Cartel Enforcer Security," Tuvok announced. "Requesting to speak to Captain Janeway."

"Don't they know she's gone to Min-Tutopa? I thought they kept tabs on everything that happened around here." Chakotay turned the portable unit. He didn't expect visual, but one could always hope for the best. "This is Commander Chakotay. How can I help you?"

The Enforcer began without preamble. "This is to inform you that a member of your crew, Lieutenant Tom Paris, was apprehended while infiltrating the Cartel computer systems."

"Paris?" Chakotay was suddenly glad the Enforcer couldn't see his face. "Are you sure about this?"

"Do not feign ignorance in this matter." The flat voice didn't change inflection. "A subspace signal was emitted from the site and your ship responded with a focused conversion beam on the subatomic level. Please explain the purpose of this emission."

Chakotay shot Tuvok a look. "I wasn't aware of any of this."

"You do have a crew member by the name of Tom Paris."

"Yes. He was allowed to go into the Hub with another member of my crew. Where is he now?"

"Prisoner 07119 is currently being held for testing, pending the interrogation."

"Hold on there," Chakotay told the disembodied voice. "You must give us a chance to find out what's happened. This could be a simple mistake."

"There is no mistake." There was a significant pause. "Will you supply information regarding the focused conversion beam?"

Chakotay usually found that lying only muddied the waters, and right now he needed some clarity on this situation. "No, I cannot do that."

"Then I must inform you that as per regulation 5569, section A, all contracts between the Cartel and the offending party are canceled. Your ship is no longer granted level-A life support. A representative of Umbilical Services will disconnect your hookups immediately."

"You can't do that!" Chakotay leaned closer to the speaker. "We paid you for three days. We've got another day and a half left."

"Your agreement has been suspended pending resolution of this matter."

"Suspended?! You already got the seed DNA from us—"

"That agreement has been suspended," the Enforcer repeated. "Trade is prohibited when a matter of Cartel security is involved. That is standard business practice."

"Not where I come from," Chakotay said grimly. "Our life-support systems are dependent on those umbilicals."

"The Cartel is aware that your ship is damaged. If you wish to resolve this matter, you may submit the requested information through this office. Your cooperation would result in reactivating your agreements with the Cartel."

"Let me speak to Lieutenant Paris," Chakotay insisted.

"That is impossible. Your crew member must undergo testing."

"What is that—"

"Will you provide information regarding the closed conversion beam?"

Chakotay frowned in frustration. "No."

"Then this transmission is ended."

Chakotay was still trying to raise Enforcer Security when Kim arrived on the bridge. The ensign's face was flushed and he had a tricorder clutched in one hand. He swallowed when Chakotay turned. "Commander! I'm sorry. I didn't mean to leave him there."

"I assume you're talking about Paris." Chakotay felt Tuvok behind him, as he went to the railing, holding on to it with both hands. "What have you got to do with this?"

Kim shifted his eyes. "Didn't you know? He came and got me . . ."

"You transported from this ship without permission?" Chakotay demanded.

"I thought you knew. He said we had to move fast."

As if his focus could wrest the story from Kim, Chakotay hardly blinked. "Paris was authorized to set up a chemical-supply contact. With Neelix. He wasn't supposed to break into the Cartel computer system, and he definitely wasn't told to take *you* with him."

Kim licked his lips. "Actually, I was the one who broke into their system. I've got the information here."

"What information is that, Ensign?" Tuvok asked.

"About the computer thefts. Paris said it was important, and he's right." Kim came toward Chakotay, activating his tricorder. "I found a file on Andross—the Cartel's been watching him. They think he's up to something, along with this Administer Fee the captain went to see."

Chakotay took the tricorder, as Tuvok told Kim, "That does not explain the fact that you left the ship without direct orders."

Kim glanced down at his nonfunctioning comm badge, but he didn't try to defend himself.

"To make matters worse, now the Cartel is aware of our transporter." Chakotay pushed away from the railing. "And they're threatening to take away our umbilicals—"

He felt the drop in pressure, and the lights dimmed as the emergency system switched on. For a moment, it felt as if his body was suspended in air, even though he could feel the deck beneath his feet.

Ensign Yarro at port environmental station cried out as she fell. "Umbilicals have been disconnected," she managed to say from the floor.

Chakotay took an instant to trigger a calming chant. "They don't waste any time, do they?"

"Power conduits are activated," Kim announced, accessing Ops control. "Attempting to switch to reserve utilities system. Gravity was affected on decks one through six."

"We're in emergency reserves," Chakotay noted. "Will our life-support systems hold?"

"I'm not sure," Kim said flatly, examining his panel.

Yarro pulled herself back up to her station. "Can't you isolate the systems from the ODN like you did with the transporters?"

Kim shook his head. "You know life support is designed for maximum redundancy. It's tied in with subprocessors and the ODN through the power distribution net, the internal sensors, everything."

"What we're facing here is the possibility of multiple systems failures," Yarro informed the commander.

"I'll try to get us into Reduced Power Mode again," Kim added. "At least that way, the systems will default into the emergency power until we can manually correct the input errors."

"Leaving us no backup during that time," Chakotay said grimly. "Like right now."

"We do have the emergency shelters," Tuvok reminded him.

Chakotay's breath hissed between his teeth. "Not in this lifetime. I'm not ready to huddle in some shelter waiting for the Cartel to decide we're worth helping. I want us back in Reduced Power Mode—"

"Commander," Tuvok interrupted. "Your ship-to-Hub communications link is being signaled."

"The Cartel?" Chakotay asked, surprised, checking his portable communications unit. "I don't understand these symbols. Oovi . . . sentix . . . denar . . ."

"Commander, I'm reading the presence of a small craft above us," Tuvok informed him.

"I know what that is!" Kim exclaimed. "The chemical-supply contact must be trying to deliver the anesthetic. Paris gave me a code check." He hurried down the ramp, as Chakotay passed him the tricorder. "I've got it in here somewhere."

"It appears the vessel intends to dock in our shuttlebay," the security chief said disapprovingly.

Chakotay watched as Kim relayed an elaborate countercode through the unit. "I know how you feel, Tuvok, but we'd better do what Paris agreed or we might not get our chemicals."

"As you wish, sir."

Chakotay took one look at Tuvok's expression and made up his mind. "Tuvok, you come with me. We'll handle the exchange."

As Tuvok followed him to the turbolift, Kim said hesitantly, "I wouldn't use the lift, sir. Emergency reserves are experiencing severe power fluctuations. . . ."

Chakotay sighed as he looked at the Jeffries tube. "I want the ODN back on-line, Mr. Kim, and I don't care how you do it."

"I'll do my best, Commander. But I never wanted to be a brain surgeon."

"Then perhaps you should go consult with our doctor. I'll meet you in sickbay once we've secured the anesthetic."

"Yes, sir." Kim nodded glumly.

Chakotay swayed as an energy surge boosted the gravity, and Tuvok had to catch his arm to keep him from tumbling into the tube. Settling his jacket, Chakotay gingerly stepped onto the ladder, wondering if maybe his worst nightmares were coming true.

"I was unable to raise my ship," Janeway told Milla.

"It happens," the assistant said vaguely. "The Cartel controls the communications in the Hub, and you never know what they'll let through."

"I've been out of touch with them for nearly a day, now. Can't you do anything about it?"

"During tournament?" Milla lifted a looking glass on a long stick, peering through the lens. Her cream-colored hair was elaborately coiled and twisted in long curls down her back. "I'll see what I can do afterward. Why don't you enjoy yourself? It's not many aliens who get to participate in our tournaments."

Janeway sighed and surveyed the tournament hall, turning almost full circle to see the round room. The ceiling was slightly concave, as was the floor, which the captain found off-balancing unless she was facing the direct center.

The Tutopans apparently weren't disturbed by the sloping floor. They gathered in small groups, watching the tournament as they roamed through the hall or reclined on the cushioned bench that ran along the great curving wall.

Janeway couldn't even tell a tournament was in progress, that is, until she looked through the visor

Andross had lent her. Then the room leapt into vivid colors and shifting light, resolving into interlocking circles. In the center was a large island of white light. With the visor on, she could also see the movable holographic icons, which shifted whenever someone stood in a link between the circles.

Janeway stepped into a link, but the icon in the circle next to her didn't shift places.

"Why isn't it moving?" Janeway asked the agent's attendant.

Milla lifted her single lens, in a practiced, graceful gesture. "It won't shift unless you're the only one standing in a link. You'll see people wait forever, acting as if they aren't participating in order to deceive the other players." She dropped her lens with a delicate shrug. "I don't usually play with Hamilt's crowd. They take it so very seriously."

Milla drifted off, her gauzy drapery making it seem as if she glided over the floor. Janeway dropped her visor to hang from the silken cord around her neck, returning the room to blandness. The Tutopans mingled together, those playing and those not, with some in deep conversation right in the midst of the circles and icons, oblivious to the images reflected on their clothing. Now she understood why Andross had insisted she and Torres wear these beige robes. She didn't think she looked particularly refined, but she decided she could look determined—a force to be reckoned with.

Torres wandered over, kicking at the long skirts. She was wearing her visor. "I don't get it."

Janeway suppressed a smile. "Come now, Lieutenant, think of how ridiculous some of our games would seem if seen from an alien perspective."

"At least someone wins when you play croquette," Torres pointed out.

"I'm sure there are winners in this game as well, they simply aren't obvious by our standards."

"It seems pretty senseless to me. For people who are so crazy about rules, it's played completely at random. No one even knows who will be the next to move something."

"Perhaps it's a necessary antidote to their structured way of life. They must need some sort of chaotic release, and this is actually fairly tame compared to what they could be doing." Janeway gestured to a nearby group, lowering her voice. "There are other reasons for this setup. Have you noticed how sound doesn't carry in this room?"

Torres cocked her head. "I hadn't realized. It's true, I hear voices, but they're muted. I can't make out any words."

"Each of these circles creates an isolation buffer. They can converse in complete privacy within arm's reach of each other. That must be very convenient in a society that values information so highly."

Torres nodded, gazing around with new interest.

"Think of this as a lesson in diplomacy," Janeway told her.

"It's a test of our survival skills," Torres replied bluntly. "These people smile at each other, then they attack."

Janeway smiled at the young woman, knowing this was something that Tuvok couldn't understand—the way Torres complemented her, as if a more impetuous part of herself had been given freedom to express the things that she was constrained to hold back.

"Whatever it is," Janeway finished, "keep your eyes on those two." She gestured to the Tutopans wearing the distinctive Board Member signet on their foreheads. "Milla tells me they're the Cartel supporters on the Board, Hobbs and Sprecenspire."

"Keeping their distance from everyone else," Torres commented. "Especially Member Hamilt."

"Aside from someone called the Eldern, there's a fifth Member, Calvert." Janeway watched Calvert, who was stooping, almost as if he didn't want to tower over Hamilt, and eagerly nodding at something he was saying. He dashed off to snare Andross and draw him back to Hamilt's side.

"Follow me." Janeway didn't like to be reduced to the Tutopan level of intrigue, but with Fee still nowhere to be found, she had to assume Andross was manipulating them again. She wasn't above using Hamilt to get more information out of Andross.

She ignored Torres's muttered complaints about the unwieldy robes as they crossed the room. They intercepted Andross before he could get away from Hamilt.

Janeway didn't waste time. "Where's Administer Fee? I thought she was supposed to be here."

"She'll arrive shortly." Andross seemed preoccupied, his eyes constantly shifting as if calculating the effect of every movement, noting who was talking to whom, who was watching whom, who played, who didn't. . . .

Janeway noticed he paid more attention when Hamilt greeted her. "You're not playing?" Hamilt asked.

"Not at the moment," Janeway replied.

"Neither is Andross here." Hamilt had a lens perched in one eye, making him squint slightly. Calvert echoed his dire expression. "I don't know what the tournament is coming to, these days."

Andross dipped his head in a gesture of respect. "Perhaps later."

"I see one of your important business associates has joined in," Hamilt added, with a polite nod in

Torres's direction. The Klingon kept her visor on, a slight sneer pulling at her upper lip. Thankfully, she said nothing this time.

Janeway asked Member Calvert, "Do all the board members participate in this tournament?"

"Most of the high officials play," Hamilt said for the other man. "Even the Eldern, though he couldn't be here physically this evening. I believe his projected image was near at hand a moment ago."

"The Eldern is very ill," Andross said, irritated. "He shouldn't be making an appearance after sitting on the Board all day."

"What is that?" Janeway asked, ignoring Andross in favor of Hamilt. "Sitting on the Board?"

"The Board makes the administrative decisions for the House while in the Council Chamber." Hamilt gestured matter-of-factly to the silver disk implanted behind his tiny ear. "We interface directly with the network."

"All administrators above the level of agent are required to directly interface," Andross agreed. "While the rest of our citizens are not allowed that privilege."

"Not true, my boy," Hamilt mildly chided. "There are numerous researchers and scientists who are granted direct interface, as well as those who create the tests—"

"Only those who are approved by the Board," Andross countered.

Hamilt gravely removed the lens from his eye. "The Eldern himself addressed the dangers of direct interface for the general populace. Our latest reports indicate addiction rates are rising, and illegal operations are sending hotheads to the emergency wards every day."

"You're talking about criminals—I'm advocating

interface for hardworking citizens whose lives would be enhanced a thousand percent, both in their work and their personal pursuits."

Janeway was watching their exchange with interest, noting that Andross spoke much more passionately than she'd ever heard before.

Hamilt waved his stick, as if to say his complaints were unimportant. "If you wish to make your opinion known, you are free to submit a review of the Eldern's report. But as you can see from the reviews we did receive, a large percentage support the House in taking a sterner stance on interface."

"Naturally!" Andross snapped. "Who would dare write a favorable review of interface? They might be sent to Harn-Tutopa to live with the waterbugs, or worse, to the Alleganey Crevasse."

"Agent Andross!" Hamilt rebuked, drawing back. Even Calvert seemed amazed. "I'm shocked by the implications of your statement."

Janeway thought this entire conversation was very revealing. "Do you mean to say, Agent Andross, that your government suppresses dissidents by interfering with their livelihood? I thought you said careers were chosen for everyone according to psychological and aptitude testing."

"Tests are devised by the system," Andross said righteously. "They support those who fit the system, winnowing out those who are unusual or innovative."

"You tested magnificently," Hamilt murmured regretfully. "Yet there were those incidents of nervous disorder during your training. You've always stressed yourself unduly, my boy. Take advantage of your current position in the Hub to learn Cartel policies," the older man advised.

"I know enough already. We must control our ties

with the Cartel before it's too late." Andross's words rang out, and started drawing attention to them.

"We'll need agents such as yourself, my boy, to keep the House from falling into Cartel hands. Don't you agree, Administer Fee?" he asked, turning to the woman who was approaching.

Janeway recognized the tall woman as the one Andross had been following through the Council Chamber. She was sinewy under her drapes, with her elbows and neck jutting out awkwardly, as if she was nothing but large bones and taut muscle. Her formal greeting, a triangle of her two huge hands, had none of the grace of Hamilt's polished gesture in return.

"I believe Agent Andross will always be an asset to House Min-Tutopa," Administer Fee replied plainly. "He has accomplished a great deal for one so young."

"Yes, of course," Hamilt agreed. "Giving away training on his estates, bleeding his holdings dry to support these good-for-nothings who complain it's the system that oppresses them, when the House provides an equal chance for everyone."

"Hardly equal!" Andross protested.

"Equal, I say," Hamilt retorted. "Fee here is proof enough of that. Born from nothing, trapped in the backwater sludge of the borderlands, she was raised to become an administrator of a province."

Fee's features were relatively angular for a Tutopan, revealing the flash of painful self-consciousness that passed through her. Andross visibly bridled at the attack.

"It's true, I came from nowhere," Fee said quietly. "It's also true that I merely fit certain criteria at certain times in my life. The fact that I was able to develop to my full potential does not necessarily mean others have the same opportunity."

"It's this idealism of the individual that will bring

down our House," Hamilt insisted. "You and the Eldern conspire to destroy the very structure which protects us. Only if we stand united will we keep the Cartel from taking control of our business."

Fee shook her head decisively. "The only thing that can destroy the House is to deprive our people of their natural right to chose for themselves."

"We shall see," Hamilt said coolly "This situation cannot continue much longer."

Fee smiled in the direction of Eldern's projected image. "The Eldern refuses to die, and for that I am grateful. I would not want this dispute solved by the death of a wise and compassionate man. He knows better than you or I, that the individual is the heartbeat of our House."

Hamilt abruptly turned away. "Don't let me take any more of your time, Administer. Those people have come all the way from the Hub to speak with you—an important piece of business, I am assured by Agent Andross. One that takes him away from his regular duties."

Fee gave Janeway a surprisingly sympathetic smile. "I understand there is some urgency in this matter."

"Yes, there is." Janeway glanced at Board Member Hamilt, who was listening expectantly. Calvert hovered behind him, also watching them. "May I have a moment with you in private, Administer?"

"My pleasure," Fee agreed. "Come walk with me—"

"Agent Andross!" Milla called out, bustling up with unseemly haste. "We've received a message about that computer. Prog says it's an emergency."

"I'll have to take this," Andross told Fee. "If you'll excuse me."

Janeway stopped him. "Does this concern *our* computer?"

Andross shot Milla a look. "I had word before the tournament started that there might be a problem with the linkage."

Milla was busy patting an errant curl back into place. "Prog says they're doing what they can, but they may lose the whole system—"

"Don't tell me you're trying to operate the processor!" Torres protested.

"I—I'm not sure. You'll have to talk to Prog."

Janeway was glad they had an audience of three board members. "Take us there right now."

"Do we have your permission, Administer Fee?" Andross asked. "The processor has been installed in the Seat's communications tower."

Fee drew in her breath, glancing at Hamilt, who was listening as if he couldn't quite understand where this was leading. After a brief hesitation, she agreed. "You have my permission."

Andross's face lit up. "I'll have an aircar ready immediately."

"Just when this was getting interesting," Hamilt commented, obviously intrigued.

Janeway wished she had time to try to figure out what all these undercurrents implied, but they had to make sure their processor remained intact.

"We'll need our equipment," she told Andross, and he gave Milla a series of orders as they left the tournament hall.

Torres trotted after them. "How can they install the processor without the flowchart of the procedural sequence? Unless they altered the operating system . . ."

Janeway tightened her lips. "Your ship better be fast, Andross."

CHAPTER
12

"I KNEW IT WAS A BAD IDEA TO COME HERE," NEELIX SAID
to himself. "I told them so, but did they listen to me?
Of course not, why should they? It's only Neelix—
only the *expert* on this area of space. But does that
make a difference? No . . ."

Neelix peeked around the corner, trying to keep his
breath from rasping in his throat. He figured he must
have finally lost Bladdyn and Rep, but the last time he
started to relax, both of them had appeared in front of
him blocking the only exit from the marketplace.
He'd gotten away by jumping the expressway at the
last instant, almost breaking a finger when he forced
the door open to get inside. The car had taken him to
the far side of the Hub, leaving him searching for the
past few hours for a way back to the ship.

Neelix edged forward, certain he was almost home.
He could almost smell Kes's hair, and the way her lips
felt against his skin. All he had to do was go through
the hall link to the next pointed room, Lobby 58,

where the lift would take him up the docking spire. He could see the lobby through the toroidal tunnel, so safe and sedate. There were even a few red Enforcers wandering among the tourist crowd, not that he wanted to call attention to himself from the Cartel.

Neelix straightened his shoulders and started toward the hall link.

Rep burst out of a waste-reclamation chamber in front of him. All Neelix saw was the blurred arch of something slashing toward him. The razor edge tugged at his shoulder as he spun away.

In a sheer blind panic, Neelix ran right over the top of the beaked hominoid. The hall link was his only goal, his only hope, driving him right through Rep's frantic jabs.

His mouth was open but he didn't realize the high-pitched squeal that accompanied his flight across the lobby came from his own throat. As he skidded around the lift depot, one of the Enforcers called out, "Hey, you! No running in public spaces!"

Neelix dove for the open lift door, having barely the presence of mind to call back, "In a hurry! My mate's waiting. Lovely time . . . I had a lovely—"

The door slid shut in front of him, cutting him off.

Neelix collapsed against the wall. *I can't believe I did that!* But he'd spent so many hours lost and looking for the ship, and the hall link had been his only way back. He could still see the outrage in Rep's eyes as he was bowled over, and the way his beak thrust forward as if to punch him in the chest.

Neelix felt around the back of his jacket, letting out a shaky sigh. Just as he thought—it had been cut by Bladdyn's knife. He had known something was behind him, a native sense of everything around him that had saved his life before. This time, he was lucky he hadn't tried to retreat. They had gotten *that* close to slicing him into bite-sized pieces, all because Paris had left him behind.

Just wait until he got hold of Paris.

Paris woke cramped and slightly nauseated. He tried to stretch and bumped into the walls.

"Blast!" he exclaimed, rubbing his hand. He'd hit it on an airlock handle.

He sat up. That was as far as he could go—the metal globe was barely three meters across, with an airlock hatch at either end.

The implications sent a surge of adrenaline through his body. Instinctively, he struck the comm badge on his chest. It responded with an open channel.

"Voyager! This is Paris. Can you read me?"

He shifted to see out the tiny window in one side. His panting misted the lower half of the clear surface, but it was clear he was in a small blister on the outside of the Hub. His view was blocked by docking spires thrusting up from the hull.

"Lock on to my coordinates, and get me out of here!" Paris called frantically, keeping an eye on the outer airlock.

Bursts of static responded, unlike anything he'd ever heard over a comm badge.

He hit the badge again. *"Voyager,* this is Lieutenant Paris. Can you read me?"

Another stream of static was his only answer.

Paris smacked his fist against the wall next to the window. Even if the ship's communications systems were functioning properly, the juxtaposing gravity bases in the Hub distorted subspace, preventing a clear signal from getting through.

He slumped down, leaning back against one of the

curved walls. His neck was throbbing, his eyes were burning, and those two airlocks were bothering him quite a bit. One obviously led back into the Hub and the other apparently opened into space. The hatch was too small for most common airlocks on ships, and he wasn't able to see if there were grapples or any extensions for docking. Still, he tried to tell himself this could be a relay station, and he was being transferred someplace else off the Hub. He'd heard about the Cartel "bonding" people to their jobs for certain periods of time. Usually it was to pay back training or work off debts, but from what Paris could tell, the large majority of Tutopans were bonded until they died.

He didn't want to spend the prime of his life flying a supply ship in the asteroid fields. . . .

Actually, he wanted to believe that would be his fate, but he was basically trying to ignore the more obvious reason for his being here. The automation of the outer airlock left little doubt in his mind. It looked like he was on a one-way trip to vacuum and instant decompression—the only way to die.

He'd gotten trapped once in a Tellarite life pod after the ancient freighter he was piloting on an "easy" one-way run suddenly developed spontaneous combustion of many of its necessary systems. It fell apart so fast Paris hardly had time to make it to the life pod, and he wasn't sure that it wouldn't suffer the same fate as the ship. It had taken two days before someone ambled out to find him. Apparently, the owner had been too busy collecting insurance money to bother with him.

Waiting for his rescue, Paris's fear had plenty of time to disintegrate into philosophical musings on the futility of life, and then into screaming boredom. The first thing he'd done when he finally made it back to the planet was to find the owner of that worthless hunk of metal, and when the Tellarite tried to buy him off for his "trouble," Paris had punched him in his hairy snout.

Paris almost smiled, shaking his head. He'd gotten out of that one, all right. He had even convinced the insurance company to pay for his way off planet. He remembered he'd taken passage to Malhalla, where he met that Palusion who'd been stuck on a communications relay station for over a year. And boy, was she ready for a *real* good time. . . .

But that wasn't helping him get out of this situation. He removed his comm badge, and turned it over to examine the back. What if he could boost the power somehow? Maybe he could make a blip on *Voyager*'s sensors. By now Kim would have told them what had happened, and they must be looking for him.

He checked his pockets—he had a small fibroknife, and a couple of silver bar passes left. Not much in the way of tools, but it was a start. He quickly searched the cubicle for anything else he could use. The inner hatch was smooth with a grooved seam, and he couldn't even force his fibroknife into the crack. The outer hatch had both an automated locking system and a manual wheel, but he wasn't ready to mess with that hatch. Not yet. That was it, except for a tiny waste-processing system in the wall across from the window.

"Great," Paris muttered. "Were you planning on keeping me here for a while?"

There were no spy-eyes or scanning devices that he could see, but that didn't mean anything. They could probably hide an entire diagnostic array in the manual locking wheel. The shiny nub in the center would be perfect for recording opticals.

Paris leaned forward and spoke into it. "I hope you're enjoying this, you sadistic butchers!"

He tried the communicator a few more times, but static was his only answer. Using his fibroknife, he pried off the outer casing. It wasn't easy, until he figured out exactly where to apply pressure. When the casing finally separated, he wondered why Academy survival training hadn't told him there was a trick to it.

He stared down at the microprocessors and circuitry in his hands; an intricate maze of electron transfers etched into silicon slivers he could barely see. The communicator was so unassuming when it was on his uniform, its slight weight familiar and reassuring. . . .

"Who am I kidding?" he sighed. If he was one of those legendary Starfleet heroes they told you about all the time in the Academy, he'd know exactly which circuits to reroute to turn the tiny thing into a beacon that would call the entire Federation across the galaxy to his rescue. But he wasn't a hero, he was Tom Paris, and he'd have just as much luck performing heart surgery on himself.

When he tried to put the comm badge back together, it didn't connect correctly. He had bent the casing getting it open. Now he when he tapped it, it couldn't even access an open channel anymore. That must be why they didn't teach cadets how to open their comm badges.

Paris tossed the pieces onto the floor and crossed his arms, brooding. He had only wanted a little excitement, something interesting to do, he hadn't intended for this to happen.

After a while, he realized he'd forgotten how truly awful it was to be stuck in a three-by-three cubicle with nothing to do. In the interests of making things as hard as he could for his captors, he could try to slit his own wrists with the fibroknife. That might get their attention. . . .

Instead, he decided that inflicting property damage would be less harmful to himself. He wedged the two halves of the comm badge into the waste-processing unit. Using the tip of the fibroknife, he opened the tiny subspace generator. All he needed was some water, and he'd short out the field. It might create sparks, and it might even affect the waste processor. Then again, nothing might happen.

"What the heck," he said out loud. He started spitting at the comm badge.

The generator sputtered, and a thin line of blue smoke trickled up. *What do you know, it's actually working.* He wet his tongue and spit again. Maybe if he really got it wet . . .

Before he could adjust his position, the automatic lock on the outer hatch was triggered. He could hear the faint sound of locks releasing inside the frame.

Paris grabbed the manual wheel, trying to keep it from rotating. It slipped, moving a few centimeters.

"No!" he cried out, hanging his entire weight from the wheel, trying to brace his feet against the wall.

The wheel turned, lifting him up as if he weighed nothing. As the pressure seals broke and the door cracked open, Paris cursed the fates that had brought him to this sorry place.

After everything, is this how it ends?!

Never one to turn his back on the inevitable, Paris let the door carry him with it as it swung open.

Expecting the blackness of space and instant oblivion, Paris blinked stupidly up into the faces of two Tutopans. "Spray him," one of them said.

Paris cringed as the gas hit him, but a wave of relief almost made him laugh out loud. He had never blessed the sight of a plain white corridor more, and he could have kissed the two handlers, even as they roughly pried his fingers from the locking wheel.

Light-headed from the gas, Paris heard one of them say, "He did it too. Did you hear him? He said something when he thought he was going to die."

"Calling for help," the other dismissed, getting a better grip on Paris's sweaty arm. He was being dragged, face down.

"No, it's more than that," the first one insisted. "Most of them act like they're angry, like they've been cheated. Like there's something important they have to say before they die . . ."

The other guy let out a snort. "You better leave the psych-behavior to the experts. You and me, we tested out for hauling waste-cases like this one."

Paris tried to lift his head, protesting their unnecessary roughness.

"Hold it, he's awake!" one of them cried out, as they dropped Paris. His neck burned even more, and the chemical taste of a sedative flooded his system. Everything blurred as he lost consciousness.

"He left me there!" Neelix wailed, as he slumped against the door of sickbay. He was a little disappointed that only Kes was there to see his dramatic entrance, but the concern in her beautiful eyes more than made up for the lack of audience.

She ran to help him, putting her shoulder under his arm and supporting him as he stumbled into sickbay. "What happened to you?"

Neelix let her guide him into the examining room. "I was brave, my dear, you would have been proud of me. But they were almost too much to handle alone." He fell back on the table, rolling to his side to reveal the torn coverall at his shoulder. "How bad is it? You can tell me the truth, I can take it."

Kes quickly sliced open the coverall. His handsomely patterned skin was marked by a thin slash that curved across the fleshy pad of his shoulder.

"This isn't bad," she murmured soothingly. "The one in the back didn't even touch you."

"It wasn't for lack of trying, let me tell you."

"Let me get a regenerator, and I'll have you healed in no time."

Neelix reared up, too indignant to be placated. "That idiot pilot left me there! With those two murderous thugs he cheated. They attacked me! As if I had any part in his nefarious schemes . . ."

"Shush, my darling. There's bad news." She held the regenerator over his shoulder. "Paris was caught breaking into the Cartel computer, and the Enforcers have thrown him in jail."

"Good! He deserves it."

"Neelix! Don't say that." She fastened a reproachful gaze on him. "Chakotay can't even find out where they're keeping him, and they're planning to do some kind of terrible interrogation on him to get our transporter technology."

Neelix rolled over on his stomach, grimacing at the soreness in his shoulder. "I don't care. I was almost gutted by that big miner. It was pure luck I got away. He had arms the size of my thigh, I swear—"

"Well, well, what do we have here?" Dr. Zimmerman asked as he entered the examining room. He sniffed delicately. "Kes, I think your patient needs a bath."

Neelix wasn't about to take any criticism from a computer program. Kes had explained it to him when he worried about her being around the man for days on end. "You wouldn't know about space stations," he said dismissively. "They aren't the cleanest places in the galaxy."

"Perhaps." The doctor glanced at Neelix's bare shoulder. "That's only a scratch. Clean it up and get him out of here."

"I'm almost done," Kes assured him, shaking her head at Neelix to be quiet.

The doctor examined the diagnostic reading for a moment. He entered a few notations, then turned back to Neelix. "Well, well, what do we have here?"

"You already asked me that," Neelix said, giving him a sideways look.

"I did?" The doctor vaguely turned away. "Ah, yes, I did. Carry on."

The doctor wandered out of the examining room, muttering to himself.

"That's one sick doctor," Neelix said.

"I know. Ever since we administered the anesthetic, he's been like this. He can't keep track of anything."

"Is it dangerous?"

"Only if he treats someone."

"What about you?" Neelix sat up, putting his arm protectively around her. "It's not safe for you to be in here alone with him. There's no telling what he could do."

"Neelix, there's nothing to worry about. The doctor would never hurt me."

He cast a wary look toward the outer office. "I'll stick around for a while just in case."

"Really, I'll be fine," she assured him. "Besides, here's Ensign Kim. He'll be here."

Neelix wasn't reassured, as he suddenly realized Kes was wearing one of her nicest outfits. She always looked beautiful, but he'd told her many times that this dress brought out the blue of her eyes and the blush of her cheek. Why had she chosen to wear it today? She had been spending quite a bit of time lately with that young officer. . . .

Ensign Kim glanced into the examining room. "I'm here to pick up your chemical requests."

"I just finished gathering the latest readings," Kes told him with a smile, putting away the regenerator. Neelix was even more convinced he ought to stay for a bit. He trusted Kes to the ends of everything, but even nice young men could start to get ideas around such a gorgeous creature.

"Are you going?" Kim asked him.

Neelix narrowed his eyes, sliding off the table. "No. I won't be in the way."

Kim shrugged as he turned to the doctor. "According to my latest report, the erratic impulses are continuing, and we're still experiencing major system malfunctions."

"The anesthetic doesn't seem to be having effect," the doctor agreed, preoccupied with the data Kes had given him. "Except for starving the neural tissue."

Kim whistled when he saw the numbers. "If we adjust the nutrient any more, we won't have a problem—we also won't have an optical data network."

"This is quite perplexing," the doctor agreed.

Neelix frowned as Kim shifted closer to Kes, pointing something out on the monitor. "Look at that. What if this is latent addition? Supposedly, a subthreshold shock can affect the core conduits without causing a direct impulse. But if subthreshold shocks are repeatedly applied, the cumulative affect is a shock artifact—indistinguishable from a stimulating impulse."

"What's providing the energy for these subthreshold shocks?" Kes asked.

"Maybe it's the inherent energy flowing through the ODN. It could be stimulating the neural tissue until it builds into one these shock artifacts."

"Maybe you should stick to technical manuals," the doctor advised dryly. "And leave the diagnosis to me."

Kim shut his mouth, his brows drawing together at the doctor's preemptory tone. Neelix wondered if the placid ensign was finally going to give someone a piece of his mind, even if it was only a holograph.

But Kes quickly drew their attention to another part of the analysis. "According to this, the transmissions are no longer polarized, allowing impulses to travel both ways through the conduits."

Kim nodded. "That must be one reason we're getting delays. When an echo meets an opposing signal, they cancel each other out."

Zimmerman sharply brought his hands together, making Neelix jump. "Echoes! That sounds like phantom pain."

"What's that?" Kim asked.

"Basically," the doctor told him, "it's an illusion experienced by amputees involving sensations in limbs that are actually missing."

Neelix stared at the doctor. "What are you talking about? What amputees?"

Kes was nodding. "Phantom pain occurs when the severed ends of the nerves continue to be stimulated, just as the ODN continues to react as if it's receiving impulses from the processor."

"How?" Kim asked, finally getting a word in edgewise.

"The phenomenon occurs in the sympathetic nervous system . . . I mean to say, there's a reflexively activated cell in the spinal cord . . ." Zimmerman trailed off, shaking his head. "What was I saying?"

"You were explaining phantom pain," Kes reminded him.

"Oh, yes, phantom pain . . . one of the mysteries of the medical world for centuries. Paskallon did an entire series on nerve tissue response in 2246."

Neelix shook his head. "Is there another medical program you can call up?"

"Don't I wish," Kim told him. "This is the only one."

"This a complicated biophysical phenomenon!" Zimmerman snapped at both of them.

"The point is," Kes said patiently. "We can try an effector inhibitor, which will destroy the impulse during transmission."

"I get it—just like the enzymes in the bionutrient," Kim agreed. "They destroy the chemical compound that transmits the impulse, keeping the effect localized. Perhaps we can enhance one of those."

"I don't get it," Neelix said, but the others ignored him.

The doctor was consulting his monitor as if nothing untoward had happened. "There are biogenic amines, such as noradrenaline, adrenaline, isoprenaline, and dopamine. Their chemical base is very similar to the nerve gas that was used against the crew."

"Good, then at least we know there's supplies readily available." Kim considered the long list of possible compounds. "Which one should we use?"

"Which . . ." The doctor scrolled through, seemingly at a loss. "Drugs that produce synaptic and effector blockade. Ammonium compounds, as well as ether, nicotine in high concentration. Reserpine, inhibits monoamine oxidase. Guanethidine, combats high blood pressure and prevents the release of transmitter. Ergot alkaloids block the alpha receptor directly at the sites, as well as thymoxamine. Also Pranolol . . ."

"Which one?" Kim asked again, more insistent.

The doctor froze, his eyes fixed and his mouth curled as if ready to speak.

"I think you overloaded him," Neelix offered.

"That keeps happening," Kes said. "He'll snap out of it in a moment."

The holograph flickered, disappearing from the chair, and appearing in the middle of the room as if his program had just been activated.

"Please state the nature of the medical emergency!" Zimmerman demanded. It reminded Neelix of the way he used to act, before Kes had talked him into being more human.

Kes touched his arm. "We were working on an effector inhibitor for the computer."

"I am not a technician," the doctor instantly replied. "For computer repair, please consult the engineering department."

"He's a goner," Neelix told them. "Better get someone else to help you."

"Access your special memory file," Kim suggested. "We've explained this situation to you already."

The doctor was starting to look confused again.

Kes patted his arm. "Relax, there's been computer malfunctions and they're interfering with your systems—"

"We don't have time for this!" Kim exclaimed. He pushed himself up, almost knocking over the chair.

"Hey, don't talk that way to Kes." Neelix shifted as if to protect her.

"It's important to reassure concussion victims," Kes tried to tell Kim, shifting to see past Neelix. "Their mental confusion can aggravate the situation."

"Frankly, *his* situation isn't the priority here!" Kim almost shouted.

"That's enough—" Neelix started to say.

But Kes interrupted him. "Wait, dear." She turned to Kim. "Something else is the matter, isn't it?"

Kim stopped and stared at Kes. "How did you know?"

"You don't usually get this upset about things," Kes told him. Neelix wondered just how well Kes knew this man.

"You're right," Kim sighed. "I've been analyzing the information I got from the Cartel computer, and I'm afraid the captain and B'Elanna are in trouble. I've found evidence that links Andross to every one of the other computer thefts—for some reason, he's been disabling ships for the past year."

"Why would he do that?" Neelix asked.

"I'm not sure," Kim said, with an edge of irritation. "That's why I don't have time for this. I've got to see Chakotay and finish my analysis—except that the chemical supplier is going to return any minute, and we have to know what compounds we need."

Kes nodded, sitting down at the monitor. "These are the ones the doctor was considering. Let me see which might work best with our system." After a few moments, she picked up a tricorder, entering one of the chemical formulas. "Reserpine. It inhibits monoamine oxidase, but it's a less brutal drug than the others. We don't want to completely stop the transmission of impulses."

"Reserpine it is, then." Kim seemed relieved, taking the tricorder. "I'm off to see the commander now."

Neelix wasn't sure he liked the way Kim smiled at Kes on his way out. "Are you sure he's as innocent as he looks?"

The doctor snapped to attention, turning uncomprehending eyes their way. "Please state the nature of the medical emergency!"

Neelix threw up his hands. "Has everyone gone crazy, or is it just me?"

Kes patted his arm sympathetically. "It's just you, dear."

CHAPTER
13

"HOW FAR IS IT?" JANEWAY ASKED, LEANING OVER Andross's shoulder as he piloted the aircar. Several of the moons cast a silvery glow across the sky, but the lights of the Seat were much more brilliant, sprawling as far as the eye could see in every direction. Only the hilltops and crevices of the vast plain were left dark and untouched by the interlinking complexes.

"There, in the communications tower," Andross pointed. "Your computer was being installed as an auxiliary processor for the network control of the Seat."

The tower rose on the horizon, its bulbous top ringed by a series of purple lights. The long, slender neck flared at the base, with the structural framework exposed in cleanly functional lines, reminding Janeway of a starship.

Getting there seemed to take an agonizing amount of time, yet she could tell that Andross was finally in a hurry from the way he was piloting the aircar. She was well aware that once again she'd been prevented from speaking with Fee. She could only hope that Andross was indeed taking them to *Voyager*'s processor, but she wouldn't know that until she'd actually touched it with her own hands.

Andross had enough authority to get them immediately admitted into the tower. As the lift carried them to the upper levels, Janeway was almost on her toes from anticipation. Torres was chewing on a thumbnail, her other arm wrapped around her stomach in an effort to keep still.

When the door opened onto a round room, Janeway first noticed the main computer control terminal with a series of interactive panels. A woman was working frantically over the monitors, and she hardly acknowledged their arrival except to cast an urgent look at Andross. Without a word, the agent gave her a cautioning gesture, before moving on.

As they circled the computer network facility, Torres kept bumping her tool case into the back of Janeway's legs in her haste.

"There it is."

The familiar gray casing of *Voyager*'s computer was wedged between two unfamiliar processing units. Their processor looked smaller than Janeway remembered—hardly bigger than the table in *Voyager*'s conference room—yet it was responsible for coordinating all the activity within the three levels of the main computer core. Right now, it rested on half a dozen hydraulic pillars with readouts at their base.

"It looks intact." Yet Janeway's hands clenched at that sight of the ragged metal edges where it had been cut from the bulkheads.

"What idiot thought this up?" Torres demanded,

pushing past Janeway. "You can't integrate these systems!"

The Tutopan straightened up from the main control terminal. She was a spare, no-nonsense sort of woman, well into middle age. "As a network analyzer, that unit is compatible."

Torres knelt down next to the readouts in the hydraulic support. "I don't know who you are, but according to your own interface, this unit isn't compatible."

Andross waved a hand at the technician. "This is Prog. She's been supervising the installation."

Torres unclamped the maintenance panel, checking the clusters of registers and operational circuits through the containment field. "None of the hardware seems to have been tampered with. Subspace field generators are on-line, and the nanoprocessor units are engaged. But all functions are locked."

"Obviously, our processor isn't suitable for your needs," Janeway told Andross as evenly as she could. "Disconnect it immediately."

"Impossible," Prog said for him. "The translation program is currently loading. To interrupt would confirm systems failure in that unit, and it might initiate a cascade failure throughout the communications network. We'll have to wait until the program has completed its routines."

Janeway drew in her breath. "Where is the converter? Or have you created a direct interface?"

"The translation is carried through the assemblers supporting the unit, it's not a conversion function." Prog hardly looked up from her monitors.

Janeway moved in next to Torres. "That means the operating system was left intact."

"That's one thing we don't have to worry about."

Torres quickly opened the tool case. In one corner was a portable interface normally used for subprocessor maintenance. "Will it work on the main processor? There's no access port."

"You'll need to manually splice into an input line."

Andross stepped forward. "What are you planning to do?"

"We'll try to use this unit to access the operating system of the processor."

Andross checked with Prog. When she nodded, clearly desperate for any help she could get, he agreed. "Give it a try."

"I almost didn't bring it," Torres said, preparing the interface unit. "I didn't expect anyone to try to install the processor." She glared up at Andross who was hovering over her shoulder. "Would you back off? You're making me nervous."

Janeway could understand why she felt that way. Both Andross and Prog were as jittery as she'd ever seen Tutopans, but then again, if the processor was capable of causing a failure of the Seat communications network, that could be reason enough for them to panic.

"Maybe we can tap the main input line," Janeway suggested, moving around to the rear of the module. "We'll have to take the casing off so we can see what we've got to work with. Do you have a cutting tool we can use?"

Andross fetched a laser himself, handling it gingerly, as if he was afraid it might go off accidentally. Janeway found the tool so simple to operate that she concluded Andross was one of those beings who was not mechanically inclined. She remembered what Hamilt had said about Andross's mismanagement of his "holdings," and wondered if he was a member of the Tutopan version of aristocracy. Whatever he was, he apparently wasn't living up to his society's expectations. She still didn't trust him, but she had to admire his courage.

Cutting a neat slice through the casing, Janeway tried to tell herself she wasn't mangling their computer further—she was attempting to repair it. Torres removed the cover plate on the interface unit so they could directly link the optical cable to the main input line of the processor.

"Accessing main control unit," Torres said, manipulating the interface sequence. "Reading general system failure . . ."

"Let me try." Janeway accessed the subprograms in the interface and ordered a level-three diagnostic to be performed. The unit warned that all data currently engaged would be lost. Janeway hesitated, not sure if that meant the Tutopan translation program or the operating system itself.

"It might permanently fuse the registers on the isolinear chips," Torres warned the captain under her breath.

"The only other option is a system shutdown, and that's almost guaranteed to polarize those circuits. No, this is the only way." Janeway initiated the diagnostic program, and held her breath.

"Microprograms engaged, elementary operational steps beginning," Torres announced, relief clear in her voice.

"Good." The captain anxiously leaned closer to read the monitor. "Timing signals activated, very good . . ."

"Is it working?" Andross asked.

As the system checks continued to clear with no program errors, Janeway looked up. "I believe so. The operating system is initiating the sequence of elementary operational steps supplied by the interface."

Prog called out from her terminal, "Our link is being interrupted by their unit." She shook her head at Andross. "I've lost access to the processor."

Andross considered the two Starfleet officers. "Can you use that interface to access our network?"

Janeway quickly got to her feet. "We're taking our processor back to the ship."

Prog joined Andross, leaning over as if to examine the interface. "We may be able to use this unit."

Torres blocked her from getting any closer. "This is our computer."

Janeway also took a defensive stance. "What's going on here?"

"Andross, I can do it," Prog said, craning her neck to see. "That interface unit directs data through the system for processing and output, activating the functional elements of the operational system. My automated setup program can be loaded directly through it."

"Good work," Andross told her quietly. He nodded to Janeway and Torres. "You've been a great help."

He casually stepped back, raising a small cylinder in his fist. Torres growled low in her throat, tensing as if ready to lunge at him. But before either of them could move, a fine mist shot into their faces.

Janeway felt the same throat-crushing sensation she remembered from the attack by the *Kapon.* As she went down, Andross was ordering, "Get that interface working. We're running out of time."

Janeway slumped back against one of the Tutopan processors, her chin sinking into her chest. The room was blurry but she could make out Prog and Andross working over their computer. The sedative fought with the antidote Tuvok had given her, yet she had to strain to stay awake.

Andross spoke into his wrist communicator. "This is it, compatriots. Get into position."

Prog's voice came from somewhere above Janeway. "Automated setup initiating. Standby for operation."

Andross stood over Janeway. She feigned unconsciousness while trying to get control of herself. She might not get a second chance.

"I'm truly sorry for this," Andross said. "But it's time my people took action to claim the rights that belong to them."

Prog's voice was tensely eager. "Program ready for input and operation."

Janeway slit her eyes to judge her position. As Andross turned to give the order, she braced herself and slashed her leg into the back of his knees. The small man flipped into the air, letting out a cry of amazement. Janeway rolled away as he hit the floor with a solid "Oofff!"

Janeway was on her feet, disoriented but moving. She was glad to hear Torres behind her, scrambling for position. Andross was gasping and wheezing in a crumpled pile.

"I've got him," Torres called out.

Prog drew back in alarm as Janeway lurched toward her. The nerve gas seemed to trap her like a tangled net, making it hard to move or see. Yet the sequence on the panel was clear enough, with the abort command blinking on the upper right.

Janeway reached for the panel just as Prog realized what she was doing. The Tutopan grabbed hold of her arm, but didn't seem to know what to do next. Any other time Janeway would have had no trouble shaking her off, but the gas made every move take three times as long. Behind her, Andross pushed Torres away from him. She could hear Torres curse as she fell.

With all of the command authority Janeway possessed, she stared right into Prog's eyes and ordered, "Don't do it!"

Prog almost obeyed, an instinctive reaction that said a lot about Tutopan society. But she caught herself just as the door to the lift opened. "Andross!" she cried out.

Several House guards emerged from the lift with their gas guns held ready.

Janeway slumped slightly in relief, as the gray uniforms stomped closer.

"We came when we didn't get the signal," one of the guards said. His gun was leveled directly at Janeway. "We thought there was trouble."

"Smart thinking." Andross clutched an arm across his stomach, hunching over. He pointed to Janeway, breathlessly ordering, "Take her away from the main terminal."

The guard motioned, and Janeway eased back when Prog let go of her arm. The twin ejection tubes of the gun were aimed directly at her face, and she wasn't sure what another dose of the gas would do to her. Or to Torres, who was already down on her hands and knees, mumbling to herself.

"Sit over there," the guard ordered Janeway. She awkwardly lowered herself next to Torres.

One of the other guards was helping Andross to the main control terminal. "Begin the operation," he said hoarsely.

Janeway leaned closer to Torres. "How are you doing?"

"Na . . . s' good," Torres slurred, her head hanging.

"Better sit down," Janeway advised.

Torres lowered her hip to the ground and kept right on going, ending up sprawled out on the floor. She blinked at the ceiling, obviously too drugged to try to get up again. Janeway wondered if the bit errors in the medical replicator had caused the antidote to malfunction, or if B'Elanna's half-Klingon metabolism was especially vulnerable to the neural toxin.

"We have switching networks and relay stations online," Prog announced. "Satellite communications, educational and entertainment database systems, as well as electronic-funds transfer conduits are available."

"That's everything we need." Andross leaned against the main terminal, still bowed over. "Terminate the links to the other processors."

The guard standing over Janeway spoke into his wrist communicator. "This is it! Take your places."

The other guard let out a shout of approval, thrusting his fist into the air. Janeway could hear more people arriving in the lift.

The distinctive sound of machinery powering down accompanied Prog's voice: "Processors off-line."

Andross swayed into Janeway's view, and she tried to focus on his face. He was obviously in pain, but his voice held grudging admiration. "Thanks to you, years of planning and effort are about to pay off."

Janeway tried to protest, but her mouth wouldn't obey. *What have we done?* She had to stop him before it was too late—

"Ready, Andross?"

"Shut down the main power grid," Andross ordered. "And open the official House broadcast channel. It's time everyone knows—the revolution has begun!"

CHAPTER
14

ZIMMERMAN STOOD IN FRONT OF THE SMALL VIEWSCREEN in sickbay, watching ships moving over the Hub while the starfield glimmered in the background. Kes had told him about the large viewscreen on the bridge that he himself sometimes appeared on, and she had described what it felt like to look out the windows on the observation deck, or through the stasis field of the huge shuttlebay doors. . . .

It was beyond his comprehension. He had created a personal subroutine to deal with sensory images and events that didn't pertain to his activities as chief medical officer, and yet . . . he didn't know what it was like to look out a window.

"At last," Ensign Kim announced. "Something is finally going right." Kim finished his examination of the latest diagnostic of overall systems performance. "The reserpine treatment seems to be having some effect. Efficiency is up eight percent."

"Just as I predicted," Zimmerman assured him, exactly as if everything were functioning normally.

He was aware that his response was at odds with his current status, but the patient-interface program was capable of a certain amount of leeway in regards to the truth. Hypocrisy was occasionally necessary during treatment, but that was usually to cover the severity of a biosystems failure on the part of the patient, not the doctor.

"Perhaps the dosage should be increeeeee—" he started to suggest.

"Uh-oh," Kim exclaimed, covering his ears with his hands. "Not again!"

Zimmerman immediately engaged a manual override, deleting the intended comment and ending vocalization. Performance errors were unacceptable in a medical unit, yet he had been forced to install an override on the termination sequence of his self-diagnostic program. Otherwise, his projected image would be constantly terminated while he was in the midst of his research on the bioneural tissue.

"The delays in his system are getting worse," Kes pointed out. The doctor wasn't accustomed to seeing that worried expression directed at himself.

Kim leaned over the medical terminal. "I don't understand it. He's apparently having some sort of systemic reaction to the reserpine treatment."

The doctor deliberately gestured to himself, reminding them that he was self-aware even if he wasn't corporeal. "I am here, Ensign."

Zimmerman wasn't satisfied by Kim's apologetic glance. Actually, there was nothing satisfying about the current situation. His self-maintenance program had attempted to compensate for the system errors by creating multiple backup memory files, updating them continuously, while his decision tracks were routed through logic-error routines for triple redundancy. In fact, he had done everything that could be considered reasonable in order to prevent malfunction, but the performance errors continued to occur. And that . . . bothered him.

"Reserpine does act as a sedative," Kes agreed. "A system depressant."

Zimmerman could tell his projected image was moving five nanoseconds slower than usual parameters. "How is it possible that reserpine applied to the neural gel packs of the computer core is affecting my program?"

"You yourself compared the computer network to an animal's nervous system," Kes told him. "If the missing processor could be considered the cerebral cortex, then the memory core would seem to function in a similar way to the brain stem, receiving sensory input and preparing the ship's systems for intense activity necessary in offense and defense."

"The 'fight-or-flight reaction.'" Kim noticed her curious expression, and quickly added, "I've been reading those neurological files you gave me."

"Humph," Zimmerman replied, finding vagueness to sometimes to be beneficial during patient interface. "It is true that most of the malfunctions appear to be responses to nonexistent emergency scenarios."

"I've seen how the ODN pathways interconnect," Kes said. "Even in living organisms, we aren't sure exactly how the nervous system harmonizes with the other physical systems of the body, but it does. The doctor is reacting no differently from any other patient whose body has been injured."

Kim shook his head. "I can't believe that—it sounds as if you're saying *Voyager* is alive. . . ."

"The keystone of a living organism is a single focus of action, with the internal regulation integrated successfully with the environment. Isn't that was the computer system does for the ship?" Kes hurried on before he could interrupt. "B'Elanna was correct—theoretically the auxiliary processor and subprocessors have no reflex connections established between them, yet they're reacting as if there is a physiological unity."

"I guess you could put it that way," Kim grudgingly agreed.

"We have the evidence in front of our eyes." She turned to study Zimmerman, who drew back slightly at being the object of attention. "The doctor's program is a direct manifestation of the computer systems, exactly the same way that emotions are a direct response to sensory input."

Kim also turned to consider the doctor. "His reaction does confirm the effect that the reserpine treatment is having on the ODN. He's functioning again, but his alertness is reduced because the impulses have been inhibited."

Zimmerman held up his hands to stop them. "I believe I understand." There was no decision track to cover these circumstances; however, his self-maintenance program had long ago installed a special decision tree to handle contingencies that were directly related to his own well-being. It had seemed a necessary step in light of the slow crew response to his needs. "You indicated that the impulse transmissions are traveling both directions along the neural pathways."

"That's correct," Kim said. "But what does that have to do with anything?"

"If it's true that I am a direct manifestation of this . . . organism you call *Voyager,* then it stands to reason that *I* am capable of controlling the functions of the ODN."

He saw no need to give them any more warning than that. Zimmerman updated his memory files, then accessed his direct link to the main computer core.

Chakotay was running over the snow-covered hills of ancient Earth, with the cold air rasping in his throat, and the branches of evergreens whipping past his face. It was a cleansing run, as he pushed himself to keep up with his spirit guide—

"Commander Chakotay, this is Tuvok."

Chakotay broke from the meditation, taking only a moment to recover from his disorientation. One good thing about the recent chemical treatment: at least their communicators were working again. "Chakotay, here."

"Sorry to interrupt, sir, but I am reading an unusual energy surge through the power conduits."

"I'm on my way." Chakotay tapped his comm badge to alert the computer. "Chakotay to Ensign Kim—what's happening with the EPS?"

"I'm not sure," Kim's voice answered. "Maybe there was damage we didn't detect when the umbilicals were connected. Whatever it is, it's affecting the doctor, as well. He isn't moving."

Chakotay felt an uncharacteristic urge to curse the fates that continued to test them so relentlessly. "I'm on my way to the bridge. Keep me informed."

Kes waited until the channel was closed before she asked Kim, "Why didn't you tell him?"

Kim accessed the Ops control system through the medical terminal. "Tell him what?"

"That the doctor is trying to take control of the ship." Kes politely averted her eyes from Zimmerman, standing motionless near the desk.

"What?" Kim asked.

"You heard what he said. He's attempting to access the ODN."

Kim gave her a strange look. "He was just rambling again. He isn't capable of doing that."

"But what if he is?" Kes slowly circled the doctor, wondering if he had chosen this for himself. "What if his program can act as a control unit, diverting the input away from the main core?"

Kim didn't bother to answer. His fingers flew over the panel, attempting to initiate a level-five diagnostic. "Something's blocking my input."

"It's him. He's doing something." She didn't add that she could sense activity within the doctor, knowing Kim wouldn't understand. He would just say that Zimmerman was a holograph, a machine projection, but she'd always believed that Zimmerman was more than sum total of the bytes of his program, just as organic life-forms were more than their tissue masses.

The lights gradually faded. Kes was glad she'd convinced Neelix to go back to their quarters after his ordeal—this was exactly the sort of thing that made him nervous about living with the Starfleet crew. She hoped he was deep asleep.

"Well, if Zimmerman's doing this, he'd better stop." Kim was unable to make his terminal respond. "The power conduits are off-line, and systems are locking down."

Chakotay climbed the last Jeffries tube, breathing much harder than he had been during his meditation. The turbolift hadn't responded to his summons.

"Report," he ordered as he stepped onto the bridge. The air felt markedly drier than usual, and the resolution of the viewscreen was reduced.

"Auxiliary fusion generators are off-line, and all

environmental systems are cycling down. Emergency utilities have not initiated."

Chakotay spoke into the tricorder tuned to sickbay frequency, not trusting the comm badge to carry his words. "Ensign Kim—we're living on borrowed time."

Kim stared at Kes. "We've got to stop him."

"End program," she instantly ordered. But Zimmerman's image didn't so much as flicker. "Computer, end program."

"It's not working." Kim shoved himself out of his chair. "I've got to get to the core."

Kes saw it coming but she didn't have time to call out as Kim ran smack into the door, face-first.

"Yow!" he exclaimed, holding his hand to his bloodied nose.

She ignored her instinct to render aid, going instead to the doctor's projection module. That was the source of their problem.

With a few quick motions, she opened the rear panel and disconnected the optical cables that joined the holographic projection module to the computer. Zimmerman's image disappeared.

"Power conduits are responding," Tuvok announced.

"I can't control the linear induction conduits," Ensign Yarro said frantically. "It's routing the entire system to the umbilical ports."

"Lock those ports down!" Chakotay ordered. "We can't afford to lose those resources—"

He broke off at the sight of millions of flashing pinpoint lights enveloping the viewscreen. The cloud of particles expanded rapidly in the vacuum, turning and sparkling as they bombarded the ships docked next to them.

As if to complete the picture, the lights surged back to their normal level.

"Tuvok?" Chakotay asked.

"The computer has returned us to Reduced Power Mode." Tuvok tightened his lips, still working. "However, we lost approximately five thousand liters of wastewater before the port could be closed."

Chakotay slumped back. "Almost ten days' worth of valuable resources." The particles continued to expand, colliding with the Hub. The lazy swirling motion reminded him of a dance, but it was a show he couldn't afford to enjoy.

"We are being hailed on the Cartel frequency," Tuvok announced.

"I'm not surprised," Chakotay replied with a sigh.

"Don't reconnect him!" Kim shouted from across the room.

Kes hesitated. "Why not?"

"He could do it again."

"I'll tell him not to," she said mildly. Ignoring Kim's protests, she reattached the optical cables.

Zimmerman appeared. "How may I help you?" Then he frowned, obviously following the dictates of a special start-up program. "I was attempting to access the main control unit of the core. Was I successful?"

"No!" Kim said.

"Yes," Kes contradicted. "You were able to affect the ship, but it blocked the other systems from functioning."

"Don't try it again," Kim ordered darkly.

Kes could understand his irritation, but she also

sympathized with the doctor. Both of them were relatively inexperienced life-forms compared with everyone else on board the ship, and sometimes she felt exactly the way Zimmerman looked right now—lost.

"It's all right," she told the doctor. "You proved that your systems are integrated with those of the ship."

"If my attempts to help are becoming detrimental," Zimmerman said, regarding Kim with an expression of hurt pride. "Perhaps you should terminate my program until the problem is resolved."

"We can't do that," Kim said bluntly. "We need to use your condition to help guide our treatment of the bioneural tissue."

"*Use* me?" Zimmerman repeated dryly.

"Yes, and that means you have to stay away from the computer," Kim insisted. Kes winced at his tone, but the young officer was adamant. "Don't touch anything, and don't *do* anything without our approval. Understand?"

Zimmerman seemed reluctant to answer. "Yes."

Kes wished there was something she could say that would help, but it looked as if this was one of those times when a person had to be restrained for his own good. She gave him an encouraging smile, but the doctor turned away, his expression stricken.

"Your ship has been fined 10.000 credits for contaminating shipping lanes," the official told Chakotay.

"Our utilities systems malfunctioned." Chakotay didn't intend to let this opportunity slip by. "And unless you agree to reconnect the umbilical attachments, our systems will probably *continue* to malfunction."

The official acted as if she hadn't heard a word. "How do you intend to pay the fine?"

"First, you tell me what's happening with Tom Paris."

There was a pause as she accessed the pertinent files. "Baseline reaction had been recorded, and the testing is under way. You may pay your fine by cooperating in the interrogation procedures of Prisoner 07119."

"How could we help you?"

"By providing another subject of the same species to undergo testing. This subject would also be used during the interrogation to obtain a collaborative reading of the data."

"You still haven't explained what's involved in this testing procedure."

"Testing is the generation of a simulation matrix that corresponds to the subject's biophysical and behavioral responses. Chemical analysis of these responses provide the factual data during interrogation. Will you provide an additional member of this species to undergo testing?"

"I can't allow that. Will you let me speak to Tom Paris?" Chakotay countered.

"I will note your refusal to cooperate in your file. If you have any information you would like to provide—"

"Yes, I know—I can submit it through your office." Chakotay closed the channel, adding, "You've been a great help."

Chakotay rested his head in his hands, wondering if it was worth it to try to return to his quarters so he could finish his meditation. The way things were going, something else would probably interrupt.

"I still have not been able to reach the away team,"

Tuvok informed him in a low voice. "It is not like Captain Janeway to remain out of contact for over twenty-seven hours."

Chakotay glanced over. "What about Andross?"

"I have spoken to his associates in the Hub office, but they have been unable to provide me with a link to Min-Tutopa. I am currently attempting to deal with Cartel communications on this matter."

"But they won't do anything until we give them our transporter technology, or another member of our crew so they can render them down for their chemical parts." Chakotay forced himself to stop. It didn't do any good to spread his frustration to the rest of the crew. "Keep trying, Tuvok. I don't know which of them I'm worried about more—Janeway and Torres, or Tom Paris."

STAR TREK: VOYAGER

CHAPTER
15

PARIS FELL TO HIS HANDS AND KNEES. THE JOLT SEEMED to clear his mind, and he felt the scrape of sand against his palms.

Sand?

He lifted his head with effort, but there was nothing to see in every direction except for a plain of sand. Overhead, two suns burned in the white-hot sky.

Drawing the back of his hand over his parched lips, he looked behind him. A short trail of his own footprints led back to a transport container. The hatch was open, where he'd obviously crawled out and gotten this far before his mind had finally caught up with his body. He figured that last dose of gas must have been a tad too much for him.

"Where am I?" he asked out loud. But there was nothing around that could answer.

Besides, he already knew the answer. That airlock cubicle had transferred him to a ship, and they had dropped him off on one of their waste asteroids. Maybe this is what they did to all the aliens they caught messing around with their computer files. They certainly did take their information seriously, but if that warranted a death sentence, why didn't they simply eject him into space and get it over with?

Paris stood up, looking back at the transport container. Maybe he should stay with it. The metal must be salvaged at some point. But that would mean he'd have to sit there doing nothing, and anything would be better than that.

Turning, he caught sight of a distant smudge on the horizon. He'd been heading toward it.

Paris figured he was probably right the first time, and started walking over the hard-packed sand. The heat was so dry it made it difficult to breathe. He took off his jacket but that did little to help. His sweat evaporated as soon as it hit the air, and his skin felt taut. He wondered how long it would take before he was lying prone on the endless plain, his body wrinkled and dried into a tough, desiccated shell of his former self.

The longer he walked, the less sense everything made. But he'd given up a long time ago trying to make sense of alien cultures. They had to have some reason for putting him here.

Uneasy, he glanced behind him again. He couldn't see the transport container anymore, but directly ahead, the smudge was getting darker.

He focused on the horizon, trying to ignore the vast emptiness around him. The first rule in survival courses counseled against panic. He was supposed to assess the situation and the resources available to him. He checked his pockets—his fibroknife and the pieces of his comm badge were gone. That wasn't reason to panic, he told himself. Neither was the fact that he had no water, and no way to get any in this arid landscape.

He decided it was time to count his blessings. He was unharmed and moving—always a good sign. And thankfully he wasn't agoraphobic like some truly hardened space-cases he'd met in his travels; otherwise he'd be curled into a screaming ball right about now. He could also tell by the angle of the suns that he was in the polar region of the asteroid. That meant there'd be almost continuous sunlight, but at least the powerful rays were deflected at an angle. He didn't want to imagine what sort of hell existed near the equator.

His blessings lasted until he could get close enough to make out the smudge through the distorting heat waves. It was another transport container.

He hurried, not sure if he would find another desperate alien or a mummified corpse. Yet caution made him slow on the final approach. There was no telling what kind of dangerous criminals the Tutopans were in the habit of depositing on this godforsaken asteroid.

A form was huddled in the meager shadow cast by the transport container. Paris waited until he saw it move. It was alive, and hardly looked threatening, so he went closer.

Flat Tutopan face, familiar somehow . . .

"Tracer!" Paris exclaimed when he realized it was the janitor. "What are you doing here?"

Tracer started in surprise, apparently unaware of his approach. He hunched one shoulder, looking up at Paris warily. "I haven't decided yet. What are you doing?"

Paris wasn't sure if Tracer was taking him literally, or being evasive as Tutopans typically were. "I'm trying to figure out what's going on. Last thing I remember, I was being dragged out of an airlock. Then I woke up here."

Tracer glanced around, his expression vacant.

"Why are you here?" Paris pressed.

"I committed a crime against the Cartel." Tracer sniffed, wiping his bud of a nose against his sleeve. "I'm already bonded to the Hub as a maintenance worker for twenty-nine more rotations. I don't know what they'll have me do now. Maybe deep-space work."

"What crime did you commit?" Paris asked sharply, hoping it didn't have anything to do with him.

"I let you into the Auxiliary Waste Management Control room."

"You didn't let me in," Paris denied. "I held your wrist badge to the sensor pad to open the door."

"You did?" the janitor asked, turning his mottled face toward Paris. "I don't remember."

"You were practically unconscious." Paris wasn't used to feeling this guilty, but Tracer was just sitting there like a kicked dog. "I don't understand why they're punishing you. It was my fault."

"I helped you get into that section, past the Enforcer on guard." Tracer thought about it a moment. "I think the Enforcer is in trouble, too."

Paris took a few steps away. "I can't explain it to you, but you didn't help me."

"There was no other way for us to get into that section," Tracer insisted doggedly. "That's why I'm here."

Paris groaned, kicking at the sand. "Take my word, you had nothing to do with it. This is a big mistake, you being here." He looked closer at Tracer. "I can understand it if you're angry."

"I'm not angry," Tracer said.

"Why not? I would be."

"It's not your fault I trusted you."

Paris turned away, telling himself that he had only intended to do his duty and protect his captain. Somehow that didn't make him feel any better. "I'm sorry. I wish there was something I could do. . . ."

Tracer shrugged as if that was a moot point now.

"Is breaking into their computer a good enough reason enough to leave us here to die? I didn't even get a chance to defend myself."

"You'll get to say whatever you want during the interrogation," Tracer said matter-of-factly. "First, we have to go through the testing."

Paris stared around at the empty waste. "This is a *test?*"

"Didn't you know? You *are* from a long ways away." Tracer pulled his foot into the tiny slice of shade cast by the smashed transport container.

Paris shook his head. "I thought testing was only for Tutopans, to determine your place in society. I didn't know it was like this. . . ." Slowly, understanding was dawning. "Those boasts I heard in the bars—people surviving incredible catastrophes—were those tests, too?"

"Probably."

Paris shook his head. Maybe that's why Tutopans were so bland—they got enough excitement through these tests. "Have you been through something like this before?"

"Growing up, we get tested all the time. It's why I was chosen to be sent to the Hub, as part of Griir-Tutopa's allotment of maintenance workers." Tracer grimaced. "I've never been tested by the Cartel, only my House."

"What are they testing us for now?"

"To prepare a matrix simulation of us for the interrogation."

Paris looked around. "That means they must be watching us, right now. Keeping scans focused on us."

Tracer acted as if that was an absurd question. "They record everything, heartbeat, body temperature, brain waves, chemical reactions . . ."

"Why would they want to create a simulation of our responses?"

"To compare it to your reactions during the interrogation, to know when deviations occur. That way, they can find out anything they want."

"What do you mean, find out?"

"They ask, and you tell them what you know. Like I said, I've never been tested by the Cartel, but I've heard you can say things that you didn't even know you knew."

Paris thought of all the technical manuals he'd been forced to read during his Academy days. If the Cartel could make him recall that information, they'd find out everything they needed to know about transporter technology. And anything else they stumbled across in his mind.

He shuddered, but tried to focus on the problem at hand. "If they're making a matrix of our behavior and physical reactions, they must be somewhere nearby."

Tracer nodded. "If this is Faltos, one of the moons of Griir-Tutopa, then they could be in a test ship in orbit. It looks like Faltos. Not much atmosphere and no life."

Paris lifted his face to the endless sky. "Tracer didn't do anything, you hear me!" he yelled. "You don't have to do this to him. It's all my fault, not his!" His voice rang out, swallowed by the still air, too vast for him to fill.

Tracer winced. "You don't have to shout, they can hear you fine."

"Well, let them listen to this." Paris shook his fist at the sky. "I'm not playing your games anymore!"

Tracer cast a handful of sand into the air, watching it drift back down. "I like to play games."

Paris wiped his forehead and wearily sat down next to the janitor, wondering if he was going to turn into an unmoving lump just like him. "How long before they come get us?"

"If this is a simulation, it could go on for days."

"What simulation?" Paris demanded. "I thought you said we were on a moon."

"This could be Faltos, or it might be a simulation of Faltos," Tracer told him. "Some people say they can tell the difference, but I never believed them."

"This might not be real?" Paris snorted. "That's a fairly important point, don't you think? If this is just a simulation, we might as well sit here until they bring the lunch cart around."

"I don't understand."

"Why work so hard? I mean, they can't let us *die.*" Paris didn't like the expression on the janitor's face. "I'm right, aren't I? People don't actually get killed on these tests, do they?"

Grimly, Tracer stared down at the sand. "It happens all the time. My mother was killed in testing when I was barely walking."

CHAPTER
16

BOTH SUNS HAD RISEN OVER THE HORIZON BY THE TIME Janeway woke. She had fought the effects of the gas as long as she could the night before, watching the rebels take control of the tower and the communications network of the Seat. From the orders and reports she overheard, the rebels had a ridiculously easy task taking over. Apparently, the House had never anticipated this sort of revolt. Then, shortly after Andross's guards had moved her and Torres to an underofficial's office and locked them inside, she had passed out again.

She checked Torres's pulse, inadvertently waking her in the process. She blocked the engineer's first blow, and ducked the second. "At ease, Lieutenant!"

Torres blinked up at her, resembling nothing more than a frightened child. "Captain. What happened?"

Janeway checked the door. "We're still locked in."

Torres pushed herself up and staggered over to the desk. Rubbing her eyes, she tried to access the computer terminal. "It's not working."

Janeway touched the light pad, but the room stayed in darkness. "They must have disconnected the power." She tugged open the blinds, to let in more sunlight. There seemed to be little activity in the complexes of the Seat below, but there was no way to tell if that was unusual.

Torres checked under the desk and came up with nothing. Aside from a padded couch and a few chairs, the office was empty. "Now what?" Torres asked.

Janeway thought that was a good question. Hostage situations were notorious for ending badly, and there was something about negotiating from this position of weakness that was abhorrent to her. "I'm open to suggestions, Lieutenant."

"I say we bust out of here." With her hands on her hips, Torres paced over to the window. It went from floor to ceiling and bowed out slightly in the middle. Bracing herself, the Klingon grunted as she gave it a solid kick. The clear material vibrated.

"It looks unbreakable," Janeway said. "But we could try shoving the desk into it. Why don't you help me?"

Together, they managed to move it a few centimeters.

"I wouldn't try that," someone said behind them. "You may hurt someone below."

Janeway jerked her head around in time to see Administer Fee sit down on the bed where she had been lying a few moments ago. She let go of the desk. "You! Are you responsible for this?"

"Not entirely," Fee said.

Janeway saw the concern and regret on the Tutopan's face. "What do you want with us?" she asked warily.

"I apologize most sincerely for this," Fee told them. "I didn't realize Andross would involve you so deeply. And I want to assure you that I will do everything in my power to make reparations."

"Good." Janeway hardly batted an eye. "We'd like to go now."

"I'm afraid that isn't possible."

"Why not?"

"As you may have gathered, we've used your processing unit to override the communications network of the Seat." Her gray eyes were steady, betraying an unexpected strength of character. "Until the Board approves my nomination as Supreme Arbitrator, your processor must remain here."

Janeway narrowed her eyes. "You and Andross, you planned this all along. You never intended to return our computer, you just wanted to keep us quiet until you executed your coup."

"Your computer will be returned as soon as this situation is stabilized."

"You mean once you gain control." Janeway was disgusted. "Would you really subvert the laws of society for your own gain?"

"Not for my gain. I do this for the people of Min-Tutopa."

"I've heard that one before," Janeway bit off. "Was it also for the good of the people that you ordered those pirates on the *Kapon* to steal our computer?"

"Andross has been purchasing computer processors for some time, hoping to find one that would be compatible. Finally, yours was brought to us."

Torres moved forward. "No—you stole it from us, plain and simple."

Janeway reached out, but wasn't able to stop Torres. It was just like her to attack the first person who tried to talk to them, but Janeway didn't order her to stop. She actually wanted to see what effect a physical threat would have on these people.

Fee glanced nervously between them as Torres approached her. "I think you should hear me out," she warned.

"I think you might be wrong about that." Torres lunged at Fee. "You're undefended—"

She stumbled forward when she met with no resistance, her arms flaying at thin air. She hardly disturbed the remarkable image of Fee as she sprawled through it onto the floor.

"I'm trapped in the Seat complex," Fee told them. "Along with the other Board Members. I wanted to appeal to you in person, but that wasn't possible."

"I wondered how you managed to sneak up on us," Torres muttered, rolling away and getting to her feet. She let one arm swing wide, swiping through the image. "Nothing's real in this place."

Fee sighed. "Your presence here is very real. However, there is a way for you to take your processor and return to your ship. If you help us."

Janeway braced herself. None of these Tutopans ever did anything unless they got something in exchange. "What is it you want?"

"Your processor is not integrating properly with the other province networks. As of right now, my people only have control of Seanss and the Seat. With your help, we can utilize your computer to its fullest capabilities and put an end to this situation."

"We can't help you," Janeway told her.

Fee didn't seem to understand. "Andross has informed me that you provided the interface between our systems. If you don't have the necessary tools, a courier can be sent to your ship. I assure you, we would make your efforts worthwhile."

"You can't pay us to overthrow your government." Janeway didn't even try to explain. "It goes against every principle by which we operate."

"What sort of system is that?" Fee asked startled. "Don't you believe in fair exchange?"

"Certainly, but you're asking us to help you violate the laws of your society. We are oathbound to not interfere with the natural development of alien species."

Fee sat very still for a moment, considering this. "Don't you believe that progress is made through cooperation?"

"What you consider progress may actually be detrimental to your people."

Fee seized on that. "You aren't convinced my position as Supreme Arbitrator would be of benefit to our House. Let me explain—"

"My answer would still be the same," Janeway interrupted.

"I know you can understand my point of view." Fee gazed at them thoughtfully. "When your communicators were examined—"

"You took our comm badges?" Torres interrupted.

Janeway touched her comm badge, wondering why she hadn't noticed it had been moved. "You know they're useless at this range."

"Andross had them examined after your unexpected resistance during the takeover. We had to make certain they didn't contain weapons of some sort." She smiled wanly. "I must say, Captain, your species hides its aggressive tendencies very well. Andross had no inkling you could react with such physical brutality."

Janeway returned the smile. "I'm glad I knocked some of the wind out of that young man. I'm sure it wasn't the grand moment of victory he had always envisioned."

"No, it wasn't," Fee agreed. "A point, you can be sure, he appreciates." She shifted. "However, I was pleased he went to the trouble when I read the report. Your devices are equipped with homing beacons capable of pinpointing the location of each individual."

"That's correct." Janeway didn't add that the beacon was a key component in locking coordinates for transport.

"Such a concern for the individual is unheard of among Tutopans," Fee said with wonder. "Our lives are geared toward the grand view of society, toward the development of our culture, with individual desires subsumed into communal efforts."

"Theoretically, that is one ideal," Janeway told her. "As you said, progress is made through cooperation."

"I understand the ideal, but the fact is strangling my people." Fee gestured to the window behind the two women. "Look out there. Tell me what you see."

Janeway didn't turn. "I've already seen it."

"It's a huge city," Torres said impatiently. "What's your point?"

"It's an even bigger world. And I'm no fool," Fee said frankly. "I realize I'm challenging a system that has a certain inertial weight, sustaining itself, even creating itself. But there are times when our direction needs to be shifted in a fundamental direction, times when a few individuals can take significant action to make sure that shift is positive, toward progress and growth, not fragmentation."

Torres jerked her head. "Fancy words for saying you know what's best for everyone else."

"I'm not alone," Fee said quickly. "I first became aware of the rebellion when I was in training. A network had sprung up between the higher centers of learning, and students were exchanging information. Since I was on track to a high-level administrative post, I was privy to much more history, law, and physics than the typical trainee. I had no need to link into this informal network. I sometimes wonder, if I *had* linked in once I received my direct interface, out of curiosity if nothing else, would I be here now?"

In spite of herself, Janeway was curious. "What happened to the network?"

"It was terminated, and the key participants . . . they disappeared from the learning boards." An old sadness showed around her eyes. "What frightened me most was the way it was done. Swiftly, fearfully, as if our way of life has become so microspecialized that we are threatened by general knowledge."

"How ironic," Janeway told her. "That you are a people who pride yourselves on your acquisition of knowledge."

"We also pride ourselves on our testing, but that, too, is a terrible trap. Hamilt was correct when he said I would have stayed among the poor growers of Province Larran without the testing to recognize my innate abilities. Yet who is to say I would not have been more fulfilled if I had been able to chose my own direction? We are given no choice, except during the testing, and our reactions are judged by preset standards, dictating where we should go and what we should do."

Janeway felt the tug of sincerity in Fee's voice. "Who determines the standards for these tests?"

"The Board—that is their primary duty while sitting in Council. The Supreme Arbitrator has veto power over any Board decision, as well as the ability to create policy, dictating how and when tests are given."

"That's why the position is so important." Janeway narrowed her eyes at the woman. "You could change the system from the top, single-handedly. I'm surprised it hasn't been tried before."

Fee actually smiled at that. "How do you think we got to this point? A narrowing of choice, generation after generation, all working toward the goal of one individual. We eliminated strife, and every other independent form of thought along with it. I believe that it is our biological right to develop and prosper according to our unique characteristics. We must be allowed to transcend the cultural boundaries of our age."

"Noble sentiments, but I must use your own example." Janeway pointed to the window. "Your society seems to be prospering quite well."

"The Cartel already subjects us to many of their testing standards, and they continue to gain power. Not only do they set the exchange rate, but they are increasingly privy to private House information."

Torres let out an exasperated sound. "All this fuss about the Cartel! We were doing fine until *your* people came along."

Fee seemed distressed by her show of anger. "I dislike disputes. I would have chosen to stay in the background, fighting through my reviews and the small indulgences I could slip to my province. But the time has come for our people to take control of themselves, before we let our House fall completely into the hands of the Cartel."

"I wish you luck with your endeavor," Janeway said, successfully keeping the sarcasm to a minimum.

"But we need your help," Fee insisted. "I don't want my people to destroy your processor in the attempt to link it to the other networks."

Janeway took a few measured steps closer to the image of Fee, leaning in close. "Can you see me through this transmission?"

"Yes."

"Good." She stared the administer right in the eye.

"Then let me make one thing perfectly clear—we aren't going to lift a finger to help you. It doesn't matter how much you try to threaten or bribe us."

"I am simply explaining the situation."

Janeway held out her arms. "I understand the situation. You're holding us hostage."

Fee seemed weary but unbeaten. "I cannot allow you to leave. The Board would seize you for testing and interrogation in an attempt to destroy us."

Torres laughed. "Why should we believe anything you tell us?"

"Perhaps you would believe the crew member who was arrested by the Cartel. Tom Paris could tell you how severe the testing can be."

"What are you talking about? What's happened to Paris?" Janeway demanded.

"He was taken into custody by the Cartel for unauthorized entry into their database. Right now, he is undergoing testing prior to interrogation. The Cartel is allowed to access anything that relates to the crime he committed."

Janeway was reminded of the last time an alien culture decided to punish Tom Paris—they'd almost lost him to those neural implants. "Is Paris being harmed by this procedure?"

"My latest report indicates he is still alive." Fee looked straight at Janeway. "I cannot help you from my current position, but I would do everything I can to repair the damage we've done—and to help your crew member—if I was in the position to do so."

Janeway clenched her teeth. "This sounds like just another ploy to convince us."

"I will arrange with Andross to allow you to speak to your ship," Fee said, surprising her. "They will confirm everything."

Torres glanced sideways at her. "Captain . . ."

"No, Lieutenant." Janeway didn't take her eyes off Fee.

"But if it's true that Paris—" Torres protested.

"I'd like to talk to my ship immediately," Janeway interrupted, watching Fee closely.

Fee nodded. "Perhaps then you will be convinced that it is in everyone's best interest to cooperate."

It was some time after Fee's image disappeared before several of the guards arrived to escort Janeway and Torres to the central command room. The guards' sleeves were torn where the Cartel insignia had been removed, leaving only the rising sun symbol of House Min-Tutopa. Janeway detected the euphoria of first battle among them, and they were keyed up so tightly that a wrong word could set them off. If these guards were under her command, her first task would be to curb their extreme optimism before someone stumbled over his own shoelace and destroyed everything.

Stepping into the command room, Janeway was greeted by a 360-degree view of the Seat. It was even more impressive than the narrow slice she'd seen from the office below, and again she wondered how this meager band of believers could shift the course of something so entrenched as this system.

Andross didn't seem daunted by the sight. He was on fire, as if all his pent-up energy had been boiling just beneath the surface, ready to be channeled into this coup d'état.

Andross drew up one corner of his mouth, and there was extra meaning to his nod of greeting to Janeway. He was moving stiffly, and she wondered if his ribs had been broken by the fall.

"I understand you wish to speak to your ship," Andross said politely.

"Yes." Janeway refused to beg.

Prog glanced up, harried at her post. "I have to shut down auxiliary systems again, Andross. The servos are overloading."

Andross muttered something under his breath. "Do it, but this time, I'll broadcast an announcement first. I'll tell them the power will be on reserve for the next cycle as a small warning of what we could do."

"How much load is our processor carrying?" Janeway demanded.

"Nearly five thousand megabits per second," Prog replied.

"No wonder the servos are strained. . . ." Torres whistled. "Why aren't you using those other two processors?"

"Their firmware includes an override command that the Board could initiate from the Council Chamber." Andross turned away from the broadcast channel, having sent his warning to the Seat. "That's why we needed the outside hardware."

"If this system goes down, what does it take with it?" Janeway asked.

"The power and communications grid of the entire Seat and most of Seanss province." Prog tightened her lips briefly. "Since we're partially linked in with the networks, there could be a relay affect in the other provinces, as well."

Torres edged in closer to Prog to see the monitor. "Why don't you disconnect from the other networks, at least that way—"

"No," Andross said quickly. "It's taken us all night to get even a partial link."

"You'll lose everything if you don't take something off-line," Torres said, in a tone that was all too familiar to Janeway. She was pretending to be reasonable, while she really thought she was dealing with idiots.

"We need the links to the other provinces," Andross said as if that was final. "We don't have enough access to their networks as it is. They've managed to interrupt our broadcasts every time."

Janeway thought he was too confident for his own good. "Why haven't the other provinces moved to help the House Seat?"

"They've interrupted our broadcasts, and they've already tried infiltration and gas attacks. But House guards are equipped to deal with isolated incidents, not mass resistance. There is little harm they can do to us."

"They could blow up this tower," Torres put in darkly.

Prog seemed shocked. "They'd never do that."

Andross wasn't nearly as surprised by her suggestion. "The House did use force during the commune uprising several rotations ago—cutting off power to parts of the lower Seanss Province. With no water, no food services, no climate control, it wasn't long before people began returning to work."

"You call that force?" Torres asked doubtfully. "Was there any bloodshed?"

Andross shook his head. "None to speak of."

"Don't give me that," Torres told him. "You people scanned our ship from top to bottom for weapons and defense systems. You must be experts when it comes to combat."

"That's the Cartel," Andross corrected. "They were created for defensive purposes and keeping the peace, particularly when dealing with alien species."

"The Board would never call in Cartel Enforcers against their own House," Prog agreed vehemently. "It would be tantamount to admitting the House is in such disorder that they can't control it themselves."

"While the Cartel would take over under the guise

of protecting the House," Andross finished. "Placing the Board under their jurisdiction."

Janeway paced a few steps closer. "Then it seems to me you have a stalemate, here."

"We have the option of cutting power to the Seat. We took over the communications network this time to prevent the Board from strangling our efforts, but it can be used as a way to convince them."

"So why don't you do it?" Torres asked, ever the advocate for action. "Get it over with."

"That would cause harm to service and support personnel long before the effect reaches the higher officials. Then people would get hurt." Andross did a good job of sounding sanctimonious. "I would rather not let this degenerate into violence, but I will do what it takes. Fee's nomination will be confirmed before I return the systems to their control."

"It must be nice to be so sure of yourself," Torres snapped, almost as if reading Janeway's mind.

Andross must have seen Janeway's agreement in her face. His cold glance included them both. "Make the call to your people. They'll tell you about the Cartel."

Tuvok was dealing with yet another underofficial of the Cartel in an attempt to obtain a subspace communications channel to Min-Tutopa. As was consistent among the officials, the clerk persisted in countering his direct requests for services with offers for "information exchange" that were unacceptable.

The underofficial closed the channel, as Tuvok received a signal on the frequency he associated with House Min-Tutopa. He signaled the ready room. "Commander, we are being hailed."

Despite his control, there must have been some indication in his voice. Chakotay was on the bridge in seconds, showing an uncharacteristic tension. "Put it through."

The resolution of the viewscreen was below acceptable standards; however, the image was unmistakably Captain Janeway.

"Captain," Chakotay said in relief. "We've been worried—"

"I was unable to contact you earlier." She glanced to one side as if to indicate wariness of her present company. Tuvok's frown deepened when he noted that her hair was in slight disarray, as if she had pinned it up without the aid of a mirror. "Our situation has changed. Apparently we've been caught up in a revolution, and our computer processor is being used to hold the legitimate government hostage."

"Are you in danger, Captain?"

"Not at the moment. But we are not allowed to leave this building." Her voice was grim. "And I don't intend to leave without our processor."

Carefully, Chakotay said, "We've received information that concerns Agent Andross and numerous computer thefts that have occurred."

"Yes, Andross was responsible," the captain informed him dryly. Her gaze rested on Tuvok for a moment. "You were correct, as usual."

"I had hoped I was mistaken," Tuvok replied.

"I don't intend to cooperate with Andross's demands." Janeway nodded to Chakotay. "Commander, give me a report on your situation."

The captain received Chakotay's report with her chin propped in her hand. Her eyes began to glaze over as the first officer went through the list of complications that accompanied Paris's arrest, including the umbilical disconnection and the extensive systems failures throughout the ship.

"We're holding in Reduced Power Mode, but we're still experiencing fault errors and delays," Chakotay finished.

"And Paris?" Janeway asked.

"I'm worried. From what I've been able to find out about the testing and interrogation, it can be deadly. In fact, the chemical risks these people take with alien biology astounds me."

"You've had no luck dealing with Cartel officials?"

"None. They want technology from us, and they won't even let me see Paris unless we give them something in exchange."

Janeway shifted as Andross stepped into the line of sight. "Do you see what blind obedience leads to?" the agent asked. "You're trying to negotiate with a mechanism that has no concern for the well-being of any individual. Now do you see what we fight against?"

"That's none of my concern." Janeway's expression told Tuvok all that was necessary—she didn't trust Andross.

The viewscreen blurred as Andross moved away. From a distance, Torres called out a warning, as Janeway's black uniform slumped out of the frame.

"Captain!" Chakotay exclaimed. "What's going on there? Andross, what are you—"

"As your captain told you," Andross said, breathing faster as if from some effort, "the situation has changed."

"What have you done to them—"

"Commander, I believe you should listen to me." The threat was clear in Andross's voice.

"I'm listening," Chakotay said flatly.

"We need more power from your processor. Give us the schematics of the procedural sequence, and show us how we can link into other network analyzers."

Chakotay slowly shook his head. "That's impossible."

Tuvok refrained from mentioning that Captain Janeway had ordered them not to assist Andross.

"Once our leader is in power," Andross urged, "your people and your computer will be returned. You will be free to go about your own business."

Chakotay sounded as if he were in pain. "We do not bargain with the future of a society."

"I'll give you one day to provide the information I've requested." Andross glanced down briefly. "Your people are nothing but a nuisance at this point. Don't make me use them to prove how serious I am."

CHAPTER
17

PARIS REALIZED HE WAS ON HIS FEET WHEN TRACER actually moved out of the shade to get away from him. He knew the Tutopans didn't have transporter technology, and he couldn't understand how they could simulate deadly force without one. "How is this illusion created?"

Tracer avoided his glare. "I'm no tech, don't ask me."

"Photo-holograms are one thing," Paris muttered under his breath. "But they have no substance."

He tossed his jacket aside and calmly walked over to the transport container. He punched it as hard as he could. The metal shell made a faint resonant sound and felt solidly resistant against his knuckles, so he punched it a few more times. Tracer scrambled out of the way, as sand went flying.

When Paris finally stopped, he was flushed and warmer than before. He also felt better than he had since he woke up in the airlock globe. "There! That's real enough for me."

"Yeah." Tracer was watching him warily. "Your sleep-journeys seem real too. But you can't die from dreaming."

It took Paris a moment to realize what he said. "You mean simulations are like a hallucination?"

"They create it in our minds. Sort of the way misto-tripping happens after you've had too much."

Paris wanted to crawl right out of his own skin. But it felt real—his hands were throbbing from the pounding. He watched as a single drop of blood welled up on one knuckle, forming a perfect dome of red that reflected the brilliant suns overhead. Then it slid down the back of his hand, leaving a faint trace of blood as another drop started to form. Was it real, or was it only in his mind? It was enough to send him right to the edge—

"Okay, let's not panic," Paris reminded himself. "First rule, don't panic. Anything can be dealt with . . ."

Tracer inched back into the shadow of the container. "What are you going to do?"

His mouth curled up in distaste. Any way you looked at it, his mind was being invaded. They were watching him, evaluating his choices, recording every flicker of energy that went through his body. Even if he had broken their law, he didn't deserve to be punished like this.

"How long can Tutopans go without drinking fluids?" he asked for lack of anything better.

"I don't know."

Of course Tracer didn't know. Paris wasn't sure Tracer knew about anything except for cleaning floors and going to some dive for the few hours of relief he could find in the bottom of a misto bottle. "Well, humans can last for a couple of days, tops, in this kind of dry heat. Maybe not even that long if we're walking. I bet Tutopans aren't much different."

Tracer settled down in the sand. "If this is Faltos, they could be using us to establish a baseline for simulations. That means it could go on for days. They often use criminals to get the baselines."

"Criminals!" Paris snorted. "You're hardly a criminal, and I never even had a trial. What kind of people are you?"

"You mean you didn't steal information from the Cartel computers?"

Paris abruptly shut up, remembering the spying eyes. "I didn't touch their computer," he said honestly.

"You didn't?" Tracer asked, wide-eyed.

"Besides, aren't there such things as extenuating circumstance?" Paris asked. "I only wanted to find out what would be common knowledge anyplace else."

"What was that?"

"Docking manifests, tracing merchandise," he said vaguely. "I wanted to know if Min-Tutopa had something to do with the theft of our computer processor."

"Did you find out?"

"I was caught almost immediately." Paris wasn't sure if they knew about Kim, or if Tracer had told them about another man. "What exactly do you remember?"

Tracer chewed his bottom lip. "It's hard . . . there's the bar, and that other place we went . . . your ship, was it?"

"Yes."

"I must have been out of my mind," Tracer sighed, shaking his head. "I knew it as soon as I saw that Neelix guy. You weren't looking for a good time, you were running some kind of scam."

"What do you mean?"

"I thought that's why you came over, that you were one of those weird aliens who likes unusual women." Tracer gestured self-consciously to the mottled patches on her face.

"What?!"

"I'm a female."

Paris knew his mouth was open, but he couldn't help it. "You're—"

"Female." She turned her mild eyes away. "I thought you knew. But you called me 'him' when you were yelling at the Cartel."

Paris sat down, hard. "I didn't know. . . ."

Tracer shrugged, that same laconic gesture Paris had seen a dozen times before. It didn't look any different, but a filter seemed to slip over his vision and all of his protective instincts rose.

"I'm sorry. It's just that you Tutopans look so much alike," he added lamely. He kept remembering the way he had pummeled her into the closet. "I've acted atrociously."

She squinted up at him. "You're not so bad."

If he felt guilty before, now it was a thousand times worse. Why hadn't he figured out that Tracer was a woman? Now that he knew, it seemed obvious.

"Come on," he told her, holding out his hand to help her up. "We can't just sit here."

She stared at his outstretched hand. "Why not?"

"Because, the least we can do is try to help ourselves." He shaded his eyes, checking the horizon. "There's got to be something around here."

"You want me to come with you?"

He leaned over and took her arm, pulling her up. "I got you into this. I'll get you out."

She flinched at his touch, quickly moving away when she was on her feet. "You will?"

213

"I can try." Paris got his bearings. "Over there. It looks like there's something in that direction."

Tracer actually gave him a little smile. "Thanks."

Paris let out a short laugh. "Sure, any time you want a one-way trip to nowhere, just call me."

"I've never been on a test with someone like you before." Tracer slogged through a patch of soft sand, avoiding his offer of help.

Paris figured he might as well find out what he could. "This testing of yours seems pretty severe. Don't you lose a lot of children this way?"

"Children don't get survival testing. Only those who are destined for command or exploration or some sort of high-level position. That way the weak and unfit are winnowed out." She smiled again. "I read that someplace."

"It seems like a lot of effort to go to just for us."

"People give away valuable information when they're trying to save themselves."

Paris thought back on what he might have said, then decided that worrying about that wasn't high on his list of priorities. "I don't know what I hate more—having them so deep inside my head they could create a simulation that feels this real, or really being stuck in a desert with no hope of rescue in sight."

"It could be worse," Tracer said philosophically enough. "Once my hands were tied behind my back. That time, it turned out to be real."

His tongue felt as if it was sticking to the roof of his mouth, and his lips were starting to crack. This couldn't be a simulation. "You know, I'm getting tired of always comparing my situation to the worst case scenario."

Tracer was obviously trying to be helpful. "I heard of one guy who drew the same test someone else at work had been talking about. He thought it was a simulation until the very end, when he realized it was real."

"What happened?"

"He broke his legs in fourteen places. He said he shouldn't have jumped off the roof."

"That's probably a safe bet anytime." It was getting more difficult to walk through the deep sand. "Do you have any more horror stories you want to share?"

"I—" Tracer stumbled to one side, just as Paris realized his boots were sinking into the sand.

"Keep walking!" Paris cried out, prying one foot out, then leaning forward to pull the other free. He tried to turn around, but everywhere he stepped, there seemed to be nothing but liquid sand, drawing him down.

"Help me!" Tracer called out, flailing her arms as she went over on her side. Her legs were buried up to the knees.

Paris couldn't stop and he couldn't turn around. His only object was to get back to firmer ground. With each step a superhuman effort, he could barely see Tracer flopping around on the sand.

"I'm sinking," she gasped out.

Paris fell forward as he hit the edge of the quicksand, rolling to see Tracer half covered. Her muffled cries and frantic movements got him moving.

"Turn over!" he called out. Testing the edge, trying to find a way around, he circled in closer as the sand shifted over the top of Tracer.

There was a terrible inevitability to the struggle. As Paris stretched out, trying to reach for her, the last bit of her coverall sank beneath the sand.

"Tracer!" Grains of sand continued to slide into the depression where Tracer used to be.

Rolling onto his back, Paris shouted, "No! Get

down here before she suffocates! Before it's too late—"

Staring up at the blinding sky, his eyes blurred, maybe with tears.

When he blinked, he saw an unfamiliar face. The flat features immediately identified him as a Tutopan.

"An excellent reading on that one," someone said outside of his vision.

The Tutopan leaned over him, barely reacting. "We can begin the interrogation tomorrow. Notify his ship."

Paris struggled to sit up, but thick bands were secured over his arms and chest. Even his legs wouldn't move. It was as disorienting as waking up in a hospital, with everything too clean and bright and cold. Dispassionate hands removed a strap from his forehead and he saw electrodes gleaming with conductive gel.

"What are you doing to me?" he cried out, even as the other Tutopan returned. He felt the burning contact of an injector against his neck.

"You are undergoing testing, Prisoner 07119."

CHAPTER
18

KIM RIFLED THROUGH THE STACKS OF ISOLINEAR CHIPS that covered the top of Zimmerman's desk. He knew the one he wanted was around here somewhere, but he couldn't find it.

In frustration, he banged the desk with the flat of his hand, making some of the isolinear chips slide off. It didn't make him feel any better. Kes was right, this wasn't like him. He couldn't think straight anymore—not while the captain and B'Elanna were being help captive. Not while Tom Paris was confined in the bowels of the Hub, paying for a crime that Kim had actually committed.

Kim slumped back down in the chair. If only he hadn't been envious of Tom and B'Elanna, then his judgment wouldn't have been impaired when Paris asked him to go into the Hub. If he had refused, or checked with Tuvok first, Paris might still be here. . . .

Then again, maybe he was wallowing in his misery in order to avoid the fact that he'd failed to fix the computer network.

But how can I fix something that always keeps changing?

He wondered if the scientists at Utopia Planitia were also finding out just how tricky their new wonder-computer was. It integrated with the other systems in a way that was certainly as unpredictable and complex as a living organism. And he had realized that the neural gel packs weren't accessing faster than nanoprocessors, they were learning patterns and interpreting them without having to go through the processor every time. Even then, the patterns that the impulses followed were a loose guideline. From moment to moment, though the end points were fixed between certain isolinear chips, the pathways through the neural tissue changed to suit passing requirements. Each cell apparently had hundreds of thousands of possible synapses, or paths of transmission. He couldn't pinpoint and isolate the problem areas or determine which systems would be affected next by the erratic impulses. And he couldn't stop the neural gel packs from processing information according to past scenerios.

To make matters worse, clusters of the nerve cells seemed to be migrating. There was no other word he could use to describe it—and nothing about the phenomenon made sense. No matter how many adjustments they made to the chemical infusions, efficiency had risen only another three percent. He didn't need Chakotay to tell him that wasn't good enough.

In the outer room, Kes glanced up from her tissue analysis. Her smile was completely sympathetic. Kim knew she'd already forgiven him for being so mean to the doctor when he had tried to access the ODN, and he added that to his list of things to feel bad about.

He called through the glass. "Found out anything yet on those cell clusters?"

"You were right," she said, pushing back from the monitor as he joined her. "They're migrating within the core, and I think I've found evidence of a few clusters that are forming in the bridge main subprocessor."

Kim let out a groan of disbelief. "That's the last thing we need!"

"I'm not even sure why it's happening." Kes glanced in the direction of the examining room. "When I tried to ask the doctor, he wouldn't talk to me."

Kim could see Zimmerman lying prone on the table. "What's wrong with him now?"

"There's been a rash of new symptoms—" Kes stood up and stretched, extending her arms as high as she could and raising onto her toes. "Oh! That feels good."

Kim didn't want to think about how good it looked. "Let's go examine our patient," he said, perfectly serious.

The doctor's eyes were open, but he didn't acknowledge their entrance. His hands were loosely clasped over his chest. It reminded Kim of ancient movies of the undead, waiting to rise and seize control. He tried to banish the thought as unworthy.

"Doctor?" Kes asked.

As if the effort was almost too much for him, Zimmerman turned his head. There wasn't a flicker of recognition.

"How do you feel?" Kim asked, determined this time to keep his temper.

Zimmerman sighed, lifting one hand as if there was nothing he could say. His hand shook with a slight tremor.

"He has all the signs of depression," Kes said quietly. "With intermittent manic episodes."

"I didn't even know he had emotions," Kim said.

"Of a sort," Kes said. "In organic beings, emotional reaction is simply the chemical impetus for decision making. He was programmed to recognize situations that are frustrating or advantageous, and to act accordingly. And his patient interface contains emotional reactions to help deal with patients."

The doctor displayed no overt interest in her diagnosis. Even Kim was starting to get worried. "Why don't you sit up?" he suggested. "We'd like to examine you."

It took a moment for the doctor's image to form the words. "Must you?"

At Kim's nod, Zimmerman heaved a deep sigh and slowly started to move. Kes reached out as if to help him, but Kim stopped her. She gave him a wounded look, but he silently watched as Zimmerman fumbled his way up. His legs dangled over the edge, and his forearms were loosely resting on his thighs. His hands were trembling again.

"Do you remember what's been happening?" Kim asked.

"I'm not brain-dead," the doctor replied, raising his head for a brief glare.

Kim held out his hands, placating him. "I know. But lately your mental processes have been . . . deranged."

"So that's it," Zimmerman said. "Is that why you won't let me work anymore?"

"You erased half the ion readout the last time you got on the monitor. We can't afford that to happen again."

"You're helping us right now," Kes reminded him gently. "Just by letting us examine you."

"You don't need me," the doctor said bitterly.

"You're our chief medical officer. You know we need you," she insisted.

"You don't," he denied, turning his head away. "Once you're through with me, you'll just program up a new doctor. I know you people! You'll probably make him look like me . . . only it won't be me."

"Shh . . ." Kes murmured. "You'll be fine. Less than two percent of people who suffer injuries to the head actually die."

"How many had their cerebral cortex ripped out?" the doctor countered. "I'm at the mercy of this ship . . . my body lives in a vacuum, endlessly traveling with no place to go. . . ."

Kim noted the new symptoms—self-pity, depression, suicidal thoughts—and he wondered if *he* was crazy, treating a computer system as if it were a mental patient. But they didn't have many choices.

"Come on," Kim said, trying to sound encouraging. "You know the drill, so let's get it over with."

Zimmerman allowed Kim to go through the examination: he touched his toes when asked, then his nose with alternating hands. He missed several times, which seemed to upset him even more. And when Kes tapped the tendon below his kneecap, his foot kept bouncing until Kim reached out and stopped it.

"Are you going to stick pins in me next?" the doctor asked faintly.

"Not this time," Kes assured him, warning Kim off with a look.

Kim didn't see any reason to push it. "What do you make of this?"

"I found a reference in one of the pharmacology texts that describes symptoms of Parkinsonism that can be induced by reserpine. The stooped posture, slow movement, lack of facial expression . . ."

"Looks like what we've got here."

"Parkinson's syndrome is usually caused by lesions in the basal ganglia. But the same symptoms can arise when there's a decrease in concentrations of dopamine in the neural tissue."

"Can't we add dopamine, then?"

Kes gave him a wry look. "That's what we're destroying in order to inhibit nerve impulse transmission."

"Oh." Kim didn't like the doctor's dour expression. "Is there anything else we can do for him?"

Kes shook her head. "Not until we can return the bioneural masses to their normal function."

"You could try freezing part of my thalamus," the doctor suggested. "Oh, that's right, I'm only a holoprogram. I don't have a thalamus."

"Don't be that way," Kim said. He wished he hadn't been so hard on the doctor earlier.

Kes put a hand on his shoulder. "I know you don't want to hear it, but maybe we should unhook your subprocessor from the main core. It's not like it's a regular junction node, so even though it has neural gel packs, it might not react badly."

The doctor tried to straighten up, his brow furrowing. "Perhaps, but then you wouldn't have me to give you feedback on the effects of the chemical therapy. No, I'll stay on-line with the ODN."

"But what if this is causing permanent damage?" Kes asked.

"How could it?" Kim countered. "His program isn't being altered."

"I checked his programming. He's designed to learn from experiences and adapt to situations. This psychotic behavior could be imprinted onto his associative behavior patterns—in the same way that your Doctor Pavlov was able to make dogs salivate by ringing a bell."

"Conditioned responses?" Kim asked. Kes nodded. He may be permanently affected by this treatment."

Kim wasn't sure what to say to that. They needed the doctor's feedback, but he didn't want to cause him any harm.

"Perhaps I'm just like any of you," Zimmerman sighed. "I'll survive, but I might not be the same. I'll have to deal with the consequences of my . . . illness. Now I understand the subroutines I am directed to initiate when treating another doctor. We do make the worst patients."

Kes smoothed his hair back from his forehead. "It's not fair for you to have to suffer this way."

"Fair?" Zimmerman tried but wasn't able to smile at her. "I'm a member of this crew, and I'll do what needs to be done to solve this problem. Only why don't you let me *do* something?"

Kes gave Kim a worried glance.

Kim didn't want to be the one to disappoint him again. "Maybe we can set up a terminal that's isolated from the rest of sickbay's systems. But that will take almost an hour—"

"I'll help," Kes instantly offered.

Kim was doubtful, but one look at the new hope on the doctor's face was enough. "Okay, let's see what you can come up with," he agreed.

"Finally, I can get to work." The doctor clasped his shaking hands together, actually smiling for the first time. "Physician—heal thyself!"

A loud buzzing woke Torres to a murky light. She rolled, automatically reaching for the phaser under her pillow, thinking she was caught in a raid in a Maquis outpost.

When she came up empty-handed, landing in a

heap on the floor, she remembered she wasn't fighting Cardassians or Starfleet anymore.

Groaning, she used the bench to try to get up.

"Better rest and let it wear off gradually," Prog suggested from her post. She seemed harried, and was surrounded by piles of square tapes.

"How . . . long?" Torres managed to get out.

"You were unconscious all day. It's almost sunset. Andross left you here so I could keep an eye on you. Your resistance to the sedative was much lower this time."

Torres didn't tell her about the antidote that Tuvok had given them. Apparently it only lasted for one attack—she'd have to tell him about that little oversight when she got back to the ship. If she got back.

She dragged herself over to the adjoining bench where Janeway was lying. It looked as if someone had taken the time to carefully position her rather than dumping her down haphazardly. Torres reminded herself to be grateful about that as she checked Janeway's pulse. It was steady and strong, but she was still unconscious. She had been closer to Andross and must have gotten a heavier dose of the gas.

"Neither of you have suffered permanent damage," Prog added.

"I'm getting tired of hearing that every time I wake up." Torres tried to get up and settled for sitting on the foot of Janeway's bench.

"I don't blame you," Prog told her. "But Andross says it's inevitable that some people will become involved even though it's not their struggle."

Torres leaned her elbows on her knees, resting before her next attempt at rising. "I remember I told somebody that once."

Prog immediately looked interested. "When?"

Torres wanted to laugh, but it got caught in her throat. "When I was fighting for a rebellion."

"You did? Did you win?"

"I don't know." Torres stared into space. "I wonder what happened. . . ."

"You left." The accusation was clear in her flat voice. "You didn't believe in your cause anymore?"

"Not exactly." Torres carefully got to her feet. "It never was *my* cause, not really. Sometimes I think I fought because I had nothing else to believe in."

"*I* have nothing else to believe in." Prog glanced down at her hands. "I'm one of the senior computer technicians for the communications network. I've risked everything, my entire life, in this attempt."

"So why are you doing it?" Torres asked. "What could be worth such a risk?"

"Worth it? Anything would be better. I couldn't stand another cycle, not another interval of living that way."

"Was your life so difficult or unpleasant?" Torres knew what it was like to be a misfit, to have nothing left to risk, but this woman didn't seem to fit that stereotype. Torres gestured to the sleek surroundings and advanced equipment. "It looks like you were doing well for yourself."

"My life is not mine to live. I'd rather be in the free commune where I grew up, but when I opted to get my professional skills, I gave everything away. They need skilled workers back home, and I want to work with the people I love, to help build our community."

"You're saying they won't let you leave?"

"I'm bonded to Seanss Province for another fifteen rotations. They decide where and when I go. If they want to transfer me to Ellosian, they could. One of my friends, Marrt, had to leave her mate and go to

Tangir. They say she'll only be there two rotations, but who knows?"

"So you threw in your support with Andross?" Torres glanced around the empty control room. "Where is the little guy with delusions of grandeur?"

"Who?"

"Andross. He doesn't strike me as the type who could lead a revolution."

Prog actually seemed shocked by that assessment. "I would chose to test with Andross any time."

Torres stretched as she got up, feeling the muscles strain from the long periods of inactivity. Swinging her arms and kicking out her legs to get the blood moving, she wandered over to Prog. A gas gun was right next to her hand, but she seemed more interested in reviewing the tapes that surrounded her. She noticed that the guards by the lift were more alert, watching her closely.

"I don't even know your name," Prog said apologetically.

"B'Elanna Torres." She squinted at the labels on the tapes, marked by red warning tags—QUANTUM MECHANICS ONLY, and RESTRICTED.

"That's pretty." Prog's gaze lifted to her forehead ridges, but she seemed embarrassed. "What are you?"

"My father was human and my mother, Klingon." She jerked her head back at Janeway. "She's human."

"You say that like . . . I don't know, like you're envious."

"Maybe." Torres hadn't expected that much perception from the woman. "Maybe I should be glad I've got some Klingon fire inside of me. I see what pacifism has done for you people. And it's pacifism that inspired the principle of noninterference, which isn't doing me much good right now."

Prog shook her head at that. "Would you really

stand by and watch your processor be destroyed when you could do something to help?"

Torres blew out her breath. How could she explain the Prime Directive when she didn't completely understand it herself? Instead, she settled for saying, "I don't do anything under coercion."

"No one is forcing you."

"No? Then we'll be going now."

"You don't want to do that. The tower is surrounded by House guards, waiting for a break in our defenses. You'd be taken to the Board and mindsucked so fast you wouldn't know what was happening." Prog shook her head. "None of us is leaving until we have control of the House."

"If you think I'm going to help you after the way you've treated us, you're very wrong."

Prog's eyes were steady. "Didn't you ever have to hurt someone when you were fighting your rebellion?"

Torres almost didn't answer, but honesty compelled her. "Yes."

"Then you understand."

Torres fingered one of the tapes. "It's just making me more confused."

"I can give you some reviews to read—"

Prog broke off as a warning signal pierced the quiet. She reached the monitor in two strides, ignoring Torres, who came up behind her.

"The synchronization is off again," Prog explained. "I can't get the patterns to stabilize within the interface control unit."

"You're rotating loads to minimize losses," Torres said approvingly.

"I've rerouted what I can, but the system continues to overload. Could there be transients or fault defects in your processor?"

Torres nudged her aside. "No, look at this indicator. The varied operating speed is coming from the control unit itself."

Prog shook her head over her readouts. "I've never seen a pattern like this, except during testing simulations when the neuron networks are compared."

"That's because of the neural gel packs in the memory core. They act as an independent variable-function generator, calibrating a continuous input of data and changing operations to suit current conditions even during the processor's calculation of a problem solution."

Dismayed, Prog stared back. "How can I integrate with a system like that? I would need a complete flowchart of the circuits of the prior memory core. Even then, I'd somehow have to copy it into our database through an invasive subroutine."

Torres shrugged. "I would never have tried to integrate in the first place without the procedural sequence."

Prog fastened her eyes on her. "You know what needs to be done to bring the processor up to speed."

In spite of herself, Torres had already figured out that they needed to input a parallel operation program to improve performance. The processor had the capacity to allow data to pass through many lines simultaneously to accommodate the neural gel packs.

"You do know!" Prog said triumphantly. "Why won't you help us? We could take over the entire network of the planet, and the Board would have to give in. You could be back on your ship, with your processor, by this time tomorrow."

"You heard what my captain said. We can't help you."

"What about your crew member with the Cartel?"

Her eyes narrowed. "He's a friend of yours, isn't he? Don't you want to help him?"

"I do." Stricken, she couldn't say more.

"Then tell me," Prog insisted, her voice lowering. "I'll do the work, just tell me."

The temptation was almost overwhelming. Torres braced herself against the monitor with one hand, bending her head. Conflicting desires swirled together, until everything resolved on the image of Captain Janeway's face the last time she had disobeyed orders—after she and Seska had installed the transport device in Engineering. Nothing had been as excruciating as confessing her transgression to Janeway, not even during those terrible moments when she couldn't detach the destructive device from the ship.

"I know what needs to be done," Torres said, her throat tight. "You'd better disconnect our processor from the network."

Prog let out her breath sharply. "You won't tell me?"

"I don't know what to do." Torres turned away, hoping she hadn't already given the rebels the information they needed.

"I thought you were a fighter!" Prog called after her. "You're weak like everyone else."

Torres silently shook her head, refusing to look back. Prog didn't know how hard it was to walk away.

With a sigh, she sat down on her bench, her shoulders slumped. When she looked up, Janeway's eyes were open, watching her. "Captain! You're awake."

"I've been awake." Janeway stiffly pushed herself up. Her voice lowered. "You lied to her."

Torres gave her a sharp glance. "How do you know?"

"My mother is a theoretical mathematician. I've been immersed in computer programming ever since I can remember. I know they need to time-share the program, and I know you're aware of how to do that."

"Why didn't you say something?" Torres demanded. "I almost told her."

Janeway seemed surprised by the question. "You're one of my senior officers, Lieutenant. I trust you to obey my orders."

Torres felt uncomfortable. "It was a test? To see if I'd obey orders this time?"

"Not at all. I must believe in my crew, or we're all in bigger trouble than this." Janeway gestured to Prog and the guards. "It's only by working together within a common system, toward common goals, that we'll survive to return to the Alpha Quadrant."

Torres shook her head. "I don't understand that. All I know is that I couldn't let you down again."

Janeway relaxed ever so slightly. "I didn't think you would."

CHAPTER
19

AFTER ANDROSS HAD MADE HIS THREAT, CHAKOTAY
spent the rest of the day going from one department
to the next, talking to the officers and getting a feel for
the atmosphere on board. It was not the sort of thing
Starfleet usually advised captains to do. But he was
discovering just how many of Starfleet's recommen-
dations relied on the fact that your ship would be
somewhere in Federation space. If you could hang on
for long enough, someone would inevitably come to
investigate.

That's what made this situation so insidious. Their
strength was being sapped in a thousand unforeseen
ways. He could sense that in the crew—even as they
brought systems back on-line and improved reaction
time, there was a desperate feeling that time was not
on their side.

As Chakotay quietly moved among the crew, he was
aware that he had fallen back into Starfleet mentality.
He had learned from the best strategists and tacti-
cians at the Academy; then his skills had been honed

even more when he left to fight Starfleet. He didn't intend to oppose the principles that guided their crew, but he determined that their execution must be molded to suit their needs.

By evening he was ready.

"You're all aware of our situation." Chakotay clasped his hands on the conference table, addressing the group of sadly diminished senior officers, including Neelix, who'd been inside the Hub, and Kes, who took the place of the chief medical officer. His visit to sickbay had revealed the extent of Zimmerman's malfunctions, but the doctor had been back at work, analyzing the reflexive effects of the neural tissue. "Now I want to hear your opinions."

Tuvok's raised brow acknowledged the unorthodox beginning. "I believe our most immediate concern is Agent Andross. In so many words, he has threatened to kill the away team unless we provide him with the computer information by midday tomorrow."

"We have to give him what he wants," Kes insisted. "Nothing is worth the life of Captain Janeway and Lieutenant Torres."

Tuvok told her, "To render aid to an insurrection would be a direct violation of the Prime Directive."

Neelix rolled his eyes. "Not that again!"

"Yes, that again," Chakotay immediately replied. "We're all aware that both problems could be solved by giving the Tutopans what they're asking for. And then what?"

"Then we get out of here," Neelix said, as if that was obvious.

"Leaving behind repercussions that would have drastic consequences for millions of people. Do you want that responsibility?" Chakotay straightened up, meeting the eyes around the table. "I don't."

"We must find another option," Tuvok agreed.

"Why don't we just go in and get them?" Kim asked.

Chakotay had already considered that possibility. "The Cartel has refused my request for permission to take a shuttle in-system."

"Did they give a reason why?" Kes asked.

"They know our missing processor is somehow involved in the rebellion. I explained that our only interest is to retrieve Captain Janeway and Lieutenant Torres, but again, they want more information about Min-Tutopa. Apparently, they have a vested interest in what happens."

Neelix grimaced at that. "The captain is a smart woman. Perhaps she'll be able to work things out for herself."

"Hostages are rarely able to resolve the situation," Tuvok informed him.

"Well, we can't just sit here," Kim said.

"Do you suggest we go in-system without permission?" Chakotay shook his head. "Our shuttles haven't the speed or the shielding power to withstand an attack by the Cartel."

"Then why don't we use *Voyager?*" Kim suggested.

"We would not get far in a malfunctioning ship," Tuvok said flatly. Chakotay wasn't sure how he managed to sound so snide without an inflection in his voice. "A shuttlecraft would be the more viable choice."

"We can't just sit here," Kim repeated doggedly. "We might as well use the leverage we've got while we still have it."

The conference room was silent as everyone considered that.

"Bold thinking, Mr. Kim," Chakotay finally told him. "I can't say I disagree."

"Voyager is incapable of warp or impulse propul-

sion," Tuvok pointed out. "Deflectors and shields are unreliable without computer control. In addition, power fluctuations continue to adversely affect every system on board."

"Let's try this from a different angle," Chakotay suggested. "What systems are working?"

"Well, we've got life support stabilized," Kim offered. "And we do have thrusters."

"Phasers and photon torpedoes are functioning," Tuvok added. "However, targeting systems are unreliable."

Chakotay pushed away from the table, frustrated by the pile of negatives that seemed to keep burying them. Pacing over to the window, he stared out at the Hub, facing the fact that there was no way they could win in a fair fight. That meant he couldn't allow it to be a fair fight. Which left guerrilla tactics again— deception and unexpected movement, with just enough terror thrown in to demoralize the enemy.

When he finally turned, their faces were expectant. He took heart in their faith. "In my experience, I've found it's better not to fight your limitations, but to use them to your advantage. I believe that is particularly true in this situation."

"How can we use a crippled ship to our advantage?" Neelix demanded.

Chakotay finally smiled. "By being as crippled as we possibly can."

Kim slowly began to nod. "Just like the way we scared off the scavengers outside Gateway Pol."

Kes didn't bother with the specifics. "If we're leaving, we have to take Tom Paris with us."

"We have pursued every line of negotiation," Tuvok pointed out. "Our efforts have been unsuccessful."

Chakotay figured it was inevitable. "If we're flying in the face of reason, we might as well go all the way."

"How do you suggest we deal with the Cartel?" Tuvok asked.

"I'm thinking about something more direct. Something Tom Paris himself would approve of."

A smile started to spread across Kim's face. "You're thinking about breaking him out of jail."

"Yes."

Neelix seemed astounded. "You'd really do that?"

"At this point," Chakotay said, "you'd be surprised what lengths I'd go to."

Tuvok shifted uncomfortably. "Paris is guilty according to the laws of this society."

"He was only trying to help the captain," Kes said on his behalf.

"Besides," Kim said defiantly. *"I'm* the guilty one. I copied those files, not Paris. If you want to make someone pay for it, then turn me over to the Cartel."

Chakotay instantly shook his head. "I won't allow anyone else to be subjected to their testing methods."

"People, please!" Neelix held up his hands. "Before you argue ethics again, you better figure out if you can do it. You're talking about the Cartel, here. What makes you think you can take Paris away from them?"

"We have been unable to locate his whereabouts," Tuvok agreed. "In addition, the sensors are unreliable. It would take time to conduct a thorough scan."

"If we can find him, we could use the transporter," Kim reminded Chakotay.

Chakotay narrowed his eyes. "The transporter would be the ideal method, providing we can punch through their shields *and* keep from giving them too much information about transporter technology while we do it."

"In order to achieve a transporter lock through the gravity bases," Tuvok told them, "a beacon must be placed with Paris.

"We could use a subcutaneous transponder," Tuvok continued thoughtfully. "The mechanism is inert, so it would pass their scanners. However, implanting the transponder would require physical contact with Paris."

"I tell you what," Neelix said, reluctantly. "I'll go into the Hub again. Maybe I can find out where the holding cells are."

"Good." In spite of all the ifs and buts, Chakotay was pleased. There was a charged feeling in the room, as if everyone had been given new life. "Tuvok, you and Kes get to work on the beacon. Ensign Kim, I want a full report of the status of each system. We have until noon tomorrow to make this work."

Kes returned to their quarters not long before Neelix arrived. He was flushed and agitated, but no more so than usual. "How did it go?" she asked.

"I take my life in my hands every time I step into that station," Neelix replied, falling back on their couch with a sigh. "I keep expecting that miner and his friend to jump out from every corridor."

"Did they?"

"No." Neelix groaned, rubbing the shoulder that had been injured. "But never again! I got what the commander wanted."

"You know where Paris is?"

"Weeellll . . . not exactly." He fished a receiver chip from his pocket. "But I did find a map that shows where the Enforcer Security Block is."

Kes kneaded his shoulders. "I'm sure the commander will be pleased."

"It wasn't easy getting it, let me tell you." He

twisted his neck. "Ah, yes, right there! That feels wonderful. . . ."

"It's late," Kes told him. "Why don't you take a bath and go to bed?"

He accepted her help getting up. "I'm too tired even for a bath."

Kes walked him to the bed, pulling off his shoes for him and unbuttoning his coverall.

"You're so good to me," Neelix mumbled.

"And you're good to me," Kes told him with a kiss. She pulled up the covers. "Now, sleep."

He caught her hand as she turned away. "What about you?"

"There's something I have to do first."

Neelix yawned hard enough to crack his jaw. "The beacon?"

"Yes, I've created a microinjector that will release the transceiver." She patted his hand, putting it back down on the cover. "Don't worry, I'll be back soon."

Neelix made a halfhearted attempt to protest, but by the time she picked up the receiver chip he'd brought back, she could hear his snores coming from the other room. Quickly, she scanned the chip with her tricorder, and examined the map of the Hub. It didn't look to difficult to get to the security block from their docking pylon.

When she reached sickbay, the doctor was still hard at work. "Are you sure this isn't too much of a strain on you?" she asked.

Zimmerman mumbled something about helping those who helped themselves. "What are you doing here so late?"

"The same as you—I'm helping." Kes smiled as she implanted the microinjector into the tip of her finger. All she had to do was touch Tom, and the release mechanism would send the beacon into his skin.

"Keep up the good work," Zimmerman told her absently.

"I will." Kes waved goodbye, but the doctor didn't notice.

When she tried to open the docking port, the monitor requested a security access code. She used the one that Tuvok had given Neelix. After all, Neelix always said that everything that belonged to him, belonged to her.

As she left the ship, she was careful to make sure the lock shut behind her. Tuvok probably didn't want anyone to get on board without him knowing about it.

CHAPTER
20

FROM THE MOMENT KES SAW LOBBY 58 WITH ITS HIGH, pointed ceiling, she thought the Hub was a marvelous place. Everywhere, there were more things than she could possibly see, while endless streams of exotic people crisscrossed around her, hurrying to get someplace else. So many frightened, lonely people. She smiled at them, nodding as she moved among them, letting them know that things weren't as bad as they thought. She let them know that she wished she could do more to help them.

What with talking to everyone and looking at all the new things, it took longer than she had intended to get to the Security Block. But the experience was well worth the time.

"You're early," the Enforcer told her when she requested to see Tom Paris. "The interrogation is scheduled for tomorrow morning."

"I'm not here for the interrogation. I'm here to see Tom."

The Enforcer turned away, accessing another

monitor. He talked for a few moments, and Kes heard something about "refusing to cooperate" and "maybe we could use this."

When the Enforcer returned, there was a new look in his eyes. "You can go through that door," he told her. "Someone will escort you to a room where you can see Prisoner 07119."

"Thank you," she said politely, wondering why the rest of the crew had been worried. Nothing could have been easier to arrange.

Another Enforcer was waiting behind the door. "Would you like to participate in the interrogation?"

"I'm sorry, but I'd need permission to do that."

The Enforcer shrugged, opening another door. "I haven't been able to find your species on file, anyway. You can wait in here."

There was another door in the opposite wall, and the shimmer of a forcefield separated the two halves of the room.

"Can't you turn off the forcefield?" Kes asked. "I'm a friend of Tom's."

"That's not possible. Direct contact is only allowed during interrogation."

"Oh." Disappointed, Kes didn't say anything more as the Enforcer left. There was no place to sit, so she leaned against one wall, wondering where Tom was.

Humming to herself, Kes waited as only she knew how—going over the physiology of the Bajoran respiratory system, her latest anatomical study.

After a long time, the door opened in front of her, and two white-garbed Tutopans dragged Paris into the room. They dropped him facedown and quickly retreated.

Kes went right up to the forcefield. His jacket was gone, and his gray shirt was torn and stained with sweat. "Tom, wake up. It's me, Kes."

Paris groaned, reminding her of Neelix when he had returned from the Hub. His hand scrubbed through his hair, as he finally focused on her. "Kes . . . ?"

"It's me," she said simply. "Are you all right?"

"Kes!" he exclaimed, staring at her, his mouth falling open. He didn't even try to get up from the floor. "What are you doing here?"

"I came to see you."

"How?" Paris demanded. "You didn't come alone, did you?"

"I wasn't alone, there were people all around me. I had to ask for directions on the expressway, but everyone was very nice."

Paris pushed himself up, shaking his head as if he couldn't believe it. "Do you know how dangerous that is?"

"No." She tilted her head as he managed to get to his feet. To her practiced eye, he was trying to shake off the effects of sedation. It also looked as if his hand had been injured. "Why?"

"Because someone could kidnap you and take you on a long voyage to nowhere, that's why! Or they could kill you, or try to hurt you, just because you happened to cross their path. You're lucky nothing happened."

"You and Neelix came into the Hub."

He let out a short laugh. "Yeah, and look what happened to me."

Kes drew her brows together. "Neelix was hurt, too, but he said that was because of you."

"Neelix got hurt?" Paris came closer. "Is he all right?"

"The cut has been healed. He said you left him behind so those two men could attack him."

Paris avoided her eyes. "I thought he'd be okay. I

didn't know . . ." He looked down at his cut hand. "I don't even know what's real anymore. I thought I was on that moon, and then Tracer, she sank in the sand . . . but maybe I wasn't really there. . . ."

Suddenly, Paris raised his head. He stared right at her, his eyes widening with suspicion. "No . . ."

"What is it, Tom?"

"No, it can't be!" he cried out, turning away.

"Tom . . . tell me," she urged. "What's wrong?"

He jerked his head around, almost spitting the words out—"You aren't *real!*"

Kes drew back at his bitter anger, sensing it like a physical force tingling through the air.

"I should have known!" His fists clenched. "You're just another one of their mind-twists, aren't you? They're trying to get more information out of me."

"Paris, that's not true—"

"Don't! Don't even try," he warned, as if holding himself back. "I should have known when I first laid eyes on you. They'd never let Kes come into the Hub alone."

Kes gazed at him silently, her alarm sinking into sadness. She knew the sympathy in her face must be achingly transparent.

"Don't!" Paris shouted, leaping for the forcefield. His blows sent static racing through the transparent wall. "That's just what *she* would do!"

His fists hit the forcefield as if he was trying to break through, trying to break the spell. Kes couldn't do anything to stop him, even though she could see the burns he was getting from the field.

Finally, panting and holding his limp hands away from himself, Paris stumbled back in pain. He retreated to one corner, his eyes closed as if he was trying to hang onto his sanity.

Kes went as close as she could to the forcefield, letting the tips of her fingers graze the static charge.

"It's me, Tom," she whispered. An overwhelming empathy rose up inside of her, seeming to swell until it burst from the bounds of her body, arrowing straight for Paris as if to enfold him in her protection. "You know me."

Paris shuddered as if a wave snapped through him. He met her eyes.

She said, "You can trust me."

Paris nodded, dazed.

"We'll get you out of here," Kes told him. "I promise."

"You what?" Neelix shrieked. "Kes, you didn't!"

"I did." Kes was sitting calmly on the couch in the ready room, her hands folded in her lap.

From the way Neelix paced back and forth, tightening the belt of his garish robe, Chakotay could tell he'd known nothing about this wild scheme. It was a relief to know Neelix wasn't that irresponsible. Yet when Tuvok first woke him up with the news that Kes had just returned from the Hub, he had to admit it reminded him of an old Indian saying—the gods protect fools and little girls. He didn't think he'd mention that to Neelix.

"You were lucky," Chakotay told Kes.

"I was never in any danger," she insisted.

"Danger!" Neelix flung one hand in the air. "You could have been killed! Or thrown in prison too!"

"Indeed," Tuvok agreed. He seemed to have difficulty looking at Neelix, but maybe it was the way the purple and yellow swirls of his robe clashed with the spots on his skin. "From what Kes has told us, I am sure they used her visit to their advantage."

Neelix suddenly swooped down on Kes, clasping his arms around her and hugging her close. "I could have lost you forever!"

Chakotay sat down on the edge of the desk. "Would you please calm down, Neelix? She's back now, and she's all right."

Tuvok crossed his arms, remaining near the door. "Kes has also agreed that she will not venture into the Hub again without permission."

"You listen to him, honey," Neelix told her. "Going to the security block alone! What got into you?"

"I knew the beacon needed to be administered to Paris." She turned to Chakotay. "But they wouldn't lower the forcefield between us. They said they only allowed direct contact during the interrogation."

"Interrogation is scheduled for tomorrow morning," Tuvok pointed out.

"I suppose we could send someone in to plant the transponder on Paris," Chakotay said. "Then transport both out before the interrogation actually begins."

Tuvok raised one brow. "The Cartel indicated that it would need to test the individual before interrogation could begin. Testing would take time."

Kes immediately protested, "You can't allow anyone else to undergo those tests. I've seen what they did to Paris—he's been tortured, physically as well as mentally."

"I won't let another member of my crew be tested," Chakotay promised. Kes drew in her breath, nodding. "I have my doubts about this interrogation procedure, as well."

"What are the risks?" Kes asked him.

"From the little I've been able to learn," Chakotay said grimly, "interrogation consists of a series of chemical inducers which allows the subject to be questioned without conscious interference."

"You mean they can't lie," Kes said.

"Well then, we might as well give them what they want," Neelix said. "Paris will tell them everything anyway."

"But he's the only human they've tested," Chakotay added. "Apparently, they can't perfect the analysis without a comparison subject. That's why they've requested another human to be used as the reactor during the interrogation."

"Sending a human is an unacceptable security risk," Tuvok said flatly. "There is a thirty-two-percent possibility that we will be unable to transport Paris from the security block. If we fail, we will have provided the Cartel with the means of obtaining any technical information they wish from Paris."

Chakotay sighed. "I have to say, I agree."

Kes seemed to sense he was at an impasse. "We could send someone who isn't human, as long as they don't need to be tested. They offered to let me participate in the interrogation if they could find a matrix of my species on file."

"What!" Neelix looked at her with dawning comprehension. "No, absolutely not! I forbid it!" He appealed directly to Chakotay. "You can't send Kes in there again—"

"He's not sending me in," Kes said patiently. "I'm volunteering."

Chakotay didn't like the idea one bit. Neelix was right—it was too much like letting a teenage Joan of Arc fight his battles.

"The Ocampa have been isolated for centuries," Tuvok reminded them calmly. "It is unlikely that the Cartel has a matrix for your species."

"Good!" Neelix patted her knee. "That settles it. I want no more talk of sending my Kes in there to be tortured."

Kes smiled up at him tenderly. "I'm sure they wouldn't hurt me. They were very considerate."

"There is another possibility," Chakotay said slowly. He almost hated to suggest it. "Neelix, your species is widely traveled. They must have a matrix for you."

"Me?" He drew back. "No, sir, no way."

"That would be acceptable," Tuvok said calmly.

"Oh, yeah? Not to *me.*" Neelix was shaking his head back and forth. "You know what these people can do once they get inside of you? I could be turned into a drone just like the rest of them . . . that's not going to happen to me."

All three turned their eyes on Neelix. He shifted uneasily on the couch. "What are you looking at me for?" he asked. "You can't order me to do this."

"I don't intend to," Chakotay said.

Silence followed.

"You could ask them if they have an Ocampa matrix," Kes suggested.

"No!" Neelix blurted.

"We can't let Paris stay down there," she insisted.

"Why not?" Neelix asked. "What has he ever done for me? He left me behind, abandoning me to fight those insane maniacs." He leaped up and started to take off his robe. "I've got the scars to prove it!"

Kes joined him, putting a steady hand on his arm. "This is the only family we have. We need each other."

"Paris didn't remember that when he left me behind."

"Maybe not," Kes agreed quietly. "But that doesn't make it any less true."

Neelix looked at Chakotay, who was determined not to point out the obvious—that it was either him or Kes.

Neelix threw up his hands. "All right, I'll do it!"

Kes's face lit up, and she slipped her arms around him. "I knew you would."

"I'm crazy, I know it." Neelix hugged her, his eyes softening. "But I'd do anything for you."

"For us," she corrected.

"For all of us," Chakotay added. "Thank you—"

The door to the ready room opened, and Ensign Kim rushed in. His jacket was closed slightly askew, as if he'd dressed hurriedly.

"Commander," Kim blurted out, focused on Kes. "I heard Kes got to see Paris."

Tuvok raised one brow. "How, may I ask, did you hear this information?"

"It's a small ship. . . ." Kim seemed uneasy, as if realizing for the first time he'd burst into a sensitive meeting. "I had to find out if it was true."

"Yes," Chakotay told him, recognizing the concern prompting Kim's behavior. "And Neelix has agreed to pose as the 'reactor' during the interrogation, so he can administer the transponder."

"Let me go instead," Kim immediately offered.

"*Good* idea!" Neelix exclaimed.

"Impossible," Tuvok replied. "Sending a human would be an unacceptable security risk."

Kim turned on him. "There's nothing about our plan that's acceptable! We're crazy to be trying any of this."

"Neelix is the logical choice," Tuvok told them both calmly, apparently unaffected by the frustration in their faces. "Ensign Kim would be able to provide them with technical information."

Neelix threw up his hands. "Always back to me!"

"They've been asking for a human," Kim told Tuvok. "Knowing the Cartel, they may only allow direct contact if we give them what they want." He turned and pleaded with Chakotay. "Please let me go. It's my fault he's down there."

Tuvok said behind him, "It is not your fault, Ensign. Paris lied about his transport authorization, and he will be reprimanded if he returns to the ship."

"If?!" Kes repeated, shocked.

"Paris has a better chance getting back with me than with him," Kim said, pointing to Neelix. "He obviously doesn't want to do this. But I'll do whatever it takes to make sure Paris is brought back to the ship."

Chakotay looked around the group. Common sense told him to send Neelix, if only to cover themselves. But Kim was right about one thing. "Motivation is the primary factor in success." Chakotay nodded to Kim. "You can go, Ensign. Only don't fail."

"Yes, sir," Kim acknowledged with remarkable composure, confirming Chakotay's decision.

Neelix smacked Kim on the back as they were leaving. The last thing Chakotay heard was "Yes, sir, I volunteered, but when I heard you offer to go, I was determined to step aside. I can't be standing between two good friends, now, can I?"

As the door slid shut, Chakotay turned back to deal with Tuvok. He could understand Tuvok's frustration, but he'd found it was sometimes better to trust his instincts. Maybe it was no accident that he had been hit hardest by the neural gas—ever since then, they'd spent too much time reacting instead of acting. Now he only had to explain that to a Vulcan.

CHAPTER
21

PARIS WAS GRATEFUL THE ENFORCERS DIDN'T SEDATE HIM again—or at least that was his recollection. After they came to take Kes away, he was left alone in the room. Maybe they did it on purpose. Maybe they wanted him to think, but how could he after everything that had happened? Even that remarkable contact from Kes—in spite of how real it had felt, it could have been nothing more than chemically induced wish-fulfillment.

Paris knew there came a time when you started to think you couldn't take any more, when you felt as if you couldn't endure another moment. He'd been there before, when he had lost every hope of fixing his life or repairing the damage he'd done. Then Janeway had taken him away—farther away than any of them had expected—and he thought that he *had* been given another chance. A miraculous chance to change his life.

The only thing I've changed is jail cells.

He was right back where he started, where he

always seemed to wind up. Maybe it was his fate to languish for the rest of his life in confinement. It didn't matter that he had crossed the galaxy, or that he had tried so hard to do the right thing—he was one of those people who belonged in jail.

He remembered trying not to cry, hating the idea that Enforcers were watching him and probably knew how he felt anyway. Then he must have fallen asleep, because the next thing he knew, Harry Kim was looking down through the forcefield.

"That's a relief!" Kim sighed. "I've been calling your name for the past few minutes. I thought you might be dead."

"Harry." Paris realized he was stretched out on his side of the forcefield, when the last thing he remembered was being in the corner. "Harry. What are you doing here?"

"The pool room isn't THE same without you." Kim paced on the other side of the forcefield, examining the emission nodes.

Paris sat up, flexing his shoulders. It certainly felt as if he'd slept on the floor all night, and the room was the same—like the inside of a box, with a forcefield down the center and doors on both sides.

Harry could hardly stand still, a sure sign he was nervous. "The commander sent me to help with the interrogation."

"Chakotay?" That didn't make any sense.

Kim tapped the forcefield, wincing at the static. "We had to do something. Our life support is failing, and we're down to eighteen percent of our reserve power."

Paris didn't believe him. Kim wouldn't come in here and hand out sensitive information like that. "This has got to be another one of their simulations."

Kim's brows drew together, and his lips tightened in distress. "Kes said they've been torturing you."

"So she *did* come here. . . ." Or maybe both of them were simulations. Paris examined him through the forcefield—seeing that self-conscious dip of his head, his painful sincerity, and even the way his hair fell across his forehead—was that really Harry? Or was everything exaggerated, the exact lines of his character blurred by generalization? It was starting to make his head swim again.

Paris sighed, certain there were monitors watching every reaction. "I don't know which would be worse—if you were a simulation or actually here. I'd hate to think what they could do to you."

After a moment, Kim said, "You don't look so good."

"I bet." Paris scratched the stubble on his chin. Were those grains of sand he felt?

"I can see it in your eyes," Kim added, surprising him with the amount of concern in his expression. "They have been torturing you, haven't they?"

"They still are."

Kim lifted one hand, letting it fall again. "I'm sorry, Tom. I'm so sorry. I wish I . . . I . . . ."

Paris watched the flush rise on Kim's cheeks as he tried to control himself. Suddenly he realized Kim was blaming himself for what had happened. That would be just like him—only how did the Tutopans know that? Still, simulation or not, he couldn't stand seeing the kid suffer. "Don't take it so hard, Harry. I get myself into these situations, but I always get out."

Kim met his gaze with empathetic directness. "You can be sure of that."

Paris grinned. "Yes, sir!"

The door behind Kim opened just as Paris heard

the lock turning behind him. The forcefield vanished as two orderlies wheeled in metal tables. Paris recognized the straps and monitors from the time he woke after Tracer had disappeared. It looked fairly ominous.

"Do you know what's happening?" he asked, moving closer to Kim.

"Yes, I do." Kim slipped a hand around Paris's arm. "We're getting out of here."

At first Paris thought Kim was steadying him, then it felt as if a live wire burned into his skin. His breath hissed between his teeth. "Maybe you're not a simulation after all."

"I am receiving a response to our subspace signal," Tuvok announced. "The transponder has been activated."

Finally, Chakotay almost said, expressing the feelings of everyone on the bridge. Instead, he ordered, "Open the Cartel frequency."

"Frequency open," Tuvok replied.

The level of distortion had been carefully adjusted so that their communications system appeared to be on its last legs. "Docking control, this is *Voyager* at Pylon BVO-nine-hundred," Chakotay called out, no longer trying to hide his concern. "We're experiencing *severe* system malfunctions. We intend to maneuver to a safe distance from the Hub in order to effect repairs."

"Voyager, this is Docking Control. Do not—"

Chakotay cut the transmission line in the middle of the official's reply. "Blow the docking clamps."

Tuvok didn't look up from his terminal. "Ship disengaged." Despite the interference on the viewscreen, it was clear they were moving away from the Hub. "Explosive charge has propelled us at twenty meters per second."

Chakotay opened the communications line again. "This is *Voyager*—I repeat, we are currently experiencing system-wide malfunctions—" He cut the transmission line again. "Now gently move us away from the station. We don't want them to think we're a threat to the Hub."

"Aye, sir. Thrusters engaged."

There was a slight jolt, and some shuddering as the ship responded. As they drew back, several red patrol craft suddenly emerged.

"They're sending out Enforcers," Chakotay said calmly.

"Distance holding at twenty thousand kilometers," Tuvok said. "Deflector dish powered up."

Chakotay signaled Tala in the transporter room. "Are you ready?"

"I have a lock on both of them," she confirmed.

"On my signal," Chakotay told them, as a hush fell over the bridge. "Deflector burst and transporter . . . *Now!*"

A nearly invisible distortion wave was emitted from the deflector dish on the front of the ship, neatly concealing the transporter beam channeled through the sensor window in the center of the beam.

The impact hurled the ship away from the Hub.

"Execute evasive maneuvers!" Chakotay ordered.

The ship skipped to one side, hovered, then seemed to sway backward as if out of control. A low-level laser beam slanted harmlessly past the hull.

Chakotay opened the Cartel channel. "This is not an attack! We are attempting to gain control of our systems. I repeat—this is not an attack!"

The dizzy motions continued, taking them farther

away from the Hub. The Enforcer patrols hovered at a distance.

"Tala?" Chakotay asked.

"I have them both, sir."

"Send them to the bridge." They would need their best pilot if they were going to pull this one off. He turned to the engineering station. "Impulse reactor ready?"

"Aye, sir!" Carter said too quickly, as if he was desperately hoping they wouldn't blow the entire impulse propulsion system.

"Bleed a little deuterium from the vents, first. Let's make those patrols stand back."

A neon stain spread behind them, and the ship did another jog farther away from the Hub. Chakotay sent another garbled message to the Cartel, warning them that their reactor was about to blow.

Kim arrived, breathless, with Paris right behind him. Kim was obviously keyed up from successfully completing his mission, and he darted to his post after returning Chakotay's proud nod of acknowledgment. But Paris looked more bedraggled than Chakotay had ever seen him.

"Thanks for the lift," Paris said, his voice flippant but his reddened eyes locked on Chakotay. "I understand I'm due for a serious reprimand."

Chakotay was glad to see he understood the severity of his transgression. "Are you able to pilot, Mr. Paris?"

"Ready as ever." He took over the conn. "Did I miss anything?"

"You're just in time," Chakotay assured him. "Let's give them a real show. Do you remember the convulsions the ship experienced when the memory core was isolated?"

"In my bones," Paris said fervently.

"Then re-create something along those lines, only give us the signal when we're aimed toward Min-Tutopa. We're going to vent the impulse system and give ourselves a good hard push in that direction."

"Aye, sir," Paris said, his eyes gleaming.

Chakotay knew it wasn't often a pilot got to flex his muscles with a ship of this size. "Proceed, Mr. Paris."

The Hub seemed to drop out of sight, and the starfield streaked downward as the ship did a lazy end-over-end roll.

"Gravity holding," Kim said, obviously clenching his teeth.

"Good thing," Chakotay murmured. He could feel the difference in the way Paris handled the ship, as if they were held in a grip of casual confidence.

"Patrol ships approaching," Tuvok warned.

"Get ready," Paris warned. "Now!"

"Venting impulse engines," Carter called out.

Their ship streaked through the gathered patrol ships and was practically out of range before they could react.

"Evasive maneuvers," Chakotay ordered. "Neelix said there's an automated line of defense protecting the inner system—"

"Aye, sir!"

"There are ten patrol ships in pursuit." Only Tuvok could look thoughtful instead of alarmed. "Their weapons systems have the capability to overwhelm our shields."

"I still have some fancy footwork I can pull off," Paris tossed over his shoulder.

"According to sensors," Kim put in. "We'll be at Min-Tutopa before they can catch up." He seemed puzzled. "That can't be right. They should be able to fly rings around us."

"I thought so," Chakotay said triumphantly. "They

want to know what's happening on Min-Tutopa as much as we do."

"This could be a violation of the Prime Directive," Tuvok warned.

"Let's hope not," Chakotay said, letting it stand at that.

CHAPTER 22

ANDROSS CROSSED HIS ARMS, LOOKING DOWN AT Janeway. "The deadline is almost here. Apparently, your people didn't take me seriously."

Janeway stood up, refusing to allow him any psychological advantage over her. "I'm sure they believe you, but they are unable to comply with your request."

"Maybe they need some prompting," Andross said.

"Andross!" Prog exclaimed from the main computer control terminal. "You aren't really going to hurt them, are you?"

"I'll do whatever it takes—"

"Perimeter breach!" one of the rebels announced.

Everyone in the command room instantly went on alert.

"The Cartel has issued a general warning," Prog said. "A rogue vessel is traveling in-system."

Andross and Prog both examined the display. Janeway strained but she couldn't see it, and when she tried to go closer, one of the guards stepped in her way.

"Vectors indicate the ship is approaching Min-Tutopa," Prog murmured. "It will be here in less than ten intervals."

"Shall I dispatch fighters, Andross?" one of the rebels asked nervously.

"Vessel size, power-class . . ." Andross muttered, searching the sensor information. He looked up at Janeway, a strange smile on his face. "It seems your ship is coming to get you."

"Voyager?" The captain ignored the guard, reaching the agent's side in several strides. "My ship is traveling in-system?"

"If you can call it that," Andross said. "They appear to be damaged."

"I'll bet," Torres replied, examining the remote sensor readings next to Janeway. "Without the main computer."

"They're being followed by an entire squad of Enforcers," Andross pointed out.

"The Cartel is coming here?" Prog asked, wide-eyed. "What'll we do?!"

"Perhaps Captain Janeway's idea will work after all," Andross said thoughtfully.

"My idea?" Janeway repeated, as if brushing off an annoying insect. "I suggested nothing."

"You were asking why the Board hasn't requested the Cartel's help. I see now that the Board could sit there and starve in their Council Chamber before they agree to our terms." His eyes were burning. "But they fear the Cartel. If I threaten to bring Enforcers into this . . . that may supply the pressure we need."

"And if it doesn't work," Janeway countered, "according to everything I've heard, your people will be even worse off."

"It's a risk I'll have to take."

"You'll take!" Torres repeated indignantly.

Appalled, Janeway stared at Andross. "Are you really prepared to take that responsibility?"

He met her gaze. "This entire situation is my responsibility. And, now, it's time to put an end to it."

"Andross . . ." Prog said as if she wasn't sure about this.

"This is the man you trust?" Torres asked her.

"I know exactly what to do," Andross assured his compatriot. "This is working out perfectly."

"But I thought we wanted to avoid Cartel interference," Prog protested.

"We do," Andross agreed, hurrying over to the communications terminal. "But Hamilt wants to avoid it even more."

The Council Chamber must have been receiving reports from the other provinces, because Hamilt came on-line almost instantly. "Return control to us immediately," Hamilt demanded, "so we can defend our House against this attack!"

"It is no attack," Andross said, seeming quite proud of himself. "I've invited the Cartel to witness your endorsement of Administer Fee for the post of Supreme Arbitrator. If you refuse, I will turn over control of the Seat to the Cartel."

Hamilt sputtered in astonishment, as Janeway kept an eye on her ship's approach. Their flight pattern had stabilized, but the Cartel patrols were closing fast.

"You'd betray your own people?" Hamilt finally managed to spit out.

"I intend to save them." Andross checked the monitor. "Fee's appointment prevents the Cartel from gaining more power, and it will guarantee a vast new reservoir of information from the people who have been untapped by our House."

"Who are you to decide these things?" Hamilt demanded, echoing Janeway's private opinion about the matter.

"I'm aware I have no authority to do this, but I must insure the security of our House. The Enforcer patrols will arrive at any moment. If you don't agree to support Fee, then you're handing the House over to the Cartel."

"You wouldn't dare!"

"I would."

Their eyes locked through the monitor.

Hamilt's lips drew back in a sneer. "Never!"

As Min-Tutopa neared on the viewscreen, Kim knew they would never have made it so far without the Enforcers' cooperation.

"Keep out of their line of fire," Chakotay ordered as *Voyager* entered orbit. "Just in case they decide to start shooting again."

"Plenty of satellites to dodge," Paris agreed, sounding much better than he looked.

"Ensign, can you lock on to their communicators?" the commander asked.

"Negative, sir." Kim felt the familiar rise of frustration. "Communications are on-line—I don't understand it. Maybe their comm badges have been tampered with."

"Attempting a sensor scan," Tuvok informed him.

The turbolift hissed open behind him, as Kes and Neelix maneuvered a large containment tube between them.

"This isn't time for visitors," Chakotay warned.

"I'm delivering the new medication for the subprocessors," Kes explained.

Kim looked up in surprise. "There's nothing wrong with the subprocessors."

"That's true," Kes agreed. "But Dr. Zimmerman has discovered that the addition of a stimulant to the subprocessors excites the synapses, drawing the data impulse patterns toward them instead of the gel packs in the core." She glanced at Kim. "It worked when we added stimulants to the medical subprocessor. The doctor is doing much better."

Chakotay turned. "Ensign Kim, did you authorize this procedure?"

Kim wanted to deny all responsibility, ready to blame it on the doctor's recent psychotic episodes. But Kes's gaze didn't waver, reminding him of the determination in Zimmerman's face. Harry knew he must have looked the same way when he had asked Chakotay to let him go see Paris. Maybe being in command didn't mean he had to solve every problem—maybe he just had to know when to trust his fellow officers.

"We should do what the doctor ordered," Kim said evenly.

"Then do it," Chakotay told him. "Fast."

Kim hurried ahead of Kes and Neelix to open the bionutrient shunt, hoping he wasn't making another mistake. But this time, his decision felt right.

Paris turned from the conn. "Tutopans are fairly xenophobic. I bet the captain and Torres are practically the only two aliens down there."

"Tuvok?" Chakotay asked.

Tuvok nodded shortly. "Narrowing scanning range to isolate non-Tutopan readings."

Janeway could tell from Hamilt's expression that he would never give into Andross's threats. She could certainly sympathize with that feeling, but it wasn't much help right now.

Stepping up to the communications terminal, she attempted to mediate the dispute. "There must be some way to solve this—"

Andross cut her off, jerking his head toward his guards. They moved forward to take her, as Torres started struggling with them.

"Don't make me sedate you again," Andross warned, keeping a wary eye on Hamilt.

Torres managed to shake off the guard, giving Prog a pointed glare. "Don't even *try*—"

"Sensors have detected two non-Tutopans in the main metropolitan area," Tuvok announced. "Locking on."

"Transporter room, beam them directly to the bridge," Chakotay ordered. He turned expectantly toward the upper deck, wondering if his gamble was going to pay off.

Janeway and Torres materialized on the upper deck, as Torres took a step forward, her hands clenched. Obviously she'd been caught in the middle of an attack. "Chakotay!" she exclaimed, breaking off.

Chakotay simply said, "Welcome home."

"How sweet it is," Captain Janeway agreed.

Before Chakotay could say anything more, they were jolted forward, rocking under the impact of a laser. The starfield swerved as Paris maneuvered.

Janeway didn't go through the formality of retaking the bridge. "Report!"

"Shields holding," Tuvok said. He almost sounded surprised.

"Sensors are back on-line." Kim had no compunction about showing his amazement. "Response is increasing in almost every system—tactical, utilities,

EPS, deflector shields . . . it must be the effect of the stimulant."

"Our power remains near reserve levels," Tuvok interjected.

"It's something, anyway," Janeway said, striding down the ramp as Chakotay moved away from her seat. "In the center of that city, there's a complex with transport lines radiating in eight different directions."

"I have it," Kim said.

"Inside that complex, within in a large open space, there's a room with heavy computer feeds and direct-access terminals."

"I am reading high electrical activity," Tuvok confirmed. "There are five Tutopans within the room."

"Good." Janeway seemed to ignore the shaking of the ship. "Next time Paris ducks around that moon, drop the shields and beam those people directly to the bridge."

"Aye, Captain," Tuvok acknowledged.

Janeway nodded shortly, giving Chakotay a conspiratorial grin. He couldn't tell her how glad he was to have her back.

"Let's end this situation once and for all," the captain said. "Execute evasive maneuvers, Mr. Paris."

CHAPTER
23

FIVE TUTOPANS MATERIALIZED ON THE UPPER LEVEL OF the bridge. Their shock ranged from Hamilt's appalled recognition of Janeway and Torres, to the pleased wonder on the face of the oldest Tutopan that she'd ever seen.

"I'm Captain Janeway," she introduced herself—to the man who was apparently the Eldern, as well to as Hobbs and Sprecenspire, the Cartel supporters. Calvert was edging in closer to Hamilt. "I'm sorry to have to pull you away so abruptly, but you've involved us in a situation that cannot be allowed to continue."

"I protest this indignity!" Hamilt exclaimed. "How did you bring us here?"

Hobbs stepped forward. "Yes, how did you bring us here?"

"This isn't a simulation?" Calvert whispered to Hamilt.

Janeway held up her hands at the questions, figuring she should have known they'd want to quiz her first. Only the Eldern was silent, hobbling slowly toward the orbital view of Min-Tutopa. He was smiling with tremulous delight.

Hobbs pointed past the Eldern. "Those are Enforcer patrols."

Janeway braced herself as the ship rocked under another laser impact.

"We're under attack!" Hamilt exclaimed, stumbling into Calvert.

"Shields down thirty-four percent," Tuvok informed her.

"As you can see, we have little time for discussion," Janeway told them. "Your people stole our computer, and now we can't run and we can barely defend ourselves." She let that sink in, as another jolt shook the ship.

"Return us immediately!" Hamilt demanded, with Calvert chiming in. The Cartel supporters were starting to look concerned.

The woman, Hobbs, appealed directly to Janeway. "Let me speak to the lead patrol. I'll tell them to cease their attack."

"I believe that is a job for the Supreme Arbitrator," Janeway told the Board. "I suggest you chose one immediately."

"What?" Hamilt exclaimed. "This is coercion! You hold us on the brink of death and expect us to make a decision?"

"I refused to lend aid to any side in this dispute," Janeway told them. "But I won't allow you to manipulate us any longer. We didn't want to become involved in your domestic crisis, but now that we are, you'll suffer the same fate as my ship unless you resolve the situation."

"You could help us disable this coup—" Hamilt started.

"No."

"Attempting evasive maneuvers," Paris announced, his voice tense with effort.

Hamilt was looking at her in disbelief and outrage. Janeway determined that this was a moment in which silence said far more than words.

The Eldern moved closer to the viewscreen. "I've always loved the sight of my House from space. I could certainly die in this place, satisfied that I've done my best for my people. My choice for arbitrator stands—Administer Fee is our only hope."

"You stubborn old man," Hobbs spat in his direction, distorting her delicate face.

Hamilt turned on Janeway. "Do you see what comes of playing with the Cartel? The danger you put us in?"

"We are on the brink of success," Hobbs told Hamilt, attempting to recover her composure. "Either by your decision to back my nomination as Supreme Arbitrator, or by default when the Cartel destroys this ship and subdues the rebels. I would be satisfied that my job was done, even if I could not be present to guide the integration of the House."

Sprecenspire seemed ready to challenge her decision, but Hobbs stared him down. "I agree," he reluctantly accepted.

"Fools!" Hamilt exclaimed, his face reddening with anger. "You would die for these fanatical beliefs? Why can't you accept the way things are? Our House is strong as it is, we can survive—"

"The House is crumbling," the Eldern interrupted, his calm voice undercutting Hamilt's hysteria. "You know it as well as I. It's time that you chose the direction we shall go."

Hamilt looked from him to Hobbs, as the Cartel

woman smirked. Calvert nervously licked his lips, obviously unwilling to take a stand until Hamilt did. But his eyes pleaded with Janeway, even as another laser bolt struck the ship.

Janeway stood unflinching, as Tuvok announced, "Shields down to twenty-one percent, Captain."

"We can't take much more of this," Kim added.

Janeway was proud of her crew—their terse reports merely showed their loyalty. After one brief glance around the bridge, Hamilt didn't even try to convince any of her officers to betray her. He was smoldering, and Janeway knew he was a man accustomed to absolute control—she wasn't sure his pride would allow him to capitulate.

"You people are *barbarians*," Hamilt sneered, sweeping his hand from Janeway to her crew. "I for one will not die in this absurd endeavor. Eldern, take my support for Fee's nomination. I only hope you live to regret it."

Calvert quickly added, "You have mine, too."

"Then it is done," Eldern said, dipping his head. "Fee is the Supreme Arbitrator of House Min-Tutopa."

Hobbs was practically spitting with rage, and Janeway was glad when Tuvok stepped into her line of sight, holding a phaser. Sprecenspire had his arms crossed tightly, staring anxiously at the view-screen where the Cartel patrols weaved into sight. Calvert asked Janeway, "Now can we get out of here?"

Janeway suppressed a smile. "Open a channel to the planet, Mr. Kim. Who would like to make the announcement? Hamilt?"

"Never," he snapped, trying to hold on to his dignity.

The Eldern moved with difficulty. "I will make the announcement."

"Do it fast," Janeway urged. "So we can let the Cartel patrols know they're attacking a ship carrying the entire Board of House Min-Tutopa."

CHAPTER

24

PARIS WASN'T SURE EXACTLY WHAT WAS GOING ON, BUT
when the Cartel broke off their attack, he figured that
was a good sign. He kept fighting the paranoid
thought that this was just another simulation—and
he wondered if he'd ever get over that sneaking
suspicion. But real or not, it wasn't his place to do
anything except what the captain ordered.

He settled the ship into a more stable orbit, as
Tuvok escorted the five Board Members into the
conference room.

"We're being hailed by the lead Enforcer patrol,"
Kim announced.

"On screen."

"Audio only," Kim said apologetically.

"Of course," the captain sighed. "Very well."

Paris felt a sense of déjà vu when a flat Tutopan
voice came over the line. *"Voyager,* your departure
from the Hub was unauthorized. You are ordered to
return immediately."

"There are matters we need to clear up with House Min-Tutopa," Janeway explained. "Didn't you speak to Supreme Arbitrator Fee?"

There was a pause as if accessing. "The Supreme Arbitrator has granted permission for your ship to stay in orbit until the Board of House Min-Tutopa is returned to the planet."

"I intend to make arrangements to do so immediately."

"The patrol will wait to escort you back to the Hub." The dispassionate tone continued, "I am authorized to inform you that your ship inflicted damages to the Hub in the amount of 46.000, and incurred fines totaling 164.500. In addition, I am authorized to search your ship for Prisoner 07119."

Janeway gestured for Tuvok to cut the line, as Paris glanced back at her puzzled expression. "They're talking about me," he said. "I shouldn't have told Tala I had authorization to beam into the Hub."

Janeway looked down at him. "I understand you've been treated rather harshly. Perhaps you've been punished enough."

Paris nodded slowly. "I can't believe I risked Harry's life as well as mine. It won't happen again, Captain."

Chakotay cleared his throat. "Captain, there's also a matter of our departure from the Hub. It was rather . . ."

"Spectacular," Kim put into the pause.

"Abrupt," Chakotay corrected. "The Cartel has been demanding information about our transporter technology, and Paris was about to undergo some sort of chemical interrogation when we . . . liberated him. So we decided to go all the way, and come liberate you and Torres, too."

Paris thought the look on Janeway's face was almost

worth the awful experience. "I leave you alone for two days . . ." She was shaking her head, as she glanced around at the bridge crew, but the warmth in her voice betrayed her appreciation for the risks they'd taken to rescue her.

"We're being hailed, Captain," Kim interrupted. "From the planet."

Fee was polite enough to appear on the viewscreen. "Captain Janeway, I've informed the Cartel that your ship is a welcome guest at our planet."

"Thank you," Janeway said somewhat dryly.

"I believe we have something that belongs to you." The larger-than-life image of Fee graciously smiled. "Agent Andross is supervising the removal of your computer from our network. It will be delivered to you when we pick up our Board Members."

"That would be acceptable," Janeway replied, as coolly as if that didn't solve their biggest problem. Paris heard sighs of relief from both Torres and Kim. He knew he should be glad, but there was a sinking feeling in his stomach.

As if sensing his uneasiness, Janeway stepped forward, putting a hand on his shoulder. "There is something else," the captain told Fee. "The Cartel is demanding the return of my crew member, Tom Paris."

"I wish I could help you, Captain, but I'm don't believe there's anything I can do. That is a Cartel matter, and even an Arbitrator's powers only extend so far."

"Yet you offered to arrange for his release if we helped you," Janeway protested. "I have to admit, it was not our intention for you to be chosen, however I ask that you honor your offer."

Fee seemed truly puzzled. "Captain, I don't recall speaking to you about this matter."

"Oh, yeah?" Torres pushed away from the engineering station, striding forward. "I was there, remember? You told us you would help Tom if we fixed the processor."

Fee slowly shook her head at the young woman. "I'm sorry, but I've never spoken to you before. I did meet both of you at the tournament, but I only exchanged a few words with your captain before Andross called you away."

"It was in the tower," Janeway reminded her. "After Andross seized control."

"I've been trapped in the Seat along with everyone else since that time."

"You said it was by special transmission," Torres insisted.

Paris told himself that he wasn't being paranoid—he knew what had happened. "It was a simulation," he blurted out. "It wasn't real."

"Is that possible?" Janeway immediately asked Fee. "Could we have talked to a simulation of you?"

Fee tightened her lips. "It's quite possible Andross was using my matrix to try to convince you to help him. It's exactly the sort of thing he would do."

"That man," Janeway started, her voice lowering with distaste, "has lied to us from the very beginning."

"Agent Andross is a superior negotiator. I did not approve of his unorthodox efforts to help me obtain the post of Supreme Arbitrator, and I pleaded with him during his occupation of the tower to return control to the Board."

"Then you'll approve of this even less," Janeway told her. "Andross was directly responsible for the theft of our processor."

"Andross has informed me that he purchased your

processor," Fee said reasonably. "Now we are returning it without charge to you. I believe that covers the
extent of our responsibility."

"Not quite." Janeway nodded to Chakotay, who
explained, "When we analyzed the manifest data
from the Cartel computer, we were able to trace a
number of thefts directly to Andross. He received the
merchandise, and his office supplied both ships and
fuel for the so-called salvage crews."

Fee frowned. "Salvage is not illegal—"

"What do you call luring us into a trap?" Janeway
asked. "Then rendering us unconscious so our processor could be removed?"

"I did not authorize Andross to do this."

"Nevertheless, as his superior, you are responsible
for his actions. Andross hired the *Kapon* to trick us
into letting them on board." Janeway almost had to
laugh. "We thought we were buying star charts of
wormhole locations."

"We never even got the star charts," Paris muttered. He was surprised when Fee acted as if that was
the most horrific thing she'd heard so far.

"Your contract was not honored?" Fee asked.

"No," Janeway said.

"Do you have a record?"

Everyone looked to Tuvok, who assured them,
"There is a complete log of the negotiations."

Fee was breathing faster.

Janeway's tone wasn't even threatening. "I'm sure
an agent for House Min-Tutopa shouldn't be engaging
in information fraud."

"No," Fee bit off. "I would not like this information
to be given to the Cartel."

"I'm sure your influence will stretch far enough to
protect him . . ." Janeway mused.

Fee swallowed. "I will authorize the payment of your crew member's bond from the House treasury. It's bound to be enormous—"

"And the fines and damages to the Hub," Chakotay added. "Don't forget those."

"No, we can't forget that." Janeway patted Paris's shoulder, smiling up at Fee. "Please take care of it immediately. We'd like this settled before we start sending shuttles back and forth—don't you agree?"

Fee tightened her lips. "I will contact you shortly."

Janeway was starting to turn away when Paris spoke up. "Captain, there's one other thing." He wasn't sure if Tracer or anything else had been real, but he had to make amends where he could. "There's a Tutopan janitor who works on the Hub—Tracer. She got mixed up in all this, but it wasn't her fault. I'd appreciate it if Fee could pay her bond as well."

"Her?" Janeway asked, raising one brow.

"That was a *woman?*" Kim muttered in disbelief.

"I took advantage of her when she was inebriated, using her access to get into the computer." Paris appealed directly to Fee, self-consciously aware that everyone was listening. But maybe it wouldn't hurt for a guy like him to learn something from Harry's empathy. "It's not fair that she's being punished," he said in a stronger voice. "She was caught up in your rebellion too, only she's got no one to help her."

"Apparently, she has your support." Fee looked from him to Janeway, her irritation quite suddenly gone. "I'm reminded of why I sought the position of Supreme Arbitrator—to keep the Cartel from crushing us into a faceless, nameless mass."

Paris leaned forward. "So you'll help her?"

"I'll make sure Tracer is released from the custody of the Cartel." Fee thoughtfully considered the bridge crew. "You are an unusual people in your degree of concern for the individual. I only hope my people can learn to be the same. . . ."

"We have a word for that sort of concern," Janeway told the Tutopan. "It's considered compassion."

"It is a gift," Fee told them.

CHAPTER
25

After the processor was welded back into the computer monitor room, Janeway accompanied Torres and Kim to sickbay to hear the prognosis on the neural gel packs.

First Janeway thanked Zimmerman for his hard work. "I understand you provided the stimulant solution which enabled *Voyager*'s sensors to locate us."

The doctor modestly lowered his head, but Janeway noticed that he slyly checked Torres's reaction. "I was merely doing my duty."

It only took a moment before Torres added, "Thanks." The effort in her voice made it clear she was acknowledging her mistaken judgment of the doctor.

Kim handed Zimmerman a tricorder. "The added chemicals have been cleansed from the bionutrient of the main core."

"I see," the doctor said, examining the readings. "We should be able to bring the main processor back on-line once the junction nodes are reconnected."

Chakotay came into sickbay. "I wouldn't like to tax Min-Tutopa's hospitality much longer." At Janeway's questioning look, he added, "The doctor requested that I come down."

Zimmerman set the tricorder aside, clasping his hands in front of him. "I wanted to inform you of my findings."

His demeanor was so serious that Janeway couldn't understand why Kes was smiling in complete delight. "Is there a problem?"

"Not exactly," the doctor said. "The damaged tissue has apparently regenerated, and the computer should return to normal functioning once the processor is operational."

Janeway hid her relief, knowing there was something else in the wings. "Then what is it?"

"The protein which was added to the bionutrient to aid in regeneration has had some unforeseen side effects."

Kes was shaking her head. "You make it sound like a tragedy, when it's the most wonderful thing that could happen."

"What is it?" Chakotay asked, obviously intrigued by their behavior.

The doctor fastened his gaze somewhere near the ceiling. "I believe the computer network system is developing."

"Developing?" Janeway asked. "What do you mean?"

Kes answered for him. "It's growing, in exactly the same way an organism matures after inception."

"Neural cells have detached within the tissue masses of the core," the doctor explained, "and are coming together to form neural crest cells. We've found evidence that they are slowly migrating within the gel packs, and are instigating formation in the main subprocessors as well. It is the first stage toward complete physiological integration."

Janeway wasn't sure she understood. "It sounds as if you're saying the computer is alive."

It was Kim who answered. "As far as we can tell, the entire ship acts as a unified organism."

Chakotay drew in his breath. "Astounding."

"What will these neural crests do to the computer system?" Janeway asked, preferring to consider the practicalities first.

"It may increase efficiency as the systems become more interrelated," Kim told her.

Kes added, "It may also eventually lead to sentience."

"Sentience?" Janeway repeated. "You mean my ship could become self-aware?"

She knew the doctor was particularly sensitive about this issue. "Legally and psychologically, individuals are self-aware when they are capable of reasoning, generalizations, discovering new meanings, and learning from past experience. The neural gel packs were designed to perform all these functions."

"And now, the brain of the ship may be evolving," Kes said simply.

Janeway felt slightly stunned. "And if it is, we're helping it by providing more protein?"

"Yes. If it is evolving." The doctor seemed unduly anxious about that idea. He picked up the tricorder as proof of his diagnosis. "However, the development has currently been halted by the removal of the additional protein from the bionutrient."

Janeway took in Chakotay's surprise, and even Torres didn't have a snide comment to make. Kim was watching her anxiously.

Kes said what everyone must have been thinking.

"Shouldn't we continue to add the protein if the computer needs it to develop?"

"Do we want it to develop?" Kim asked in return.

"It seems we have an obligation to continue what we've started," Janeway told them. "Good work, Doctor. I want you and Kim to keep an eye on the effects the added protein have on our computer system. Let me know if there are any further developments."

The doctor nodded, finally reflecting the enthusiasm in her eyes. "I thought you'd be concerned."

"Like any captain, I'm duty-bound to help my ship develop its full potential."

"Even if it interferes with returning to the Alpha Quadrant?" he seemed compelled to ask.

"Doctor, we're in the business of discovering new life-forms. I'm pleased to find one right under our noses, and I prefer to believe that this will help us get home rather than hinder us."

He seemed relieved. "I was afraid you would withhold the protein once you knew what it could do."

Janeway laughed out loud. "If I tried to fight the entire universe, we wouldn't get very far, now would we? I prefer to work with whatever presents itself." She smiled at Torres in particular. "I don't intend to impose my will on any sentient being. We'll get home, and we'll do it by working together—the crew and the ship."

Chakotay added quietly, "After all, we were big enough to handle the Cartel."

ACCEPTED AROUND THE COUNTRY, AROUND THE WORLD, AND AROUND THE GALAXY!

- No Annual Fee
- Low introductory APR for cash advances and balance transfers
- Free trial membership in The Official STAR TREK Fan Club upon card approval*
- Discounts on selected STAR TREK Merchandise

To apply for the STAR TREK MasterCard today, call

1-800-775-TREK

Transporter Code: SKYD